AN AUTHOR BITES THE DUST

*Other mysteries by Arthur W. Upfield
available as Scribner Crime Classics:*

AN AUTHOR BITES THE DUST

Arthur W. Upfield

A SCRIBNER CRIME CLASSIC

COLLIER BOOKS
Macmillan Publishing Company
New York

Macmillan Publishing Company
866 Third Avenue, New York, N.Y. 10022
Collier Macmillan Canada, Inc.

Library of Congress Cataloging-in-Publication Data

Upfield, Arthur William, 1888–1964.
   An author bites the dust.

   "A Scribner crime classic."
   I. Title.
PR9619.3.U6A92 1987   823   87-13850
ISBN 0-02-054900-8 (pbk.)

First Collier Books Edition 1987
10 9 8 7 6 5 4 3 2 1
Printed in the United States of America

Contents

CHAPTER ONE

The Great Mervyn Blake

THE large room rented by the Australian Society of Creative Writers for its bi-monthly meetings was comfortably filled on the afternoon of 7th November. The Society was fairly strong and quite influential, for many of its members had arrived in the local world of belles-lettres and its president was the well-known Mervyn Blake, novelist and critic.

He was the chief speaker this afternoon, and he spoke with the assurance of the successful. His speech began shortly after tea, which was served at half past three, and it finished at four minutes to five, being followed by polite hand-clapping. At five o'clock he left the building in company with Miss Nancy Chesterfield, the social editress of the *Recorder*.

Blake's age was somewhere in the early fifties. He was large but not fat, florid of face but not flaccid of muscle, and his over-long hair still matched the colour of his dark-brown eyes. He carried his years exceptionally well, for Prosperity riding on one shoulder and Success on the other kept those shoulders well back.

"Glad you were able to make the grade this afternoon," he said when he and Nancy Chesterfield were walking along Collins Street to the Hotel Australia. "Do we pick up your case at your office?"

"Yes, please, Mervyn. I left it with the commissionaire so there'll be no need to go up for it. My compliments on your speech. But—"

"But what?"

"I wonder. Do you think if the modern novelist turned out his wares similar in length and scope and digression to, say, the novels of Sir Walter Scott and Thackeray, that they would be acceptable to modern publishers?"

"No, most certainly not. Modern publishers have to and do pander to the demands of the modern and now comparatively educated herd. Old time publishers took pride in their part of the production of fine literature. Nowadays they demand sensationalism slickly put across, for their shareholders must be given their pound of flesh. Anyway, it's a heck of a dry argument, and at the moment I'm sick of telling the would-be great how to write novels. And I am sick of literary people—which is one reason why I had Janet to ask you out for the night."

"Bored with your house party?" she asked when they came together again in the crowd on the footpath.

"The boredom even brandy won't dispel."

They did not speak again until they had relaxed in one of the lounges of the famous hotel. Then he ordered gin and vermouth for his companion and brandy and dry ginger ale for himself. She noted that he called for a double for himself.

"What were the other reasons you used to persuade Janet to invite me?" she asked. He drank the brandy as though it were a light beer and signalled to the waiter.

"The mirror in your bag will provide one of the reasons," he said. "I wish I weren't old. I wish I weren't married. I wish I were your age and yet in possession of all the experiences and the success I have today. Dammit! No sooner do we reach the top than we are old and able to enjoy only —brandy. A double, please, waiter. The lady will miss out this time."

"And the other reasons?" pressed Nancy Chesterfield. Dressed in a beautifully tailored black suit and pale green blouse with a fashionable black hat emphasizing the brilliance of her almost golden hair, she would have made any man proud to be her cavalier.

"Another is that I want you to give a full report of what I said this afternoon. Publicity is an author's very breath of life," he said with brutal candour made charming by the way he smiled. The second double brandy had been set

8

before him and he drank it quickly, then said, "That's better. Again, waiter, and another gin and vermouth. Been on the wagon, Nancy, since before lunch. A week-end party is quite all right, but one that goes on for a week becomes very wearing. I'm glad they didn't want any encouragement to stay put. I didn't want them with me. Marshall Ellis is a bore, and I am unable to understand why his face hasn't been pushed in long ago. Wilcannia-Smythe gets under my skin at times. Lubers is a humourless inconoclast whom I find irritating, and Ella is exceedingly depressing after twenty-four hours. That leaves Twyford Arundal, who is really amusing when he's properly drunk. Janet has been a little difficult, and I have been boozing too much."

"Quite a tale of woe. Poor old Mervyn! Never mind. Janet likes having people about her, and the end of the house party is in sight, isn't it?"

"Yes. Of course, I'm with Janet up to a point. One must mix. One must use people, especially influential people, and the lion of the moment is decidedly influential in London. Make no mistake, I use you, too, but then in my own fashion I'm fond of you. Your coming home with me will save my reason. Your glass is empty."

They left the Australia at five minutes past six and proceeded to a car park for Blake's car. Nancy Chesterfield suggested that she should drive, but that proposal he put aside. The evidence of his condition was not manifest in his gait, nor at first did it become manifest in his driving. His voice betrayed it to her. He spoke now very slowly and distinctly, with an accent he fondly thought was genuine Oxford.

Having called for her case, he drove with excessive caution till they were beyond the tram terminus, and then raised the speed so high that she had to remonstrate with him.

"My dear Nancy, we're not driving in a T-model Ford. My nerves are steady. My eyes are wide open."

"But my nerves are not particularly good today. I had a hectic morning with the Chief," she told him.

"Indeed! You astonish me," he said. "No one but creative writers are entitled to nerves. If this old dame in front doesn't

9

get clear in two seconds she is going to cop it, as the vulgar would say."

However, thereafter he drove with moderate speed and care the remaining thirty odd miles to Yarrabo, again being exceedingly cautious when passing loaded timber trucks coming in from the distant mountains. Just after entering Yarrabo they left the highway for a branch road and then passed through a double gateway giving access to a spacious garden in which stood a spacious house.

In the hall they were welcomed by Mrs Blake and Mrs Ella Montrose.

"It's so good of you to come, Nancy," Janet Blake exclaimed, warmly. "Ella and I have become bored with each other, and even the men are getting tired of us. Come along! I am putting you in my room. Ella will bring you a cup of tea while you are dressing. There isn't much time. Mervyn should have brought you hours ago."

"We gossiped after the meeting," Nancy Chesterfield explained, following her hostess from the hall. Behind her she heard Mrs Montrose tell Mervyn Blake that his evening milk had been taken to his writing-room, and she was aware that Blake always drank milk after a "heavy" afternoon that he could take a "heavy" evening the better.

The dinner was an informal affair. Everyone had long known each other excepting Marshall Ellis, the visitor from England. The Blakes were noted for their hospitality to literary folk, and at this time they were blessed with the services of an excellent cook and a maid with a personality. The room, the table appointments, and the efficient service made a combination altogether pleasing.

Eight people sat at the board, Mervyn Blake, well groomed, sober, and mentally alert, occupying the head of the table. On his right sat the guest of honour, Mr Marshall Ellis, one of London's leading literary critics, Nancy Chesterfield did not like him, but forbore to condemn him merely for his imitation of G. K. Chesterton. The imitation proceeded no further than the paunch, the hair fashion and the pince-nez with its attachment of broad, black ribbon. The face was like that of a punch-drunk Liverpool Irishman, but the voice was the most melodious male voice she had ever heard.

Ella Montrose sat next to him. She was fifty, dark and tragic. When in her twenties she had produced two novels; since then she had spent her time reviewing books and writing pars for the literary journals. She might have done better had she reared a family—better that than delving into mystic cults from Odinism to Voodooism.

Next to Ella Montrose was Martin Lubers, short, dapper, alert and alive, with hazel eyes, clipped moustache, brown hair, and forty years behind him. Nancy wondered how he had managed to stay for a whole week, for he heaved grenades at those likely to differ from him.

She herself sat on Blake's left, and beside her sat the cold, suave, white-haired Wilcannia-Smythe, reputed to have the most musical pen in Australia. He was slim and always elegant in dress, a rival and yet Mervyn's firm friend for many years. Beyond him was Twyford Arundal, small, wispy, weak of eye and chin, but a poet of the top flight.

Last, but by no means least distinguished, was Janet Blake, who occupied the other end of the table. *Who's Who* gave her age as forty-one, and people felt inclined to argue against that statement. Janet Blake was large but not thick, her eyes were dark and restless. Her mouth was generous and yet firm-lipped, and her chin was square and strong. She seldom smiled, and Nancy Chesterfield decided that the house party had "taken a lot out of her".

All in all, the dinner was a happy affair. The host talked well about nothing and was supported by his friends. Marshall Ellis told of famous novelists with whom he was well acquainted, and, provided one closed one's eyes, his voice was a delight to the ear.

Subsequently the party gathered in the lounge, where Mrs Blake served coffee. It was then nine o'clock, and at half past nine Mervyn Blake suggested drinks. From then on, no one but Wilcannia-Smythe was worried by an empty glass. Everyone except Marshall Ellis smoked cigarettes, and he smoked cigar after cigar so that the atmosphere became foggily dense, though every door and window was open.

The conversation veered to the subject of Mervyn Blake's lecture at the literary meeting that afternoon—"The Structure of the Novel"—and then Martin Lubers had to throw one of his grenades, the temptation being too strong to be resisted.

"Which is preferable," he asked, "an imperfectly constructed skeleton covered with healthy flesh and vitalized with good, red blood, or a perfectly constructed skeleton covered with parchment and pigment with watered ink?"

"Why be anatomical?" complained Twyford Arundal, who was fast reaching the point when his voice failed. "Don't be difficult, my dear Martin."

Marshall Ellis eased himself in his chair, lit another cigar, belched, and opened his mouth. Everyone but Nancy Chesterfield knew what threatened, but the menace was averted by the iconoclastic Lubers, who, being a Director of Talks on the A.B.C., was not a person to be ruthlessly crushed.

"You have been discussing the structure of the novel as though the novel is an established science," he said. "No art can be a science, like ballistics or material stresses. Not once have you mentioned the vital essentials of fiction, inspiration, and imagination, and the ability to believe in what is imagined. Without these essentials, the perfectly constructed novel is merely a thing of words."

Marshall Ellis's cheeks were being puffed out and drawn in. He grunted to command attention, and Wilcannia-Smythe took up the challenge in time to thwart him.

"If we may assume, Lubers, that your preference is for the crooked skeleton covered with bulging fat, give us examples," he urged.

"Very well, I will," assented Lubers. "You, Blake, were stressing the importance of deliberate analysis and the even progress of pure drama, the novelist's imagination to be subservient to the language he employs. Life is not like that. There is no such thing as pure drama, any more than in reality there are human characters who are all angel or all devil. A novel ought to be a slice of life, up in one chapter and down in another, its characters angels in the morning and devils in the evening. It's the pictures painted by the words that count, not the words that paint the pictures. The story must be paramount, and in my opinion Clarence B. Bagshott can tell a story better than some of your lauded novelists."

The room became quiet. It was as though Martin Lubers had praised the *Decameron* at a Methodist Conference. Then Blake spoke, slowly, giving exaggerated space between each word.

"My dear man, don't be a complete ass," he said. "We were discussing the novel and novelists, and you bring forward the atrocious efforts of a 'whodunit' writer."

"All right, Blake, we'll pass him by," said the unabashed Lubers. "What of the novels of I. R. Watts? No one can say he does not turn out an excellent novel. He writes with astonishing vividness and achieves remarkable suspense."

"Melodramatic trash," averred Mervyn Blake, his eyes glinting.

"They sell, anyway," Lubers argued. "And I've seen high praise of them in oversea journals. Watts gives an important something in addition to entertainment, and that addition is knowledge of history and of people."

"But Lubers, Watts's work lacks rhythm, and the writing is far from good." Mervyn Blake's lip lifted in a sneer, and he said, "It could never be claimed that I. R. Watts is a contributor to Australian literature—or any other. Our sole interest at the moment is Australian literature, and the influence we may exert upon its development."

Nancy Chesterfield observed that Blake was becoming extremely angry. He emptied his glass and almost filled it with neat brandy, drank most of that and continued, apparently knowing he was the elected champion, his words falling like small hammers upon cement.

"Your taste in broadcast talks is excellent, Lubers," he said, "but your judgment of literature is, shall we say, peculiar. You wireless people are like the film people. You cannot divest your minds of the idea that popularity spells artistic quality. There was never yet a best-seller that had any claims to being good literature, literature as understood by the cultured. We are interested, Lubers, in Literature with a capital L, not commercial fiction that receives the approval of the common herd."

"Well, before I go up in smoke and flame, I'm firing my last shot," Lubers growled. "The greatest best-seller of all time, you will agree, is the Bible, read by the cultured and the illiterate all over the world. The common herd can and does appreciate literature provided it says something worth hearing with the mind."

Twyford Arundal opened and moved his mouth to mock but not the tiniest sound issued from it. Then he fell off his chair and his forehead came in contact with the edge of a stool. When he had been picked up and put back again, the powder for Blake's next shot was drenched with the general sympathy for poor Twyford Arundal, who continued to work his mouth without result.

The unpleasantness had cleared by half past eleven, when Ella Montrose said she was going to bed. Everyone seemed ready to retire, and the party moved into the hall and broke up. There Blake asked Wilcannia-Smythe to lock the back door after he left the house for his writing-room.

"Be sure to go to bed, Mervyn," Ella Montrose advised, and softly laughed. "Don't go making love over the fence to the extraordinary Miss Pinkney."

"I would much prefer, my dear Ella, to cut Miss Pinkney's scrawny throat," he countered.

Nancy Chesterfield slept soundly all through the night until half past seven the next morning when the maid brought her early tea. She was returning from the bathroom when she met Ella Montrose. Ella was whimpering like a child recovering from punishment. Nancy asked her why she was so upset, but could obtain no explanation, and she took the distraught woman to her own room, where she pacified her.

At last Ella managed to say between sobs, "Mervyn! The men went to call Mervyn to breakfast. They say he's dead. He's lying just inside the door of his room. The door was shut, and he couldn't get out. He tried to claw the door open, but—he—couldn't get out."

CHAPTER TWO

Miss Pinkney's Lodger

LIKE a fledgling bird, Miss Pinkney was all a-flutter. Her heart was fluttering with excitement, her feet fluttered in and out of the rooms of her cottage. Once she went to the front veranda to gaze with critical eyes at the crazy pavement extending to the front gate. Once she went to the back of the cottage and gazed over the well-tended vegetable garden to the line of lilac-trees masking the rear fence and partially obscuring the cream-painted building beyond, the building in which Mervyn Blake, the great Australian author and critic, had died from apparently natural causes.

Miss Pinkney was finding life most interesting. Indeed, she had found it so the moment she learnt that Mr Mervyn Blake had rented the property beyond her own. Thereafter her sedate and somewhat bucolic life was enlivened by interest piled upon interest in the visits to the Blakes of famous authors, artists, and radio personalities.

Then came the discovery of Mervyn Blake dead in his writing-room at the bottom of his garden, the building just beyond Miss Pinkney's back fence. For days the police were all over the place. They even raised their heads above the division fence and stared at Miss Pinkney when the hem of her skirt was pinned to her waist and she was wearing old shoes and gardening gloves, being then engaged with her vegetables.

She had wanted to pay a call on the poor little widow, but she felt that it would not be appreciated by a woman who had never given the faintest sign of neighbourliness. And the peculiar thing about the matter was that it seemed the coroner could not make up his mind what Mr Blake had died of.

That was weeks ago, and then, just when life threatened to become once more bucolic, that nice Constable Simes had stopped her in the street and told her he would be much easier in his mind if she got someone to live with her, since there was a positive crime wave in Melbourne. She had told Constable Simes that she hadn't a relation or a friend who could possibly come and live with her, and at that the dear constable promised he would find a boarder for her, someone quiet and genteel.

The very next day he had called to tell her he had found just the ideal gentleman he had had in mind, and she had consented to accept this paying guest. Now he was due to arrive and she and her house were dressed in their best. But wait!

Where was Mr Pickwick? She had actually forgotten to change Mr Pickwick's collar. What a mercy she had remembered it in time. She flew to the kitchen, then out to the back garden crying, "Mr Pickwick! Dear Mr Pickwick! Where are you?"

An enormous all-black cat emerged from the shadow cast by a camellia bush and followed Miss Pinkney to the house. There she removed a stained blue silk collar looking much like an early Victorian garter, and placed about Mr Pickwick's neck a similar item of orange. It was then that someone knocked upon the front door.

Uttering a little cry Miss Pinkney rushed to the mirror hanging behind the kitchen door, patted her hair and the collar of her old-fashioned bodice, and fluttered along the passage to the hall and the front door.

"Miss Pinkney?" inquired the caller.

"Yes! Oh yes! You are—"

"Napoleon Bonaparte. Constable Simes has told me about you and that you are willing to give me a haven of rest and peace for a week or two."

"Yes, that's right, Mr Bonaparte," she hastened to assure him. "Oh, I see you've brought your luggage. Will you bring it in? I'm so sorry I haven't a domestic—please do come in."

Detective Inspector Napoleon Bonaparte had removed his hat and now smiled upward at Miss Pinkney who was standing on the topmost of the three steps to the veranda. He saw a slim woman dressed in grey, her hair greying, her small face coloured by excitement, her prominent grey eyes bright and warm.

"Thank you," he said. "I'll get my case. What a charming house you have. What a beautiful garden. Oh!"

The enormous cat appeared beside Miss Pinkney's brown house shoes.

"This, Mr Bonaparte, is my Mr Pickwick," announced Miss Pinkney.

The cat marched down the steps, tail erect, great golden eyes examining the stranger. Bony stooped and stroked the animal and Mr Pickwick purred.

"You adore cats, I can see," Miss Pinkey cried happily.

The paying guest admitted that he adored cats, and when he turned and walked to the gate for his case Mr Pickwick waddled after him. He waddled behind Bony on the return journey to the front veranda.

"Please come in," Miss Pinkney cried. "I'll show you to your room. Yes, do come in. It's so warm out in the sun today."

She preceded her guest into the hall, on the panelled walls of which hung three large pictures in oils of sailing ships. Bony's gaze passed from them to the ship's oil lamp suspended from a bracket fixed to the wall near the opposite door. Miss Pinkney halted beside a door on the right, and she smiled at him and gave a little bow of invitation for him to enter.

Murmuring his thanks, he went in. The walls were of wood stained mahogany. The bed was a ship's bunk, broad and long and inviting. Above the bunk was a ship's brass port, the inside painted bright blue to resemble the sky. The floor was polished and unspoilt by coverings. A large table and two easy chairs, an open-fronted case filled with books, a standard lamp and a brass spittoon completed the furniture. Bright cretonne curtains ornamented the casement windows.

Bony put down his case and dropped his hat upon the table. He turned then to see Miss Pinkney still standing just outside the door. She was looking at him anxiously, her hands clasped and stilled against her flat breast.

He said, "I like this room—very, very much."

The anxiety vanished, and the words came tumbling.

"Oh, I'm so glad you like your room, Mr Bonaparte," she cried. "It used to be my brother's room, you see. He loved it. He was a sailor, you know. He commanded ships. We were very happy here at Yarrabo, though he missed the sea after he retired. Poor man, he died four years ago. If you wish, I will show you the bathroom and the dining-room and the lounge. Then I'll serve you with afternoon tea. Do you like afternoon tea?"

His deep blue eyes beamed at her and he gave her a hint of a bow, saying, "Madam, I like tea at any hour of the day and of the night."

The dining-room contained additional evidence of the departed sea captain, but the lounge belonged entirely to Miss Pinkney. The floor was covered by a white and gold Chinese carpet. Books rested everywhere. Framed photographs on the mantelpiece flanked the enlarged portrait of a vitriolic-looking man in the summer uniform of a captain in the mercantile marine. It was a woman's room with its cut flowers, its soft divan, and inviting pouffes.

Mr Pickwick came in and parked on the hearth rug. Miss Pinkney entered trundling a tea wagon, and Bony rose to assist her. Fifty and lonely, celibacy had not soured her. He had expected to meet an eccentric woman who lived alone with her cat, and he was feeling the warmth of a mind that life had never defeated. She was as excited as a child of twelve, and she made no attempt to conceal the pleasure his advent gave.

The cat advanced to his feet, and he put down the fragile blue and white cup and saucer on the trolley that he might stroke Mr Pickwick. Mr Pickwick loudly purred and rubbed himself against Bony's elegantly trousered leg, and Bony said, "Mr Pickwick, you have that which few cats possess—personality."

"Mr Pickwick is a character reader," averred Miss Pinkney. "He likes you. You are doubly welcome, for the liking is dual. Please don't think Mr Pickwick takes to everyone. Oh dear, no." She spoke directly to the cat, saying, "Now Mr Pickwick, show Mr Bonaparte how to play ping-pong."

She moved her arm like a baseball thrower and the cat walked sedately from the room. Bony observed that he was expected to be silent. Miss Pinkney sipped her tea and smiled. In came Mr Pickwick, walking with the appearance of having no weight. He stared up at Miss Pinkney, and she deliberately looked out through the window.

Whereupon the cat, finding no encouragement in that quarter, approached Bony and placed on the carpet at his feet the ping-pong ball it had been carrying in its mouth. What he was expected to do was plain to Bony, and he did it. Mr Pickwick flew after the ball Bony rolled towards the door. He punched the ball into the passage beyond and there skidded and bucked and punched the ball about the bare and polished floor, watched by the admiring Bony and the proud Miss Pinkney. That the ball was a little "dead" Bony attributed to the repeated assaults upon it by claws and mouth.

"I taught Mr Pickwick to fetch and carry when he was quite young," remarked Miss Pinkney. "Another cup of tea? He just loves to play with a ball or a little wad of paper. You've made him accept you as his friend. Ah, here he comes!"

Again Mr Pickwick did his act and Bony picked up the ball. His finger-tips told him that the ball was firm and hard, but his mind was occupied with the expression of simple delight registered on his hostess's unadorned face. The cat disappeared after the ball, and Miss Pinkney rose and left the room without explanation.

Ah! Bony leaned back in his chair and sipped his tea,

sipped it from fragile china far removed from a tin panni-kin. Comfort! Comfort surrounded him, solid and real, and no man was better able to appreciate comfort than he who but recently had come back from the interior, where he had been investigating a disappearance. Mr Pickwick again entered the room and this time laid himself down beside the ball, flanks working like bellows, mouth wide open. Miss Pinkney returned, in her hands a silver cigarette-case and a silver lighter.

"I like a cigarette sometimes," she said, and then giggled. "The sometimes is as often as the ration will allow. Please offer me one."

On his feet, Bony opened her case. She took one and insisted that he should do likewise. Then he needs must take her lighter and find that it would not work, and whilst he held a lighted match in service, she said it was a shame that in these days the garage people didn't know their business.

"I have been visualizing a stern lady who would denounce tobacco and forbid me smoking in the house," he told her, smiling.

"My dear Mr Bonaparte, you may smoke when and where you like," she said. "I'd hate to think of you lying with your head in a cold fire-place and smoking up the chimney. I am glad you smoke. My brother used to say, 'Never trust a man who doesn't smoke or drink or swear when he hits his thumb with a hammer'. Mr Pickwick distrusts them, too. He hated Mr Wilcannia-Smythe when he was staying next door at the time Mr Blake died. I've seen him lying on top of the division fence and hissing at Mr Wilcannia-Smythe. Afterwards, someone told me that Mr Wilcannia-Smythe neither smoked nor drank. And, I assume, never used an inaccurate adjective."

"What was Mr Pickwick's attitude towards Mr and Mrs Blake?" Bony asked.

"Mr Pickwick hated Mr Blake," replied Miss Pinkney. "Mr Blake would sometimes throw a stone at Mr Pickwick if Mr Pickwick happened to be in his garden. Once I saw him do it, and I remonstrated with him. He was very rude to me."

Miss Pinkney smiled. "I'm afraid I spoke to him somewhat after the fashion of my brother!"

"H'm! Did you see much of Mrs Blake?"

"Very little. I used to see her on occasions playing ping-pong. They have a table on the back veranda. We can see it from the fence. They must have lost a ball when playing, because Mr Pickwick brought one in from their garden. He will wander at night, although why I don't know, because I had him doctored and he's quite, quite happy about it."

"I read of the affair in the Melbourne papers," Bony murmured. "About the sudden death of Mr Mervyn Blake. There was a house full of guests, I understand."

"Oh yes, there was a house party for a week before Mr Blake died," Miss Pinkney said. "Several well known people, you know. The Blakes often had writers and personalities staying with them. But they wouldn't associate with anyone in the district. Er—well, you know what I mean."

Bony was not sure that he did know. He said, "It was most peculiar Mr Blake dying so suddenly. I wonder if he was tired of life?"

"Not a bit of it," Miss Pinkney cheerfully stated. "No man who drinks like he did would think of ending his life. He was so well known. Someone told me that if he condemned a book the book was a certain failure, and it would be a success if he praised it. Oh no, there was no reason for him to commit suicide. Someone hated him enough to murder him. This evening, when it's cool, I'll take you into the garden and show you the little building where he died."

CHAPTER THREE

The People Next Door

HAVING eaten an excellent dinner, Bony was in the proper frame of mind to appreciate the view from the front veranda of Rose Cottage, Yarrabo, in the State of Victoria.

Before the flower-embowered house passed a main highway to the city from the vast timber country of Gippsland. Beyond the road, beyond the narrow valley, the trees marched up the steep slopes of Donna Buang. There were no clouds beheading the mountain this summer's evening, and the setting sun was painting the escarpments with deep pink which, even as he watched, was turning into cloudy purple.

Seated in luxurious ease, completely satisfied with the accommodation found for him by Constable Simes, and confronted by a puzzle promising to tax his intelligence, Bony felt calmly happy.

The Blakes had certainly chosen wisely when they purchased the property next door and called it "Eureka". Old Captain Pinkney had also been wise, though his main objective in retiring to Yarrabo was to put the sea away from him that his heart might not pine overmuch for it.

It is a far cry from the inland plains and mulga forests and gibber flats, swooning in the grip of the relentless sun, to the Valley of the Yarra, bright green and luscious and temperate even in January. The sun was setting to end this third day of the month, and deep in his most comfortable chair, Napoleon Bonaparte relaxed both his mind and his body.

For him it was another busman's holiday, and the cause of it Superintendent Bolt of the Victorian C.I.B. Bolt had written suggesting that the death of Mervyn Blake fell under circumstances sure to interest Inspector Bonaparte. The letter was waiting for Bony at his home on his return from the far west of Queensland, and the writer of it became extremely unpopular. Bony's chief wanted him to sally forth on another Inland case, and his wife wanted him to take his month's accumulated leave and herself to a South Coast ocean resort. Bolt had won—with the official summary of the investigation.

Subsequently he said to Bony, who was seated before his huge desk, "This Blake bird was fifty-six, but he was tough. He drank heavily between bouts of complete sobriety, and he suffered slightly from gastric ulcers, but the post mortem revealed no reason why he died. Take the case history with you, and thank you for coming down."

"Give me your private opinion," Bony requested, and Bolt said, "I won't bet any way—natural causes, suicide, murder—I've just got a funny little feeling that Blake was laid out. We can't discover any likely motive for suicide, or any motive for murder. I don't believe he died from natural causes just because the pathologists and the toxicologists can't find any unnatural causes sufficiently severe to have killed him. My crowd are all flat out on a series of gang murders, and I thought of you and decided that this Blake business might be right up your alley. As I just said, I'm pleased you consented to come and take hold of it because I don't want it to grow cold."

It was cold enough in all conscience. Blake had died on 10th November and now it was 3rd January. The Coroner's verdict was an open one, and the dramatis personae had scattered: one to England, another to Adelaide, the third to Sydney, the others being domiciled in Victoria. Cold and dead as the author-critic, the case was all Bony's.

His decision to "look into it" had been taken entirely on Bolt's recommendation. From the summary of the investigation he had formed no opinion, and study of the huge official file he intended leaving until after he retired to that most attractive bedroom.

So here he was a thousand miles or so from his own stamping grounds, seated at ease a few yards from a main highway instead of a winding camel pad, living in a country of flowing

23

water and green verdure instead of flowing sand and brick-red, sun-baked earth. Oh yes, a detective's life did have an occasional bright patch in it. And in this case the particular bright patch was Miss Priscilla Pinkney. She came and sat with him.

"I do hope, Mr Bonaparte, that you won't be disturbed by the timber trucks," she said. "My brother used at first to complain bitterly about the—the damn noise beginning too early in the morning. Just listen to that one coming up the hill."

His mind a little shocked by the adjective, which was so foreign to his acceptance of Miss Pinkney's personality, Bony did as requested. The road to the city began to rise just before it entered the scattered township of Yarrabo, and the driver of the approaching wagon loaded with one huge log had been quickly compelled to change to a lower gear. The engine was labouring with a steady roar, and presently they watched the vehicle pass the gateway in Miss Pinkney's cypress hedge. A similar vehicle was coming the other way, fast and loadless. As it came speeding down the long hill its exhaust issued a succession of loud reports similar to those made by a battery of light guns.

"I expect I shall become used to it," Bony told his hostess. "I sleep soundly."

"We all get used to it in time, Mr Bonaparte, but a visitor at first finds it annoying." Miss Pinkney gave a silk-clad leg a smart slap. "The traffic begins about five in the morning and it continues all through the day until about nine. It is astonishing the number of logs that pass every day."

"Do they bring them from very far?"

"From up in those mountains, in frightful places," she replied. "You should go up one day in an empty truck and return with it on its way to a mill. How on earth they ever get the logs to the loading stages I don't know. Oh my! The mosquitoes are beginning. They do bite me so. Do they attack you?"

"They do," admitted Bony, rubbing an ankle. "Will you not show me your garden?"

"Of course. I'll call Mr Pickwick. He dearly loves to walk in the garden in the cool of the evening."

She left him to go into the house, and he stepped down from the veranda and strolled to the front gate, there to gaze up and down the broad highway at the few shops and scattered houses. Then he heard her voice again in front of the house.

"Now come along, Mr Pickwick," she was saying, as though talking to a small boy. "I won't have you pretending you are too tired to take a walk. It'll do you good. If I carry you everywhere you won't have any legs to walk with."

Mr Pickwick had gone on strike. He was lying on the veranda as though trying to reach the veranda roof with his paws. His slave gave him up and joined her guest.

Together they admired the roses and the many choice gladioli, pausing here and there whilst Miss Pinkney discoursed upon them and her flowering shrubs. Eventually they came to the vegetable garden at the rear of the house, and it was here that Mr Pickwick joined them, arriving at top speed and ending up in a plum-tree.

"You don't tend all this garden yourself, do you?" Bony inquired, his brows fractionally raised.

"I do all the planting and most of the hoeing," he was informed. "I have a man who comes in now and then to dig and trim and cut wood for me. He typifies the new generation."

"Indeed! In what way?"

"In giving as little as he can for as much as he can get. My brother, however, used to manage him very well by setting him a good example. My brother used to work very hard. Perhaps if he hadn't worked so hard he would be alive today. Thrombosis claimed him, poor man. You would have liked him. So downright in his opinions. So—so forceful in his language. Let's go on and I'll show you the place next door. Mrs Blake has been away for ten days and her cook, I think, has gone to the pictures at Warburton."

Miss Pinkney led the way along the narrow cinder path separating the beds of peas and carrots and parsnips and greens of all kinds. They skirted the rows of currant and gooseberry bushes and entered the early shadows cast by the line of lilac-trees masking the rear fence. This fence was built of narrow boards and was six feet high. Here and there a board was loose, and a coat of paint was indicated.

It was comparatively dark beneath the lilac-trees, for the sun had set and the mountain rose jet-black against the indigo blue of the evening sky. Miss Pinkney tittered. She tiptoed to the fence, against which lay a banana case. Mr Pickwick caught up with them and sprang to the top of the fence. In a thrilling whisper, Miss Pinkney invited Bony to stand on the case and look over the fence.

The branches of the lilac-trees reached out into the Blake's garden, and the fence was therefore almost invisible to anyone near either Miss Pinkney's house or that next door. As Miss Pinkney had said that Mrs Blake was away and her cook had gone to the pictures, he wondered at her cautious approach to the fence and her plea to him to be cautious.

Beyond the fence, distant about twenty-five feet and slightly to his right, stood a cream-painted, weatherboard building of about twenty feet by fifteen. The door he could not see, and on that side towards the house there was a large window having a single pane of glass.

The house he could plainly see. It fronted the side road off the highway and its back faced to the east and the mountain. Of the usual bungalow type, it contained, he estimated, ten or twelve rooms. The rear side was protected by a spacious veranda, and on the veranda he could see several lounge chairs and the white net spanning a ping-pong table. A man was sitting low in one of the chairs.

Bony stepped down from the case.

"Quite a nice home," he said, and said it softly for no reason.

"Yes, it is," she agreed as softly. "I've never been in the writing-room, but I have been into the house. The previous owners were most friendly. Since then I've often come here and spied over. They used to play croquet on the lawn— well-known people, many of them. Their names were in the papers. I could watch them playing ping-pong on the veranda, and they never knew I was looking at them."

Poor Miss Pinkney! Poor, lonely Miss Pinkney. How happy she might have been had the Blakes offered to be neighbourly! Bony pictured her looking into the forbidden garden like a child looking through plate glass at a display of toys.

"Who would be the man sitting on the veranda?" he said.

"A man on the veranda!" she echoed. "Oh! I don't know. Some relation of the cook's I suppose. There's no other domestic now. Let me see."

Bony offered his hand and she accepted the proferred assistance to mount the banana case. The delighted Bony watched her as she raised her head stealthily to the top of the fence until her eyes were one inch above it. The next instant she was down again with him, her eyes big in the pallor of her dusk-dimmed face.

"That's Mr Wilcannia-Smythe," she breathed. "I wonder what he's doing there. Let's look again."

Together they mounted the case upon which there was just room for them to stand. Together their heads rose until their eyes were one inch above the boards.

CHAPTER FOUR

Concerning Mr Wilcannia-Smythe

IT was not possible for anyone seated on the house veranda to observe Miss Pinkney and Bony peering over the division fence. The evening being far advanced, the gloom beneath the lilac-trees was too profound for such observation, and consequently Bony was amused by the excessive caution displayed by his fellow spy.

Miss Pinkney became a little more daring. She raised her face high enough to rest her chin upon the hands clasped to the fence.

"What's he doing there?" she whispered, without moving her head.

"Merely looking at the mountain, I think."

"I can see that, stupid."

Before the surprise occasioned by the epithet took full effect on Bony, Miss Pinkney stood straight up and impulsively turned to him.

"Oh, Mr Bonaparte, I'm so sorry," she gasped. "I didn't mean to say that. Indeed, I didn't. It must have been my brother in me. I was so intensely absorbed in that man on the veranda."

"It's nothing, Miss Pinkney," he assured her. "Look now! He's left his chair."

Miss Pinkney again crouched and gazed towards the house. Wilcannia-Smythe, if indeed it was that well-known author, was moving towards the five wide steps down to the lawn. He came down the steps without revealing evidence of either haste or a desire not to be seen. He sauntered across the lawn towards the writing-room. It was still light enough for the watchers to see him quite clearly, and Bony now recognized Wilcannia-Smythe by the description of him in the summary.

It became quickly obvious that he was making for Mervyn Blake's writing-room, to reach which he would necessarily pass the watchers within ten or a dozen paces. Gradually the two heads sank behind the division fence, and the watchers were compelled to be content with narrow chinks between the boards.

They were unable to see Wilcannia-Smythe actually enter the small building since the door was on its far side, but as he did not re-appear beyond the building, both decided that he had entered.

"What has he gone in there for?" breathed Miss Pinkney.

"It's difficult to tell," Bony answered, actually more interested in Miss Pinkney's fierce excitement than in the meanderings of Mr Wilcannia-Smythe, which were probably quite legitimate. "I am wondering if the door was locked and he had a key. I believe you said that the only occupant of the house, now that Mrs Blake is away, is the cook."

"And she's out, I'm sure, Mr Bonaparte. I heard the picture bus stop at the corner. I know she very often goes both on Wednesdays and Saturdays. D'you think that person is up to no good?"

"I wouldn't venture an opinion just yet," Bony said, and neither spoke again for at least four minutes during which period the last of the light faded out of the sky. Then he said, "I wonder if Mrs Blake has returned home. I can see no light in this side of the house."

"She can't be home," declared Miss Pinkney. "I would have heard her car."

A speculation was born in Bony's mind as to how much of the local life was registered by Miss Pinkney's ears in addition to her eyes.

"Whereabouts are the kitchen and the maids' room, do you know?" he asked.

"On the far side of the house. The domestics' bedroom is next to the kitchen." Controlled by mounting excitement,

Miss Pinkney clasped Bony's arm. "Do you think—oh, what are you thinking? Look! Look at the window."

The window was presented obliquely to them, but they could see the reflection of an electric torch beyond the glass. Not once in two minutes did the beam fall directly upon the window, and Bony at last decided that Wilcannia-Smythe was not this time an invited guest.

"I'd like to see what he's doing," he murmured, and instantly Miss Pinkney voiced agreement with him.

"Would you stay here on guard if I went over to find out?" he asked.

"Of course. I'll caterwaul like Mr Pickwick if I see any danger. I don't know where he is. I think he went up into the trees."

"I'll go over the fence. You stay right here and don't move away."

Again Miss Pinkney impulsively clutched his arm, saying, "Don't climb the fence. It's too frail. It might collapse under your weight. I know where there are three loose boards. I'll show you."

She was down off the case before he could begin the movement, and she led him along the fence and nearer to the house next door until she halted where sagging boards offered him access to the next garden.

Recalling that he was supposed to be an ordinary citizen, he said dubiously, "I suppose it will be all right. It would be most awkward if someone found me in there. Anyway, I'll just see what the fellow is doing. You be sure to remain on guard. I'll not be long."

Bony stepped through the hole in the fence. Beneath the trees the darkness was complete, and he moved away, not towards the writing-room but towards the large house, keeping well within the darkness provided by the lilac-trees.

Eventually he came to a soft gravel path laid between the fence and the house and bordered by standard roses. This gave place to an open space which he was sure although he could not see, was the driveway from the gate to the front entrance. There was no light in any of the front rooms or the hall. He passed across the front of the house and then could make out the outline of the garage beyond it. Another path led along the far side of the house where the kitchen and the maids' room were. Still he could see no light, and he became sure that there was no one in the house.

The presence and activities of Mr Wilcannia-Smythe were now of decided interest. He proceeded to investigate.

Stepping on to the lawn he was able to reach the writing-room without making a betraying sound, confident that now not even Miss Pinkney could see him. The door was closed, an exceedingly faint line of light at its foot. He ran his hand softly over the door and found the Yale lock.

Crouching against the wall, he edged round the corner and so came to the window, drawing near to it with caution until he was able, with one eye, to peer round its frame into the room beyond.

Mr Wilcannia-Smythe was seated at a large writing table and reading what appeared to be typescript. For the purpose, he was using a small electric torch, and he was wearing kid gloves.

The window was not fitted with a blind, neither was it guarded by curtains. Bony could make out the shape of a typewriter on a small table immediately below the window. He could see several cases of books black against the cream walls. On the writing table rested a kerosene power lamp.

Presently Wilcannia-Smythe pushed aside the typescript and rose to cross over to one of the bookcases. It was obvious that he was careful not to direct the beam of the torch towards either the ceiling or the window, and, arrived at the bookcase, he moved the beam to read the titles of the books on the several shelves. There were four such cases, open-fronted, and his torch beam crossed the back of every book in the four cases.

What he hoped to find was not among the books, and he began with the drawers at each end of the writing table. Methodically he went through the contents of drawer after drawer until he paused to examine a substantial note-book.

This he placed on the typescript and took no further trouble with the contents of the remaining drawers.

Bony thought then that the reason for Wilcannia-Smythe's clandestine visit was accomplished and that the fellow would leave. Instead, he went back to the bookcases, beginning with that nearest the door and passing from it to the next, where he selected a book and looked between its covers with his back to the window and the torch set at a useful angle on top of the bookcase.

Though Bony's mind was busy with surmises as to the whys and wherefores of this visit to a dead man's room when the dead man's wife was absent from home, and the one domestic away at the local pictures, there was still room in it to wonder how Miss Pinkney was enduring her vigil. Through the silent night came the noise of a laden timber truck and the comparatively musical humming of a car approaching from the direction of the city.

The timber truck passed on its way up the long hill. Its noise was diminishing and that of the car increasing until abruptly the car was braked and its lights temporarily illumined the lilac-tree along Miss Pinkney's fence, and stopped before Mrs Blake's front gate.

Somewhere among the lilac-trees a cat began to caterwaul. Bony decided that if the excruciating cacophony was being produced by Miss Pinkney, she was indeed an excellent animal mimic. The car was being driven in through the gate, and almost immediately the lights swung right, were masked by the house, and then were reflected by trees growing behind the garage. The engine was switched off. The cat was working up to a perfectly rendered feline love-song.

Strangely enough, Wilcannia-Smythe evinced no consciousness of the caterwauling or of the arrival of someone at the house in a car. He showed no perturbation and continued with his reading of the volume he had taken from the bookcase.

Bony was compelled to divide his attention between the man inside the writing-room and the person who had arrived. The alleged cat was continuing its uproar, and then was joined by a second cat. The duet made a realistic sound record of hell, but if Wilcannia-Smythe heard it, he took no notice. The book apparently had captivated all his mind.

A light was lit in one of the rooms off the rear veranda, the white light of a kerosene pressure lamp. The cook had probably returned with a friend, Bony thought, until he recalled that the car had come from the direction of the city and that the cook had gone to the pictures at Warburton, in the opposite direction.

The feline love song continued unabated and with extraordinary verve. A door of the house was opened, and after a period of three seconds was slammed shut. That sound brought Wilcannia-Smythe from out the pages of the book. He came swiftly to the window. He must have seen the light in the house, for now he moved rapidly and with precision.

The wad of typescript he folded and slipped into an inside pocket. The note-book went into the same pocket. The reading glasses were swiftly removed and almost jammed into their case and the case into a side pocket. He went back for the torch and switched it off one second after Bony saw a handkerchief on the desk.

Bony crept to the corner of the building and waited. He was in time to hear the door being opened. Then came the sound of the key being placed into the lock, and the door finally closed gently with the key, preventing the lock making any sound.

Bony drifted noiselessly back along the wall, passing the window, stopping only when he reached the rear corner where he went to ground and turned up the collar of his coat and screwed his eyes so that their whites could not show. In this position, he saw the black form of Wilcannia-Smythe against the sky as it moved away from the writing-room to the lawn.

Wilcannia-Smythe was engulfed by the night and Bony waited a full minute before he proceeded to walk over the lawn towards the house. He was mid-way across it when the cats ceased their imitation of a torture chamber. He was at that side of the house nearest Miss Pinkney's fence when the car engine broke into its murmur of power and, hurrying forward, he was in time to see it being driven into the garage.

Its lights, reflected by the far wall of the garage, faintly illumined the driveway and the front of the house, and his keen eyes searched the scene for the presence of Wilcannia-Smythe and failed to discover him. Then the car lights were switched off, a door banged, a torch was switched on and he saw the figure of a woman walking to the doors, which she proceeded to close and lock.

There was no cause for doubting that she was Mrs Mervyn Blake. Had Mrs Blake returned unexpected by Mr Wilcannia-Smythe? It seemed obvious that she had.

Aided by her torch, Mrs Blake entered the house by the front door, closing and locking it after her. Cautiously Bony walked on the fine gravel of the driveway to the garage side of the house and proceeded along that side to where the light from the unmasked window laid a brilliant swathe across the path.

Mrs Blake was inside watching the lighted spirit heat a primus stove. She was hatless, but was wearing a light coat. Her description matched that given of Mrs Blake in the police summary. The spirit died, and she pumped the stove, placing on it a tin kettle. Then she left the kitchen and Bony waited.

The night was utterly quiet. He continued to wait, his eyes roving the dark garden and his ear attuned to catch the least sound indicative of the presence of Wilcannia-Smythe. He saw nothing and heard nothing. Presently steam issued from the kettle and shortly afterwards Mrs Blake appeared and made tea. She placed a cup and saucer on a tray, added a jug of milk and a basin of sugar, and departed.

Bony reasoned that if Mr Wilcannia-Smythe was a guest and was inside the house Mrs Blake would have placed two cups and saucers on her tray. A few seconds later she entered the kitchen again, this time to turn out the lamp. Bony decided to return to Miss Pinkney and allay her curiosity with a partial outline of what he had seen.

Without difficulty, he found the hole in the division fence.

Once inside Miss Pinkney's garden, he walked along the fence to the banana case. Miss Pinkney was not there. He called her name, softly, and received no reply.

The rear of the house was in darkness. On going round to the front he was astonished to see no light in any of the rooms or in the hall. He passed up the steps to the veranda, crossed it to the front door, and found it wide open. In the doorway he stood listening. He could hear the ticking of the grandfather clock in the dining-room, and the faint ticking of a smaller clock distant in the bowels of the dark house.

With matches, he lighted his way to his bedroom where he found his torch. With that to help him, he went from room to room calling Miss Pinkney's name, not hesitating to enter even the bedroom she occupied. He became most uneasy. Miss Pinkney was nowhere in the house. Mr Pickwick was; Bony met him in the passage.

CHAPTER FIVE

The Amateur Sleuth

HAVING found out the mechanism of the ship's lamp and lit it, Bony occupied a chair on the front veranda and rolled a cigarette. Miss Pinkney's disappearance was extremely odd, for she had promised to remain at the fence until he rejoined her.

When at the expiration of five minutes Miss Pinkney was still absent, he left his chair and took the path to the rear fence. He recalled that she had been wearing a dark-grey suit and light stockings which, he knew, would be easily distinguishable if he came across her body.... It was by no means likely, but still ...

On reaching the banana case, he proceeded along the fence to the gap through which he had entered the garden next door, and then onward until he came to the corner of Miss Pinkney's garden that was roughly in alignment with the rear veranda of the Blake's house. Beyond that corner was a vacant allotment.

The lamp was still alight in the room opening on the rear veranda, and had not the disappearance of Miss Pinkney become a matter of urgency, he would have taken a second walk round the house that evening. He returned to the banana case and as far as the opposite corner without finding any trace of his landlady.

Back again on the front veranda, he was met by Mr Pickwick. The cat wanted to be friendly, and he followed Bony from room to room when the second search was made. The grandfather clock chimed the hour of nine, and he decided that if Miss Pinkney had not returned at ten o'clock, he would call on Constable Simes.

She returned about ten minutes to ten, alighting from a car that came from the direction of Warburton and continued towards Melbourne. She came trippingly along the crazy path from the gate, and did not see him until he spoke.

"Oh! There you are!" she cried, the current of excitement in her voice. "Come along in. I've something to tell you, something terribly interesting."

When he reached the door of the lounge, she was lighting a standard lamp.

"Now you sit here and make yourself comfortable," she ordered. "I'm going to the kitchen to brew a pot of tea, and I'll cut some sandwiches, and we'll sit here and have our supper and gossip over our adventures."

"Why not allow me to go with you to the kitchen?" he suggested. "I like having supper in a kitchen. I always do at my own home. My wife says that it saves sweeping up the crumbs."

"Oh!" Miss Pinkney stared at him. "So you are married. Well, well! Let's go to the kitchen. Where is your home?"

"Johannesburg," he answered, and stepped aside to permit her to proceed from the lounge.

Arrived at the kitchen, she exclaimed, "You've been here before! Why light the hurricane lamp? Why not the table lamp? It gives so much better light."

"I lit the hurricane when I came here looking for you," he said, lightly. "You deserted your post, you know."

She pushed paper into the stove and kindling wood on top of that. Casually, she dashed kerosene into the mixture and fired it. To the accompaniment of flame roaring up the chimney, she filled a tin kettle from the sink tap. Not a word in answer to his charge until the kettle was on the stove and she had seated herself at the table. Then out came the cigarette-case and the lighter he had repaired.

"Offer me a cigarette, please, Mr Bonaparte, and then tell me all that you did and saw."

"First of all I would like to know why you left the fence," he said, his voice firm but his eyes beaming. He held her lighter in service, and because her mind was so crammed with memories she omitted to thank him.

"Well, when you crept through the fence, I went back to the banana case," she began, at first slowly, regarding him steadily across the table. "I could see nothing at all, not even you, and I couldn't even see a light in Mr Blake's room. I could hear nothing either, except timber trucks and Mr Pickwick moving about somewhere in the trees.

"Oh, my poor legs and ankles! I thought of rushing back to the house for the citronella, and then I remembered I had promised you to keep watch. I'm sure I scratched ladders in my stockings." She slewed herself sideways and stretched her legs, keeping her body between them and Bony. "No, I haven't. It's a wonder, though. Anyway, I was being a terrible martyr for your sake when I heard a car turn off the main road and then saw its lights sweep round before it stopped at the Blake's front gate.

"That will be Mrs Blake, I thought. When she comes in through the gates the light will shine along these lilac-trees and maybe the writing-room and on you. So I mimicked Mr Pickwick to give you plenty of warning. When I saw the light go on in the living-room, I wondered why you didn't come back. I kept on caterwauling, and presently, as I knew he would, Mr Pickwick joined in. He can never bear with my caterwauling. Either it's such a poor effort or it's so realistic he thinks it's a lady cat."

Miss Pinkney paused for breath and a lungful of smoke. She was thorough in everything she did.

"Well," she proceeded, "there were Mr Pickwick and I singing to each other, and we were still at it when I heard what I thought was you coming back along the fence, and on the other side, too. I stopped my caterwauling, but Mr Pickwick kept it going and I heard a voice that wasn't yours say, 'Stop your screaming, you little bitch'.

"I very nearly fell off the case, and I might have, too, if I hadn't been holding on to the fence. Instead of climbing through the hole in the fence, this person clambered over it by holding to the branch of a lilac-tree. He dropped down on my side and passed me so closely that I could have kicked him. I just saw him taking the path towards the house, and I thought if he thinks he is going to burgle my home I'll let him see that it can't be done.

"So I hurried after him. Then, just before I could reach the kitchen door, I saw him at the front gate in the lights of an approaching car. He closed the gate, and I rushed to it and was in time to see him walking down the road. He was Mr Wilcannia-Smythe."

Again she paused for breath. Rising hastily, she crossed to the stove on which the kettle was now boiling. Having made the tea, she left the pot beside the stove and returned to Bony, saying, "I followed that man all the way to the Rialto Hotel, which is this side of Warburton and three miles away. I'm sure he never saw me, not once. I saw him walk through the gateway and along the short drive to the terrace, and I saw him walk up the steps to the terrace and there talk casually with several of the guests before he went inside. The terrace is brilliantly lit, you know. He must be staying there. He wasn't wearing a hat or anything. He couldn't be Mrs Blake's guest now, and I can't understand why he didn't stop and meet Mrs Blake instead of sneaking over my back fence to get away from her. What did you see?"

"I watched him reading one of Mr Blake's books," replied Bony. "When he saw that Mrs Blake had returned, he left hurriedly and I lost him in the darkness. His behaviour is very strange. Er—don't you think the tea is brewed now?"

"Of course! How silly of me." The subject of the tea, craftily introduced, placed a brake on her interest in his adventures. She spread a cloth and proceeded to cut sandwiches, while she ran on and on in circles after a solution of the mystery.

Presently he said, "Did you see much of the Blakes?"

"Quite a lot, Mr Bonaparte," she answered, and laughingly added, "over and through my back fence. Oh dear, Mr Pickwick! Please be patient one more minute." The cat "mirrilled" and almost tripped her on her way back from the stove with the teapot. "I'm afraid I've spoilt Mr Pickwick. Don't you spoil him, too, Mr Bonaparte."

"I'll try not to," Bony promised. "Did the Blakes entertain much?"

"A great deal. They had a house party at least once a
month."

"Well-known people, I assume?"

"H'm I suppose so."

"Did you see evidence of too much drinking?"

"Oh no! No, nothing like that."

"You never overheard any quarrelling?"

"No, never. The Blakes were excellent hosts, and their
guests were always well behaved, though they were literary
people and artists and radio announcers and that kind. Now
this tea ought to be ready. And time, too."

"Shall I pour?"

She looked swiftly into the blue eyes, smiled, and might
have giggled, but didn't.

"If you like," she assented. "Plenty of milk for me. I'll
clear away the bread and things. I wonder if Mrs Blake's
cook did go to the pictures. I think she did. I'm certain the
picture bus stopped at the corner."

"If she went, what time would she return?"

"About half past eleven. We'll hear the bus coming up
the hill, and I'll slip out to the gate and see if she gets off it.
Dear me! My hair must be a sight." She flew to the mirror
hanging behind the kitchen door. "Why didn't you tell me
it's all upsidaisy?"

"I didn't like to," he confessed, chuckling. "It looks quite nice
as it is, anyway. Have you read any novels by Mervyn Blake?"

"No. I don't care for Australian novels. I borrowed one of
Wilcannia-Smythe's just because I saw the man in the next
door garden. It was all about the bush, you know, and gum-
trees and things, but the characters were just too terribly,
crashingly boring. He's frightfully clever, you know. At least
the paper says he is. I like a book that tells a story—you
know, books by Conrad and John Buchan and S. S. Van Dine."

"There was a Mr Marshall Ellis staying with the Blakes
when he died. Did you see him?" Bony pressed, and Miss
Pinkney almost snorted.

"He was English," she said. "And a big lout of a man. Mr Blake spoke through his adenoids. Mr Wilcannia-Smythe spoke like a Canberra trickster. Mr Lubers spoke like an Oxford man. And Mr Marshall Ellis spoke like an—like an angel. But, oh my! He had a face like a Manchester bargee."

Bony chuckled and helped himself to another sandwich.

"We are getting along famously, Miss Pinkney. Permit me to compliment you on the art of cutting sandwiches. What about the ladies who were at that last house party?"

Now Miss Pinkney did giggle. She said, "The Montrose woman reminded me of a picture I saw of Marie Antoinette going to the guillotine. Talks with grapes in her tonsils like some of those women on the screen. Used to make eyes at Mervyn Blake. Anyway, that didn't matter much because when the Spanish gentleman was staying there he used to ogle Mrs Blake and they'd walk arm in arm about the garden."

"Indeed! Do you think there were any marital differences between the Blakes?"

"No, I think not," Miss Pinkney replied slowly. "You see, the Blakes and their friends appear to be people who were too much in love with themselves to have any capacity to love anyone else. The Miss Chesterfield who stayed there the night Mr Blake died had often stayed with the Blakes. She's on a newspaper or something. I wish—" Miss Pinkney sighed, and then went on, "I wish I could dress as she does. I wish—but I mustn't be stupid. Hark! That's the picture bus coming. I'll run."

Bony heard her hurrying along the passage, and helped himself to another sandwich. Nowhere in the official summary did Miss Pinkney's name appear, and he wondered if her name was also absent from the official file still waiting to be read by him. He heard the bus pass the house and then stop at the corner, heard it go on. Half a minute later Miss Pinkney returned to say that Mrs Blake's cook had alighted from the bus; she had recognized her by the hat she was wearing.

CHAPTER SIX

Bony Seeks Collaboration

THE police station at Yarrabo was situated at the lower end of the straggling settlement, and the officer in charge was tolerant but efficient. His interests were few and sharply defined. Outside his official duties he had three loves, his daughter, his garden, his painting. From the front veranda one had to bend back one's head to look up at the summit of Donna Buang.

There was a picture in oils of Donna Buang, as seen through the policeman's eyes from his front veranda. The picture was a little distracting to Bony, who was seated opposite the constable.

"Anything I can do, sir, to help I'll be delighted. I assume that you read my report, among all the others, on the Blake case."

Constable Simes spoke quickly, crisply. If he was yet forty, his face belied it. He was large, hard, fair, blue-eyed and round-jawed. He was impervious to Bony's examining eyes.

"I read the entire official file on the Blake case before I went to bed at four forty-five this morning," Bony stated, as though giving evidence. "Reports and statements, however, are limited to facts, whereas the summary provides a few assumptions based on the known facts. When you and I have to make a report, we confine ourselves strictly to facts as we think we know them. When a person makes a statement, he also sticks to facts—unless he has reason to give false information. Strangely enough, the majority of cases successfully finalized have rested on the ability of the investigator to prove facts from assumption. Care to work with me?"

"Yes, certainly, sir."

Simes said it with official stiffness, and now Bony smiled, and all the little stirrings of hostility towards the Queenslander vanished from the constable's mind.

There was genuine happiness in Bony's voice when he said, "Good! Let me explain a few points that will assist us in getting together. Firstly, I am not a policeman's bootlace. We have the authority of my Chief Commissioner for that, and he is a man of astonishing acumen. Now and then, however, he does admit that I am that paradox, a rotten policeman but a most successful detective. I am glad to hold the rank of inspector only on account of the salary.

"My present task is to reveal how Mervyn Blake came by his death. No one knows that, and the medical experts seem to have agreed that he died from natural causes. I am here simply because your own C.I.B is snowed under with work, and Superintendent Bolt doesn't want the case to grow too cold. He asked me to keep it warm for him, believing it would interest me—which it does."

He lit the cigarette he had been making and again smiled. Simes looked at the cigarette, and wanted to smile.

"I would like you to banish two things from your mind," Bony went on. "The one is to forget that I am an inspector, and the other is to forget to call me 'sir'. I want you to be entirely free in your attitude to me, because I want your collaboration off the record as well as on it. I want you to have no hesitation in expressing assumptions and presenting theories, not because I want to use you up, as the current expression goes, but because if you are able to be free with me, you will, doubtless, provide valuable data which you would not do did you continue to regard me as an official superior. I have all the known facts. Now I want your opinions, your assumptions, your suspicions. Do you get it?"

For the first time, Constable Simes smiled.

"You make it easy to collaborate—er—er—"

"Bony. Just Bony. Now I want to ask questions. Ready?"

"Go ahead," Simes invited, and then added, "Of course, not remembering what you asked me to forget, I am permitted to smoke?"

"Naturally," agreed Bony. "You see already how well it works. No stiffness, no official barriers. Well, to begin. How long have you been stationed here?"

"Slightly more than nine years."

"Happy here?"

"Yes. I like these mountains and the people who live among them. I was born at Wood's Point. I went to school there, and for six years I worked among the timber."

"Like promotion?"

"Of course. It's overdue."

"It's habit with officers who collaborate with me to gain promotion," Bony said, seriously. "You do that painting?"

Simes nodded, saying, "Yes, but I'm no artist. Several real artists have told me my work shows promise, and they urged me to study. But I paint to amuse myself, and some day I may have the chance to study."

"Not being an artist, I think it a fine picture of Donna Buang. What do you know of Miss Pinkney?"

"Nice old thing," Simes said, and Bony was glad he had succeeded in getting behind the policeman's official façade. "She and her sea-captain brother settled here in the early thirties. He was a bit of a tartar, and he didn't approve when she fell in love with a timber faller. My sister knew him. Despite the captain's ruling, they were to be married, when he was killed at his work. Miss Pinkney's never been the same since, and when her brother died she stayed on and lived alone. You are her first paying guest. Treating you all right?"

"Better than a paying guest," Bony asserted warmly. "Does she associate with the locals?"

"Oh yes. Attends church and works for the Red Cross. I believe my sister is the only real friend she has. There's a particular bond of sympathy between them, as my sister's husband, who was a forestry man, was caught in the fires of '38."

"M'm! Makes a difference. I understand that she didn't like Blake because he threw stones at her cat."

Simes chuckled. "She told him he was the illegitimate

44

offspring of a shanghaied drunk. She told him that if he threw one more stone at Mr Pickwick, she would get through the fence and kick his face down to his backside."

"Dear me!" murmured Bony. "I would never have believed it of Miss Pinkney."

"I understand that she used once to sail with her brother, who owned his own ship."

"Was the unpleasantness about the cat the reason the Blakes were never friendly to her?"

"Not the real reason. They would not associate with anyone here at Yarrabo. They stood well with the local store and garage, and Mrs Blake often subscribed to the vicar's various funds. But that was all."

"Mrs Blake subscribed? Not Mervyn Blake?"

"Mrs Blake's name always appeared in the vicar's lists."

"Tell me more," urged Bony. "Tell me from the time they came here."

"They bought the property slightly more than two years ago," Simes proceeded. "They managed to get the place renovated and that writing-room built despite the chronic shortage of materials. It took—"

"Did they find the money for the purchase or was the purchase financed?"

"I'm afraid I don't know that," admitted Simes.

Bony made a memo.

"We will establish the point," he said. "Go on."

"Well, what with the scarcity of materials and the shortage of labour, the work took something like five months," Simes continued. "After it was done, they began to entertain, having several people staying over the weekend, and sometimes having a house party for a week or more. The visitors were mostly literary people, I think. Very often they were mentioned in the papers, according to my sister, who reads the social pages."

"M'm! Did you ever contact the Blakes?"

"I spoke to Mrs Blake several times. She owns the car. Seemed all right to talk to, but wouldn't relax, if you know what I mean. She might have been different had I been an inspector, or a sergeant. Blake himself was supercilious. Had a high opinion of himself. Spoke as though I were the village constable and he the squire." Simes grinned. "Might go down in England, but not in Australia."

"He was English, was he not?"

"Yes. Came to Australia shortly after the First World War —at least, I think so. I'm not quite sure about her."

"She was born in Melbourne," Bony stated. "Do you know the reason why they came here from Essendon?"

"Yes. Blake suffered from gastric trouble. I have the idea that the trouble was eased by the change."

"You have the idea!" Bony echoed.

"Yes, only that. I think my sister spoke of it."

Bony made another memo.

"He seemed to be quite well?" was his next question.

"Quite. Used to walk a great deal. Swung along as well as I. He was a well preserved man. In fact, I was surprised when I learnt he was fifty-six."

"He didn't look the suicide type?"

"He did not."

"The post mortem revealed that he suffered from stomach ulcers. Also that his heart was not strong, and that his system was saturated with alcohol. Not one of these conditions is thought to have been responsible for his death. Neither is it thought that all three in combination could have been responsible. The Government Analyst was puzzled by the condition of the dead man's liver and other organs. Did you know that?"

"No," replied Simes.

"Very well. Let us assume that you did know the Analyst's confidential report. Does it support any theory you have that Blake was murdered?"

Simes regarded Bony steadily for a full three seconds before he answered the question in the affirmative.

"I've always thought that murder was most likely," he added.

"On what grounds?"

"On something that Inspector Snook would not accept

seriously," Simes answered, a dull flush stealing into his face.

"I noted that the date of your report was five days after the date of Blake's death. Blake died on the night of 9th November. It is now 4th January. Since you wrote that report you have had opportunity to review all the data you then set down, and also to review your opinions held during those vital five days, opinions you did not express in your report but doubtless did express to Inspector Snook, eh?"

"No, I expressed no opinions, Bony. I was not invited to."

"In fact, you were discouraged from giving opinions. Well, having met Inspector Snook on another case, I can understand that. Now tell me what you did, saw, and heard following the summons by Dr Fleetwood. Relate your reactions, your own opinions. Forget that I have studied your official report. Light your pipe and let your mind relax. Begin with the weather that morning. I suppose there are more murders and suicides influenced by the weather than the detectives wot of."

Simes smiled slightly and relit his pipe.

"I can begin with the weather easily enough," he said. "It had rained the night before, and I was very pleased because the garden was suffering from a long dry spell. The morning that Dr. Fleetwood rang me was bright and, compared with the previous day, cool. I reached Blake's house about ten minutes to nine that morning, and I went straight in as the front door was open. Dr Fleetwood was in the hall waiting for me. Also in the hall were Mrs Blake and a woman I knew subsequently as Mrs Montrose. Both were crying.

"The doctor led me through the house to the back veranda, where there were several people, then down to the lawn and so to the writing-room. The door was closed. I saw that there was no handle and that it was fitted with a Yale lock. The doctor took a key from his pocket and opened the door, which I then saw opened outwards.

"Blake was lying with his head almost touching the door when it was closed. He was dressed in pyjamas. I stepped over the body and the doctor came after me and reclosed the

47

door. He spoke for the first time and said, 'There's something about this affair, Bob, that I don't like.'

"The doctor and I have been a little more than acquaintances for several years," explained Simes. "He told me that when he reached the house he was met by a guest named Wilcannia-Smythe who stated that when Blake didn't turn up for breakfast at eight twenty he went out to the writing-room. Finding the door closed and being unable to open it because of the lock, he knocked twice and received no answer. Then he went round to the window, which was also closed and fastened, and looking through it saw Blake lying just inside the door.

"He returned to the house and asked the maid if there was another key to the writing-room, and she gave him a spare key, which she took down from a hook in the hall. Wilcannia-Smythe then collected another guest named Lubers, and together they went to the writing-room. Wilcannia-Smythe opened the door. Neither went in. First one and then the other tried to rouse Blake and found that he was dead. They then shut the door and returned to the house where they told Mrs Blake and advised sending for the doctor.

"The doctor reached the house shortly after eight forty. He was taken to the waiting-room by Wilcannia-Smythe, who remained outside the building while the doctor made his examination. The examination didn't take more than two minutes, and immediately after it, the doctor left closing the door, and he and the guest went back to the house where Fleetwood telephoned to me.

"All that," continued Simes, "was what the doctor told me after he and I had entered the room and he had closed the door. Then he told me that he had given the dead man a thorough overhaul six weeks previously, and had found him quite fit, except for stomach ulcers, which were drying up. He was very doubtful of the cause of death and said he'd be unable to sign the certificate until he had made an autopsy. That, however, was not the reason why he called me, and he asked me to stand by the window and see if I could see what he had seen and still saw.

"I did as he suggested. The room was not in great disarray, and there was no evidence of a struggle. The dead man's clothes were folded neatly on a chair, and over the back of it hung his dinner jacket. The bedclothes were normal. On the writing desk was a kerosene pressure lamp, a glass jug that had contained milk and a glass that had also contained milk. There was a bottle of brandy almost half full and another glass, and an empty dry ginger bottle. In addition there were several books and papers and the usual appointments. There were four bookcases against the walls, and a couple of chairs, and a typewriter on a table. There was no wardrobe or any other bedroom furnishings other than the bed. Over the floor was thick wall-to-wall felt covering.

"At first sight it appeared that Blake had been taken ill during the night and had got as far as the door when he collapsed. He was lying in a partial huddle, the top of his head and his right shoulder about five inches from the bottom of the door. His left arm was under his chest as he was lying almost completely face downward, and his right arm was bent as though his last effort had been to raise himself. He had been slightly sick.

"I saw several distinct scratches on the paintwork of the door. They were low down and on the outer edge. When the doctor saw me looking at these marks, he told me they had been made by the dead man's fingers. The fingers of the right hand were badly lacerated when he tried to get out of the room and was too weak, or in too much pain, to reach up for the lock.

"I couldn't see anything else of significance. Not for a minute or two, anyway." Simes chuckled. "I'm only an ordinary policeman, not a trained detective. The doctor wouldn't help me, and so I went on staring at this and that, until I saw that the felt inside the closed door was damp. It was so damp that I must have been blind not to have noticed it before. The colour of the felt was rose and the wet place was much darker. The rain the night before had beaten in through the door to a limit of about fifteen inches, and on this wet patch lay the dead man's head and his shoulders and right arm.

"I went over to the corpse and knelt beside it. The hair at the back of the head was damp, and the collar and upper part of the pyjamas. Then I saw that under the body the carpet was quite dry. I could follow the edges of the dry place without moving the corpse and thus see that the rain had beaten in through the open door after he had died.

"I asked the doctor if he were sure that the guest had told him the door was closed when he went to call Blake for breakfast, and Fleetwood said he was sure. He asked him the second time about it when making the examination, and the guest asserted again that the door had been shut.

"The doctor asked me then if I worked it out as he had done," proceeded Simes. "I wasn't sure what time the rain had begun, because I went to bed about half past eleven the previous night. I knew that it had stopped when I got up that morning at six, and that it hadn't rained after I got up. So the rain on the dead man's head and shoulders and on the carpet must have fallen before six o'clock. I said, 'After Blake was dead, someone came into this room and stayed for at least a minute before going out again and shutting the door'."

CHAPTER SEVEN

Human Reactions

"That's very interesting," Bony said. "But there's nothing about rain on the floor in your report or in the summary provided for me."

"I spoke of it," Simes said levelly, "because you asked me in a decent manner to collaborate, and because I'm sure you won't regard me as a liar or a damn fool. It was like this.

"I went through the dead man's pockets and found his keys, one of which fitted the door. I got the other from the lock where the doctor had left it. I told Dr Fleetwood that I'd have to report to headquarters, which I did, and the result was that the homicide crowd didn't arrive until a quarter to twelve. They were in no hurry, because I wasn't in a position to report that Blake had been murdered.

"Inspector Snook was in charge and they were accompanied by a surgeon. Everything then proceeded according to routine. The photographer did his stuff as I was making my verbal report, backed by the doctor. The doctor then went into conference with the surgeon and they moved the dead man from the floor to the desk. I had told the inspector about the rain falling on the dead man and the felt, and told of what seemed to me the obvious theory about it, but Inspector Snook was sarcastic because by then the wetness had dried out of the floor covering. When Dr Fleetwood corroborated, he was told that the obvious explanation was that Blake in his last gasp had managed to open the door and push it wide, that the door had remained open for a little while until a gust of wind had slammed it shut.

"Such was Inspector Snook's attitude that Dr Fleetwood would say no more about it, and I went dumb. The doctor

51

wouldn't undertake the autopsy. The finger-printer dusted the entire place. There were plenty of finger-prints on the glass milk-jug and the glass that had contained milk, but the brandy bottle and the glass used to drink the brandy bore only the prints of Mervyn Blake.

"Subsequently the doctor and I talked about the wet floor and the rain on the dead man, and we discussed the inspector's theory that Blake himself had flung open the door and then collapsed, and the wind had slammed the door shut.

"It so happened that the doctor was called out to an accident that night shortly before twelve. He did not get home again until two. At half past two he was called to a confinement. He says that the rain began about midnight. It fell in showers until shortly after four o'clock, and at no time during the night was the wind gusty or even moderately strong.

"Just before we left the building—I to make my report— we both swung the door out and in several times, to test the theory about the wind, because the inspector's theory had then occurred to us. We found that the door was not properly swung. In fact, when the catch of the lock was free, its tendency was to swing open."

"Very, very interesting," Bony murmured. "The accident that took the doctor out that night—was it in the open air or inside a house?"

"It was a bad car accident. He was out in the rain from first to last. The police at Warburton had charge of it, which is why I wasn't called out, too."

Simes loaded his pipe, regarding Bony with moody eyes.

"A day before the inquest, Inspector Snook called here. He told me that the post mortem had proved nothing, no poison, no other cause for Blake's sudden collapse. He said also that Dr Fleetwood had stated that when he overhauled Blake several weeks before his death he found him to be physically sound, including his heart. Then he said that the post mortem had revealed that Blake's heart was not in a healthy condition, and added, 'That shows how these country doctors can make errors. Dr Fleetwood made one error about Blake's heart, and can therefore make another error about that door being opened by a murderer. An efficient policeman, Simes, doesn't permit himself to indulge in imagination—only facts.' "

Simes shrugged his broad shoulders, saying with finality, "That was that. Now I am wondering just how you came into it."

Without hesitation, Bony said, "Because, my dear Simes, Superintendent Bolt does indulge his imagination. Have you considered likely reasons why anyone should enter Blake's room when he was dead?"

Simes shook his head and confessed that, in view of the medical evidence, he had racked his brain without result.

"Don't continue to rack it," Bony urged. "Let's try in our respective spheres to find evidence that will lead us to the reason, or reasons, why that person entered the writing-room after Blake was dead. Now for other matters. We have had Snook's reactions and the doctor's. Let's examine the others, beginning with Mrs Blake. On entering the house that morning you found Mrs Blake and Mrs Montrose crying. Did you note the exact degree of Mrs Blake's distress?"

Simes did not at once speak. He was thrusting his mind away from a wet section of felt and an open door, and the rain pelting in through the door-frame, to this other scene, and at the same time noting the altered demeanour of the suave and affable man who had asked him to forget rank and title. Bony's dark face was stern.

Simes said, "Mrs Blake was seated on a chair in the hall, and Mrs Montrose was standing close beside her. Mrs Blake was dabbing her eyes with a handkerchief, and she was softly sobbing."

"Was it a clean handkerchief?"

"Yes. It appeared hardly used. The ironing creases were still evident."

Bony's brows rose a fraction and he smiled faintly.

"When you saw her again was she still crying? You did see her again?"

"Yes, I saw her again when I told her I would have to

report the death of her husband to headquarters," Simes replied. "She was still in the hall with Mrs Montrose."

"The handkerchief?"

"It was a little wet ball. Oh, Mrs Blake was genuinely upset, there is no doubt about that."

"Naturally, Simes, she would be upset. Now for Mrs Montrose. How was she behaving? Tell me—exactly."

"When I first saw her, she was just standing beside Mrs Blake and allowing the tears to run down her face unchecked. She was not standing when I saw her the next time, and she wasn't crying."

"You've got a good memory, Simes," Bony said. "And the artist's gift of observation. It should take you a long way. After you contacted your headquarters, you sought out every guest and the domestic staff and warned them not to leave the house. You took a statement from everyone. All that you put in your report, but into your report you did not put your private thoughts concerning the impressions they made on you. We've been studying the reactions of others, now let's have your personal opinions."

"If you think it's important—all right," Simes assented.

"Everything is important, even the most trivial occurrence or the most casual remark. Now for all the persons you met inside and outside the Blake's residence. Wilcannia-Smythe discovered Blake dead. Begin with him."

"All right, I'll see what I can do," agreed Simes, and for a little while regarded the wall behind Bony's back. Then, "Wilcannia-Smythe betrayed no emotion. He spoke precisely. He might have found a hundred dead men before he found Mervyn Blake. The man with him, Martin Lubers, was agitated. He seemed to me more natural than the other man, for after all most of us would be upset under the circumstances. The third man was Twyford Arundal, who lives in Adelaide—small, scented, a thorough twerp. Three years in the army would do him a great deal of good. He was anxious to tell me that after he had gone to bed he did not leave his room until Lubers called him with the news that

Blake was dead. Then Marshall Ellis, from England, and Miss Chesterfield.

"These two were on the back veranda. He was smoking a cigar, she was writing on a letter pad. You will recall that Miss Chesterfield is a journalist. She was nervously taut, understandable in a journalist on a probably good story. Good looker, but direct in speech and manner. Ellis was impatient when I asked him to tell me about himself, as though he were a personage to be questioned by no one lower than the Chief Commissioner. A surly brute."

"Excellent, Simes, excellent," Bony cried delightedly.

"Mrs Montrose would make a good tragedienne. She's the type who is happiest when able to give vent to emotionalism—Mrs Blake is different. She would fight the wind instead of bending to it. That's all, except for the two domestics.

"The cook's name is Salter. I don't know her personally. She came from the city. Her husband is with the Forces in Japan. Struck me as being a good type. The maid is a local girl. Name of Ethel Lacy. Parents soundly respectable. She's a bit of a gadabout, but otherwise O.K. She was engaged by Mrs Blake for the duration of the house party, and it was not for the first time."

"Good looking, I understand."

"Very. Knows it, and can take care of herself. I've often thought that, rightly handled, she could tell us quite a lot about the Blakes and their guests."

"We'll keep her in mind," Bony said, and added slowly, "It's a lovely case, one of the most attractive ever to come to me. No gore, no blood-stained knives, no pistols and sawn-off shotguns, and, apparently, no poisons. Man dies and no one can find out what killed him. Was apparently on excellent terms with wife and guests, and also with the domestic staff. By the way, was there any other domestic—chauffeur, gardener, or such?"

"No. A local jobbing man has been employed there for a day now and then. Man by the name of Sid Walsh. Whisky soak, but harmless. You'll probably meet him soon. Miss Pinkney asked me to tell him she wanted him for the day."

"Sid Walsh," repeated Bony. "I haven't come across his name before."

"Likely not," Simes said. "He wasn't working for the Blakes anywhere near 9th November."

"H'm! Did you know that Wilcannia-Smythe is staying at the Rialto Hotel?"

"I did not."

"I have reason to believe that he is. Could you ascertain when he booked in?"

"Yes, of course. I know the manager. Shall I ring now?"

"Please do so."

Simes was talking to the manager when Bony, having lit another cigarette, leaned back more comfortably in his chair to study the picture of Donna Buang. Only when the telephone rattled down on its stand did he bring his gaze back to the policeman.

"Wilcannia-Smythe booked in at the Rialto Hotel on 2nd January," Simes reported. "That was the day before yesterday. He told the manager he'd be staying for a week or ten days, and had come to Warburton to gather material for a book."

"Probably not important to us," Bony said. "Miss Pinkney mentioned that she happened to see him enter the place yesterday. You know, I wish I could write a novel, or paint a picture. Is your sister at home?"

Astonished, Simes said she was, and Bony then said, "I'd like to talk with her. D'you think she would mind?"

"Not a bit."

"D'you think she would accept me as her brother-in-law?"

The astonishment in the constable's eyes waned and there waxed gleams of humour.

"Might," he conceded. "Will you come inside to the sitting-room?"

"Thank you, Simes, I will. I'm in the mood to gossip, and I see that it's time for morning tea. Don't you suggest it, though. Leave that to me."

CHAPTER EIGHT

Mrs Farn's Reactions

THE large picture was of a forest of giant trees, white and dead and ghostly. In all his travels about Australia Bony had never gazed upon a scene similar to that presented by the brush of Constable Simes. The trunks rose from a floor of low green suckers, rose with the smooth gleam of marble columns for two hundred feet or more, thrusting out and upward white skeleton arms in mute appeal towards a cobalt sky. Ten years previously they had died by fire.

Hearing footsteps at the door, Bony turned to meet a woman who entered the room followed by Constable Simes. She was small, plump, and immaculate in a blue house frock. Her hair was black, as were her eyes, and because her complexion was sallow and she wore no make-up, her eyes were a startlingly dominant feature. Simes introduced her as his sister.

Her face was expressionless until she smiled in accordance with Bony's smile when he made his little bow. Then it became remarkably alive.

Bony said, lightly, "Once I prevailed upon your brother to forget for the nonce that I am an inspector, we thoroughly enjoyed a chat about people in whom we are interested. I expect he has told you I am staying with Miss Pinkney and Mr Pickwick?"

"Yes, he has," replied Mrs Farn. "He tells me that you wish to ask me a few questions. I shall be glad to help you, if I can. Would you like a cup of tea? I've just made it."

Bony looked at Constable Simes and laughed. Mrs Farn also laughed, and said that her brother had no secrets from her. She went away and Bony turned to the picture, asking, "Where is that scene?"

"In the Cumberland Valley out beyond Marysville," Simes replied. "When I was there two years ago I took a series of photographs from which I painted the picture."

"Don't let anyone tell you you can't paint," Bony murmured, engrossed by the scene of stark death. "Are there many trees like that?"

"There must be a hundred thousand in the Cumberland Valley alone," asserted Simes. "Nineteen thirty-eight was a tragic year. A number of people, and at least a million trees, died in the fires. Please don't forget that my sister's husband died then."

"I haven't forgotten. Tell me about that door. Why was it made to open outward?"

"Well, the place was built with unseasoned timber," Simes said. "The demand for timber for houses was, and still is, so great that seasoned timber is unprocurable. A door could not be built, and so one of the inside doors was taken and fitted to a frame made by the carpenter. After a week or two the building warped and the door could not be made to open over the thick felt laid on the floor. Because the door is of excellent quality and is intended to be returned to its original frame when a door can be bought for the writing-room, it was decided to reverse it to swing outward. That's the explanation I received from Mrs Blake."

"Did Blake always sleep with the window shut?"

"No, very seldom. It is thought that after Blake retired from the house, he sat in his room drinking brandy and dry ginger for some time before going to bed, and that when the first shower came he closed the window."

"Yes, a reasonable explanation. Ah, here is Mrs Farn with the tea. Mrs Farn, you are very kind. I confess that had your brother not suggested tea I would have done so."

Mrs Farn said, "My brother is always suggesting tea, and he couldn't resist the temptation of suggesting it first this morning. Do you take milk and sugar?"

"Milk, thank you. Sugar, no. Not with three growing boys to support, and the eldest at the University having most expensive tastes. I gave up my sugar, but conditions are going to be excessively tough before I give up my cigarettes."

Simes begged to be excused and took his cup and biscuits to his office, and Bony almost at once got down to his questioning.

"I assume that you know almost as much as your brother about the Blake case," he said over his cup. "The lack of evidence and the absence of any motive for either suicide or murder creates extraordinary difficulties. To make it even harder for me, there's the lapse of nearly two months since Mervyn Blake was found dead. However, I must make a beginning, and it seems the only way to do that is to get beneath the surface and dig up bits and pieces of the puzzle in order to prove whether Blake was murdered or not, and, if he was, who murdered him.

"I must begin at the beginning, and the beginning is not when Blake died but some time before he died—days, weeks, months before that night he died. Well now, your brother and I were talking about Mervyn Blake's health. He said that he understood from you that Blake benefited by the change to Yarrabo."

"I know nothing definite," Mrs Farn confessed. "I recollect that he was ill for about a week. Now let me think. It was when the first strawberries came in. I was in the fruiterer's shop buying two punnets of strawberries when Mrs Blake entered. We were at the nodding stage, you know, and I asked her how she was keeping, and she said she was very well, but that Mr Blake was in bed with a bout of his old trouble. She said, too, that he used to suffer terribly from stomach ulcers, but that since coming to Yarrabo he had been ever so much better. You don't think—"

"Don't you," warned Bony. "You must not let the trend of my questions make you think I have any thoughts about the case. I am like a city policeman on his beat at night— testing doors." Abruptly he laughed, adding, "You see, it's the only thing I can do. I find Miss Pinkney a very charming woman. You have known her for some time, your brother informs me."

"I knew her before she came to live here with her brother."

"There was a tragedy, I understand?"

"Yes. She was engaged to marry a man who was killed by a tree." Mrs Farn regarded Bony with steady eyes. "He was a fine man, a Norwegian. He had straight dark hair and eyes like yours, and they said he could fell a tree within an inch of the line he chose. The giants of the forest fell to his axe and saw, and one day a giant killed him."

Bony nodded in sympathy, and she went on, "He was caught by the backlash on his last trip into the mountains. They were to be married and he was to take charge of a mill quite close by. Priscilla was always a happy woman, always delighted by simple things. She wasn't particularly strong in character, but everyone overlooked that because of her joyousness in living. She was never the same again, after he was killed."

"Yet she gets along very well by herself."

"Oh yes. After her brother died she wanted to withdraw herself from the local world, but I stepped in then and prevented it. You see, we have much in common. My husband perished in a forest fire."

"Indeed!" murmured Bony.

"The forests and the trees take their yearly toll," Mrs Farn said steadily. "The pity of it is that the men who die in the forests are real men, the salt of the earth. My man was strong and a good tree faller, but Priscilla's man was the king of the fallers."

"Now all she has is her cat," Bony said matter-of-factly.

"Yes, Mr Pickwick is father and mother and husband and brother to her. She became eccentric after her sweetheart was killed, but her eccentricities are without harm."

"I find them charming," Bony asserted. "Did you ever visit the Blakes?"

"Oh, no. I think I might have got closer to Mrs Blake," Mrs Farn paused and pinched her lip. "I received the impression that she was a woman who wanted to be friendly with everyone and yet could not forget her husband's importance."

"Was he important—so very important?"

"Well, he wrote books, you know. His name was often in the papers."

"H'm, yes, I understand that was so, though, living in Queensland, I read nothing about him to fix him in my mind as an important person. I am afraid that I am not *au fait* with literary people, and it does seem that now I must become familiar with them. I understand that Mervyn Blake was a critic as well as an author, and of late years had been much more a critic than author. Do you read novels?"

"Plenty. And I am very fond of poetry."

"Ah!" Bony sighed, and yet his eyes twinkled. "I detest poetry produced after Tennyson died," he confessed. "One of Blake's guests was a Mr Twyford Arundal. He has been described to me as a puny little twerp. From the reports on the case compiled by the C.I.B. I gain the impression that he managed to keep himself much in the background. I wonder if you happen to know anything of him, saw him when he stayed with the Blakes, heard anything concerning him?"

"He was in love with Mrs Blake," Mrs Farn said.

"Is that so?"

"Yes, indeed. Priscilla Pinkney used to see them walking in the garden late in the evenings," Bony's hostess smiled swiftly. "One of Pris's little failings is a tremendous curiosity in her neighbours, especially the Blakes and the people staying with them. She's not a gossip, you know. Never one to make mischief, and I do believe she never told anyone but me what she saw and heard beyond her fence."

"I am strongly inclined to believe that, too, Mrs Farn," Bony said earnestly. "I like your Priscilla Pinkney, and through her I am going to get right into the background of that night Mervyn Blake died. There were, you remember, six guests, Blake and his wife, and the cook and the maid. Can you tell me anything of the cook, Mrs Salter?"

"Quite a respectable woman."

"Yes, I have been informed on that point. I mean can you tell me what your impressions are of her, assuming that you have met her?"

"I haven't met her," Mrs Farn said. "I have heard of her."

"What of the maid, Ethel Lacy?"

"I know her and her parents. Hard-working girl but a little frivolous." Mrs Farn paused to consider. "Ethel has always worked in neighbouring guest-houses and hotels. She likes to be among people. I fancy she liked working for the Blakes when they had guests. In fact, she told me that she was sorry she had to leave them."

"Where is she now?"

"Working at the Rialto Hotel."

"Have you ever been there?"

"To the Rialto? No."

"Would you give me the honour of having afternoon tea there with me this afternoon?"

Mrs Farn's eyes betrayed doubt, but Bony hastened to add, "I should like to see this Ethel Lacy—and another person, a Mr Wilcannia-Smythe. If you accompanied me, I could pretend to be an old friend. I suppose we could hire a car for the afternoon?"

"Ye—es."

"The proposition does not appeal?"

"Oh, it's not that," he was assured. "You see, the suggestion takes my breath away. The Rialto is a fearfully expensive place." Mrs Farn smiled and then laughed. "Thank you. I shall be delighted to go. I've always wanted to."

"Good! I'll call for you at—let me see—half past three?"

"Yes, that will do."

Bony pondered, gazing at his feet.

"I did think of asking Miss Pinkney to come along, too, but perhaps—no. Not this time. You might know other people there whom you could point out to me. You see, Mrs Farn, I haven't as yet been able to get my mental teeth into this case, and I've got to start somewhere. I may get the start at the Rialto. I may get the start during a conversation with Miss Lacy, and I rather think that an entrée through you would be of assistance. If you could claim me as a relation, now. I am not precisely unpresentable. I could be your brother-in-law on a visit from South Africa."

CHAPTER NINE

Beau Bonaparte

THE Rialto Hotel is built on a lower slope of Donna Buang, and from the vantage of its magnificent terrace the visitor may look over the tree-lined river and the Valley of the Yarra to the gum-clothed Baw Baws. At Christmas and at Easter the place is full to capacity with people who prefer pocket wallets to bank accounts in which to slip extra profits, but in the first week in January it is possible to lounge on the terrace over the teacups without being overwhelmed by vulgarity.

Mrs Farn and Bony arrived in Constable Simes's car and strolled up the white front steps to the spacious terrace fronting the entire building. There were some forty people seated at tables near the low stone balustrade, and, notwithstanding the paucity of visitors this afternoon, the scene was gay with red and white striped sunshades, the colourful frocks of the women and the almost equally colourful ensembles of the men.

A magnificent major-domo welcomed the arrivals with a bow and broken English, and conducted them to a table, where, unnecessarily, he re-arranged the chairs. They were admiring the remarkable view when a waitress in black, relieved with white apron and cap, reached them with afternoon tea.

The waitress said, "Good afternoon, Mrs Farn."

Half turning, Bony looked at her. She was an attractive red-head.

"Good afternoon, Ethel," Mrs Farn said, brightly. "I was hoping you would serve us."

"I saw you come up and so I put myself forward to serve."

She took careful note of Mrs Farn's escort, from his sleek

black shoes to his sleek black hair, with the pin-striped grey suit in between. She gazed with calm inquiry into the clear blue eyes, and at the straight nose and the finely-moulded mouth. She was twenty-nine according to the records, and Bony thought it remarkable that she had successfully evaded marriage. He liked her voice.

"This is my brother-in-law from South Africa," Mrs Farn said, having been coached on the trip from Yarrabo. "I wanted him to see the Rialto and the view. He's staying at Miss Pinkney's cottage. Have you been busy over Christmas?"

"Very. We had three hundred and sixteen for Christmas dinner," replied Ethel Lacy. Her interest in Bony, however, did not wane, and she could not forbear to probe. "You come from South Africa, sir? What part?"

"Johannesburg," Bony lied. "I am on the *Johannesburg Age*, and I've come to this country to visit my late brother's wife and to gather material for a series of articles and perhaps a novel or two."

"Oh, a writer!" Red-head was impressed. It was obvious that she wanted to linger with them, but she had noted the look of disapproval on the face of the major-domo that a member of his staff should be familiar with the patrons. With a rustle of starched clothes, she departed, and Mrs Farn began to pour the tea.

"Did I do it rightly?" she asked.

"Superbly, Mrs Farn," he told her, smilingly. "I am sure, even thus early, that I am going to fall for her. She will be worth my broken heart, and my wife's amusement when I tell her. Can you see Mr Wilcannia-Smythe on the terrace?"

Mrs Farn's dark eyes went into action, and without a hint of the conspirator, she examined their fellow guests.

Then, "He's sitting on your right—three tables away—with a blonde dressed in blue. The man with the white hair."

"A beautiful position," Bony remarked loudly. "A magnificent view, indeed. It was a happy thought to come here."

He moved carelessly so that he could examine the man with the white hair and the beautiful blonde he was entertaining. She was laughing and he was presenting his open cigarette-case.

Forty-two was his recorded age. His hair was snow-white and worn over-long, sweeping back from the broad forehead in leonine waves. His eyes were hazel, and at the moment were regarding his companion with light mockery. It was an extraordinary face, but without the strength that should have been there in accordance with his hair and the shape of his head.

"Yes, a restful place, indeed," Bony went on, and added softly, "D'you know the woman?"

"I'm sure I've seen her," replied Mrs Farn, two vertical lines deep between her eyes. "How vexatious!"

"Perhaps the Lacy girl would know," Bony suggested.

"Yes, she might. I'll try to attract her attention."

"Do. Is there anyone else here you recognize, and in whom I could be interested?"

Mrs Farn once again surveyed the company, the frown still deep between her eyes. This suddenly vanished, and she said, "Yes. Mrs Mervyn Blake is coming up the steps."

Beyond Wilcannia-Smythe and his friend, Bony observed the widow of the dead author, and his first impression was one of slight disappointment. It puzzled him why this should be, for she was dressed in a natural linen frock, wore smart shoes and stockings, and her abundant hair was correctly groomed. Wearing neither hat nor gloves, she appeared as though she were staying at the hotel. She was still handsome, still graceful as she walked from the steps towards the main entrance to meet the major-domo.

To him she said something and the man nodded and spoke, but with what he said she disagreed, shaking her head with sharp protest. The major-domo then conducted her to a table at the back of the terrace near the main entrance.

"I'd like another cup of tea," Bony said.

The major-domo seated Mrs Blake and beckoned to a boy uniformed in white. He gave an order and the boy sped away into the building. He took Mrs Blake's order and stalked to an alcove of palms where waitresses not engaged waited to serve. Neither Wilcannia-Smythe nor his companion—if she knew Mrs Blake—was aware of that woman's entry on to this stage. The boy issued from the building carrying a blotting pad and note-paper, which he set down before Mrs Blake. She proceeded to write with a silver stylograph. When the waitress reached her with the tea things, she was slipping the note into an envelope and looking round for the boy.

Under cover of light conversation with Mrs Farn, Bony watched the little play with profound interest, his insatiable curiosity sharpened. The waitress set out the tea things and the boy stood back with the envelope on a salver. People left their tables and drifted away, and others were conducted forward by the magnifico. The boy came forward, weaving between guests and tables. When almost at their table, he turned towards Wilcannia-Smythe and his friend, and they heard him say, "For you, sir."

Wilcannia-Smythe looked at him and then at the note proferred on the tray. Bony expected to see surprise registered on his face when he saw the handwriting, but Wilcannia-Smythe's smiling face indicated no recognition. He spoke to his companion, obviously begging to be excused, opened the envelope and read the contents. She looked away and towards Mrs Farn and Bony, but not quickly enough to meet his gaze.

Wilcannia-Smythe slipped the note into a pocket and asked again to be excused, saying something that changed her expression. She nodded, and he rose to follow the boy, and Bony noted that he walked with the easy grace of the dancing master.

"Please get that waitress again, Mrs Farn," Bony said urgently.

Having crossed the terrace, Wilcannia-Smythe stood before Mrs Blake. His back was towards Bony, but a man's back can reveal much, and the straight and narrow back of Mr Wilcannia-Smythe revealed his suave greeting. Mrs Blake smiled frostily and waved her hand in invitation to him to be seated. He sat with his back to Bony, which was unfortunate.

The blonde in blue was undisguisedly perplexed, her eyes puckered, her left hand nervously teasing her handbag. No longer did she smoke with any evidence of enjoyment.

The distance between Mrs Blake and the unobtrusively watching blue eyes was not less than eighty feet, but every shade of expression, every movement of the dark brows, and the slight trembling of hands were noted. She was talking rapidly and she was not in a pleasant frame of mind. The light was reflected by her glasses in dots and dashes. The white head of the man she was addressing seldom moved save now and then to indicate dissent.

Had he been a lip reader, Bony could have followed what Mrs Blake was saying. Mrs Farn's voice had become a gentle sound against the babel of over-loud voices. He had not forgotten the honey blonde and he regretted that he could not keep both her and Mrs Blake under observation. Mrs Blake had to have priority.

Mrs Blake was becoming positively angry, and repeatedly Wilcannia-Smythe was shaking his head in denial of what appeared to be accusations. Then the red-headed waitress was standing between Mrs Blake and himself, and Mrs Farn was asking for another pot of tea.

"Who's the girl who was with Mr Wilcannia-Smythe?" asked Mrs Farn. "Don't look that way. She might think we are talking about her."

"Oh, her! That's Miss Nancy Chesterfield."

Nancy Chesterfield! Bony covertly regarded the blonde. Nancy Chesterfield, indeed! One of the six guests staying with the Blakes that night he died. She was the woman who had accompanied Blake from the literary meeting to the hotel lounge, and from the lounge to his home in his car.

"I think she's the loveliest woman I've ever seen," the waitress declared softly. "She knows how to dress, and that's a gift, not an art. Wonder why that Wilcannia-Smythe left her to talk to Mrs Blake? Funny Miss Chesterfield didn't go over there as well. Must be something up. Mrs Blake's in a real tantrum. I must go. See you later, perhaps."

Mrs Blake was fumbling in her handbag. Her face was

coloured by emotion, and her eyes maintained their gaze on Wilcannia-Smythe. The hand groping in her bag seemed to be energized more by unrestrained anger than mental direction, because the result was delayed a full minute. Eventually she produced a handkerchief. It was a man's handkerchief. She held a corner of it towards Wilcannia-Smythe. He became perfectly still, until after Mrs Blake had dropped the handkerchief on the table near him.

The watchful Bony thought it probable he was now seeing the light. The very last thing he had observed inside Blake's writing-room before Wilcannia-Smythe had switched off his torch was a handkerchief lying on the writing desk. That was a white handkerchief, and so was this one produced from Mrs Blake's handbag. If it were the same then it could be assumed that Mrs Blake had discovered it on the writing desk, that it bore Wilcannia-Smythe's initials, and that, believing he had entered the building unknown to her, she had examined her husband's possessions and missed the typescript and the note-book. Now she was demanding an explanation; most likely she was demanding the return of the note-book and typescript.

The fresh pot of tea was brought and Bony had to withdraw his attention from the play. He heard Ethel Lacy remark to Mrs Farn, "I don't think they hit it off very well when he was staying there. He's a mealy-mouthed, sarcastic devil whose face I'd like to slap. He was pretty thick with the Montrose woman and Mervyn Blake."

She drifted away and Bony asked Mrs Farn what had led to the statement.

"I asked her what she thought of Mr Wilcannia-Smythe, and that's what she said," replied Mrs Farn. "I think Miss Chesterfield is going to leave."

"H'm! Interesting, Mrs Farn, most interesting. Please go on talking. I think the subject was chickens. Thank you. Yes, I will take another cake."

Once again stealthily observing Mrs Blake and the white-haired man, Bony saw that he was now standing and that the handkerchief was no longer lying on the table. Had not the interruption come, he might have been certain that Wilcannia-Smythe had taken possession of the handkerchief, instead of merely assuming that he had done so. Mrs Blake was now looking appealingly at Wilcannia-Smythe. Her mouth was trembling, and her hands were betraying her emotion. Wilcannia-Smythe sat down in the chair opposite to her, thus enabling Bony to see his face.

He began to speak, his face devoid of emotional stress, the manner in which his lips moved denoting deliberate speech. He spoke for at least two minutes, Mrs Blake regarding him intently. Then abruptly, he rose and stood smiling down at her, made a little bow of finality and walked unhurriedly, not back to Miss Chesterfield but to the main entrance of the building. When he had gone, Bony's gaze returned to Mrs Blake. She was biting her nether lip, and her left hand resting on the table was spasmodically clenching.

From the corner of his eyes, Bony saw something in blue rise up. The gorgeous Miss Chesterfield floated across the terrace to the front steps, daintily went down them, walked like Venus across the open space to the car park and there entered a smart single-seater. Its engine burred, and slowly Miss Chesterfield drove down to the highway and turned citywards.

"She'll be furious, being left like that," said Mrs Farn. "I know I'd be."

"My wife often is," Bony averred, absently. "Let us wait for the curtain. Will you have a cigarette?"

Mrs Farn declined to smoke. Mrs Blake was writing a letter, and Bony proceeded to talk of Johannesburg, where he had once stayed for a week. Mrs Blake covered one sheet of the writing pad and began on the second. She covered that, half filled a third, folded the sheets, and placed them in an envelope, which she addressed. A stamp was obtained from a little book in her handbag. That done, she rose and made her way to the post box at the top of the front steps. Two minutes later she also left, driving a car.

"Well, Mrs Farn, that was a very nice interlude," murmured Bony. "Thank you so much for bringing me here. We must come again. It has been most enjoyable."

CHAPTER TEN

The Debunker

IT was seldom that Bony felt the need of advice, for he was master in the vast pastoral lands and the semi-deserts of inland Australia. But he was experiencing the need when lounging on Miss Pinkney's front veranda on the morning following his visit to the Rialto Hotel, for now he was moving in a world in which he was not master, a world of human sophistication in a settled community.

It is often extremely difficult to bring to a successful conclusion an investigation of a plain case of homicide. Nevertheless, in every such case there is the body of the victim to announce the cause of death, be it by bullet or blunt instrument, by knife or poison. In effect, Superintendent Bolt had said, "A man named Mervyn Blake died suddenly one night. The medical men cannot tell us what killed him, only that he appears to have died from natural causes, as most of us die. Still, I've got a hunch that someone put the skids under him. My men have done their stuff, and they can't produce any likely motive for murder."

Bolt's men had tackled the circumstances surrounding Blake's death with the relentless efficiency of modern scientific detection. They placed under their microscopes much more than the dead man's viscera and under microscopes of a different kind they had placed the dead man's widow and his guests and his household staff in their search for a motive for murder.

There must be a motive for homicide unless the killer is an utter idiot. There was no evidence that Blake had committed suicide; in fact, the evidence of his death was opposed to the theory of suicide. And for all their probing, the Victorian

C.I.B. under the redoubtable Inspector Snook had not been able to unearth one fact that would lift the finger of suspicion against any person.

Inspector Snook had written the summary, and it revealed that Inspector Snook had reached the opinion that there was no proof whatsoever that Mervyn Blake had died illegally, and that being so, he did not believe Blake had been murdered. Superintendent Bolt, on the other hand, thought he smelled homicide. He was not satisfied to pigeon-hole that material gathered and, perforce, placed it in cold storage, and so in a spirit of friendship, he offered to take the case out of cold storage and give it to Bony to smell. And Bony smelled blood.

It is one thing to smell blood and another thing to find it. The only way to locate it in this Blake case was to discover a motive for killing Mervyn Blake.

Bony felt rather than knew that there was a something deep below the surface that Snook had not troubled to search for because he did not know it existed. To understand the stage, one must go behind the scenes and study the mechanism of the theatre, and Bony felt that to understand the profession of authorship and those who practised it, it would be necessary to delve and burrow into the lives of living writers and critics of literature to ascertain how they ticked.

Coming against this Blake case, he came to a world with which he was absolutely unfamiliar. How to gain entry into the world of literature inhabited by the Blakes and their friends was becoming a problem to Bony—until he remembered Clarence B. Bagshott.

Clarence B. Bagshott lived on a mountain top, and Bony had once accompanied him on a swordfishing trip to Bermagui, since when they had exchanged letters at long intervals. It had not been Bagshott's mystery tales but his feet that had gained Bony's interest in the man. His feet were exceptionally large, and the boots on them became professionally important in a case known as "The Devil's Steps". Inclined to call a typewriter a blood-drenched stone-crusher,

Bagshott had no guile, very little culture, and the vice of exaggeration.

Tall, lean and hard, middle-aged and active, Bagshott welcomed Bony in the manner of the prodigal's father. Bony's left arm was gripped and he was propelled forward into the house, and into the writer's study where he was forced down into an easy chair beside the desk. A little breathless, he was left alone for five minutes, a period he occupied by making a number of his distinguished cigarettes, and then was presented with tea and cake, and urged to "relax, Bony, relax".

Bagshott grabbed a chair, dragged it into position, and added, "You're the very last bloke I expected to see, and yet—the pleasure's all my very own. How's things up your street?"

"Quite well. And you?"

"Oh, just so-so. I've got another five weeks, three days and—let me see—yes, and nine hours to go before starting off for Bermagui and the swordies. But I'm holding out with astonishing fortitude. My launchman learnt a new tip from an American angler. Remember how we used to let the bait and the flanking teasers troll about forty feet astern of the boat? The new dodge is to increase that distance to a hundred feet astern."

Bony sighed loudly, resignedly.

"Wish I were going with you," he said.

"What's going to stop you?" demanded Bagshott.

"Work, my Chief Commissioner, and all the circumstances that keep my nose to the grindstone, my dear Bagshott. I am even now using my annual leave to work for Superintendent Bolt."

"Referring to?"

"The late Mervyn Blake."

Bagshott grinned, his hazel eyes suddenly hard.

"I've had the thought that the passing of the great Mervyn Blake might attract you," he said. "Can I do anything?"

Bony nodded and lit another cigarette. He inhaled deeply, drank half a cup of tea and then exhaled before saying,

"An extraordinary case because of its lack of clues and the absence of any likely motive either for suicide or homicide. I am finding it delightfully absorbing. Bolt and his fellows got nowhere, and so far I'm not getting anywhere, either. Actually I've come to talk about personalities. Did Mervyn Blake ever criticize your books?"

"Mine! Lord, no! I don't produce literature."

"Then what do you produce?"

"Commercial fiction."

"There is a distinction?"

"Terrific."

"Will you define it, please."

"I'll try to," Bagshott said slowly. "In this country literature is a piece of writing executed in schoolmasterly fashion and yet so lacking in entertainment values that the general public won't buy it. Commercial fiction—and this is a term employed by the highbrows—is imaginative writing that easily satisfies publishers and editor because the public will buy it."

"Go on," urged Bony.

"Don't know that I can," Bagshott said, doubtfully. "Let's get back to the starting point. You began it by asking if Blake ever criticized my work, and I said no."

"And then you added that Blake did not criticize your work because you wrote commercial fiction," Bony pressed on. "On several occasions I have felt an immovable object. I am feeling it now. Also I am feeling the current of hostility in you towards Blake and his associates. Do you think it reasonable to assume that that hostility in another would be strong enough to produce the act of homicide?"

"No," was Bagshott's answer. "I'll tell you why I say no to that. The Blake-Smythe coterie in number is very small. It's influence a few years ago was powerful, but it's rapidly on the wane now. My hostility to it isn't engendered by what it is doing to the growth of Australian literature but rather by what it's done in the past."

"Did you ever meet Mervyn Blake?"

"Never. And I've never met Wilcannia-Smythe, either."

"Read any of his work?"

"Yes. The fellow's a master of words. His similes are striking, and he knows how to employ paradox. But he can't tell a story. Let me enlarge on that by comparing his work with mine. He has the mastery of words but not the gift of story-telling. I have the gift of story-telling but not the mastery of words. The great novelists have both gifts."

"I take it that Wilcannia-Smythe's work and that of Blake is judged to be literature."

"Without doubt."

"Judged by whom?"

"By the members of their societies and by those who have come to rely upon their judgment. But not by the general public."

Bony became pensive. He lounged farther down into his chair and gazed upward at an enlarged photograph of a marlin suspended from a triangle. Chalked on the body of the fish was the name Bagshott, and beneath it the weight in hundreds of pounds. Beside it stood the angler, an insignificant dwarf.

"Ah, me!" he exclaimed and, rising to his feet, he whipped out his breast handkerchief and draped it over the picture. Sitting down again, he said, "Damn the swordfish, Bagshott."

"Yes, damn everything. Another cup of tea?"

"Thank you. Just tell me what you know, and what you feel about the late Mervyn Blake and all this literature business. I might then see the obstacle I spoke of. I want to get inside these associates of Mervyn Blake, deeper than the police seemed able to do. If there are currents running strong and deep below the surface, tell me about them."

"All right, I'll blow the gaff and the baloney," Bagshott assented. "Let's remember that our civilization in Australia is young and still has many of the silly attributes of youth. The nation came to maturity during the First World War, and during the early twenties evinced a marked interest in the work of its authors.

"In 1918 or '19, Mervyn Blake came to Australia from England to join the staff of the local university, and his first novel was published in the early twenties. He and a few friends founded yet another literary society in Melbourne, and they became affiliated with a similar crowd in Sydney, of which Wilcannia-Smythe was the leader.

"They barged into the few magazines and the city dailies as literary critics, and they boosted each other's novels no end. They caught the public interest in Australian stories at the crest, and the public bought heavily on their say-so. Alas, the public found itself with second-rate novels and, quite indignantly, said, in effect, that if this was literature, it would have nothing to do with it.

"It wouldn't, either. Immediately a bookseller or librarian offered an Australian novel, he was almost rudely told to keep it. For years public hostility to Australian fiction remained steady. The Blakes and the Wilcannia-Smythes persisted. They went on and up in the critical field. In the production field they have gone down and down despite all the mutual backslapping.

"In the early thirties, several men and three women forged ahead as novelists. They cut right away from the gum-tree and rabbit-oh era and presented Australia as she is. They—and the Australian public—were extremely fortunate that in every capital city there were some independent critics who were not novelists with an axe to grind and who were not at all respectful of the Blakes and the Wilcannia-Smythes.

"Today, the Blake-Smythe faction is still influential," Bagshott went on. "It's fascist or communist in its close preserve. You are either a member and wear the halo of genius, or you are an outsider, to be ignored or condemned to writing commercial fiction. However, quite a considerable number of Australian authors are doing very well and gaining recognition in England and America.

"There is, for example, I. R. Watts. The Blake-Smythe crowd have always been blatantly hard on Watts, but his books are selling very well overseas. If you want substantiation of what I've said, you dig him up."

"Met him?" asked Bony.

"Never. Don't even know where he lives. His publishers

will have his address, of course. You ask him this question—is there any possibility of internecine warfare within the Blake-Smythe combination? I don't regard that as improbable."

"I. R. Watts," Bony repeated. "Could you let me have one of his books to read?"

"Yes, I can. I have also a copy of Blake's last book. Take that, too. When you have read the first six pages of Blake's book you'll understand why the Australian public is hostile to Australian novels."

"But your books sell well in Australia, don't they?"

Bagshott grinned again, his eyes vacant of humour.

"Not as well as they would if the Australian readers hadn't been led up the garden path by the back-slapping critic authors," he countered.

Bagshott's hostility towards the Blake-Smythes Bony found to be an interesting facet. He accepted it with caution born of the knowledge that Bagshott was given to over-statement.

He said, "What do you know of Mrs Blake?"

"I saw her once and then didn't speak to her," Bagshott replied. "I think she's more ambitious than her husband was. Her art is the short story. She writes very well and the praise of her work by the Blake-Smythes is merited. Mrs Blake does a fair amount of public speaking, and she contributes a lot to literary periodicals in which she never fails to mention her husband's books."

"Thanks. What of Martin Lubers, the wireless man?"

"Heard of him, of course, but I know nothing about him."

"Twyford Arundal?"

"A poet. Limited outlook, but a good versifier."

"Mrs Ella Montrose?"

"Wrote a couple of good novels about twenty years ago. She's as full of repressions as a general is of bile. Husband died years ago. Nobody blamed him. She's this and that in a dozen literary societies. Does the book reviews for the *Melbournian*."

"A woman of many parts, evidently. Tell me about Marshall Ellis."

"Marshall Ellis! Read the classics less and the newspapers more. You shouldn't need to be informed about Marshall Ellis," chided Bagshott. "Marshall Ellis rose to fame by crudely insulting all and sundry, in print and out. Clever bird. Uses vitriol for his ink, and carbolic acid for a gargle. Tries to ape G.K.C. Came to Australia to study growth of our national literature, and even before he left England he was captured by the Blake-Smythe combination. During his visit here, he was never allowed to wander from the fold and, without doubt, he was thoroughly stuffed by his hosts. You can wipe him off. He was just a sucker who ate the pap fed to him."

"H'm!" Bony smiled. Clarence B. Bagshott hadn't changed a scrap since that memorable holiday at Bermagui. "Well, then, what of Miss Nancy Chesterfield?"

"Ha-a-a!" Bagshott got to his big feet and gently closed the door. Then he exclaimed softly, "What a woman! What a—a—woman! The very thought of her makes me frantic to cast off thirty years. A glorious creature, Bony, but tough. If you could persuade her to talk heart to heart you'd get something worth while. She knows all the self-crowned highbrows in all the arts, all the members of solid society, all the racketeers, and the black marketeers, all the gambling kings and sport barons. She even knows me!"

Bony's brows rose.

"I'm delighted to hear that," he said. "She is, I understand, a journalist."

"Edits the social pages of the Recorder. Writes personality pars on people who are tops," Bagshott went on. "One weakness only. She a valuable ally of the Blake-Smythes!"

"Could you obtain an introduction for me?"

"I could, Bony, old boy. But you hesitate. Be your age."

"I think she'd be interested in me," boasted Bony.

"No doubt of it. That's why I'm trembling for you. She is catastrophic to anyone having your sentimentality of heart. They talk about atomic blondes—Nancy is a cosmic blonde. She's got all the doings ten times each way, and why Holly-

77

wood hasn't snapped her up at a million dollars *per diem* beats me."

"I saw her the other day."

"You did!" exclaimed Bagshott.

"Yesterday, in fact. I'll need to remember my advanced age. Honestly, she would like to meet me. You see, I'm a South African journalist, a special writer on the staff of the *Johannesburg Age*. I'm visiting Australia to study the people and to gather material for a novel or two."

"You don't say!" Bagshott leaned back in his chair and laughed without restraint. Then, "I'll write the letter of introduction," he agreed. "But we must be careful. Nancy will be sure to check up on you by cabling the *Johannesburg Age*. You'd be sunk then."

"No, I don't think so," Bony calmly said. "Twenty-four hours before I presented your letter of introduction, I should myself prepare the editor of that journal with a message of enlightenment."

CHAPTER ELEVEN

Donation by Mr Pickwick

EARLY the wind swung to the north, and by nine o'clock the temperature was above normal and rising fast. Such a day as the morning promised could not be better spent than in lounging in the shade produced by the lilac-trees at the bottom of Miss Pinkney's garden.

Into this inviting shade Bony brought an easy chair, several books, and an easy mind. It was his own time, a day of his leave, and it was nobody's business how he spent it. He had not been seated five minutes when Mr Pickwick emerged from a gooseberry bush and laid at his feet the ping-pong ball.

"It's too hot to play ball this morning," he told the cat. "I wonder now why Miss Pinkney named you Mr Pickwick?"

Questions! Endless questions! Bony's life was a continuous effort to find answers to questions, all manner of questions. They were not unlike living creatures parading before him without cease. Some were aggressive, like "Who killed Cock Robin?" Others were languid fellows, such as "Why had Miss Pinkney named a cat Mr Pickwick?"

He was in no mood to seek answers to questions this warm morning, and yet could not withstand them. Why had Wilcannia-Smythe burgled Mervyn Blake's writing-room? Why had he taken away selected pages of typescript and a note-book?

Wilcannia-Smythe entered the writing-room that evening to obtain data he knew or suspected existed, but did not know in what form. Had he known in what form he would not have had to read the typescript and several pages of the note-book. That indicated that the things he took away actually belonged to the dead author and were not his own possessions that Blake had borrowed. And why the excessive caution in wearing gloves? There seemed to be no reason for that unless he thought it likely that Mrs Blake would discover and report the theft.

Mrs Blake had not reported the theft. Instead, she had gone to the Rialto and taxed Wilcannia-Smythe with the theft, producing his handkerchief in proof. The more clever they are, the more stupid the mistakes they make once they follow an unfamiliar path.

Convinced that a theft had been committed, the normal procedure to follow, in order to find out what data had been stolen, was to have Wilcannia-Smythe arrested and his possessions examined. That, however, would mean applying to Superintendent Bolt, for Bony could not act officially outside his own State, and he did want to reach the position of placing the completed case before Bolt, and thus putting one over the unpleasant Inspector Snook.

Then Nancy Chesterfield had not acted normally that afternoon on the terrace of the Rialto Hotel. She was in the company of Wilcannia-Smythe when Mrs Blake arrived. They had not witnessed her arrival; Mrs Blake had been met by the head waiter, of whom she had inquired for Wilcannia-Smythe. The head waiter, it was obvious, had told her that Wilcannia-Smythe was on the terrace with a lady, but he did not know the lady's name, because had he told Mrs Blake with whom Wilcannia-Smythe was taking afternoon tea, Mrs Blake would instinctively have glanced over the company to find her.

Mrs Blake had entertained Wilcannia-Smythe for a full week before her husband died, and probably often before that, and yet, following her appeal to him, was rudely left at her table. Instead of returning to Miss Chesterfield, Wilcannia-Smythe walked into the building. And instead of crossing the terrace and greeting Mrs Blake, Miss Chesterfield, who had been Mrs Blake's guest and was her friend, had quietly left and driven away back to the city.

H'm! Strange people.

Bagshott's several assertions might not be very much over-drawn. That he was given to over-statement, Bony was aware, but over-statement is not mis-statement. Were these writing people as altruistic as the public believed? Were these eight people now under review as friendly as the summary gave one to think? He was reminded of shops that have ornate fronts and frowsy backs. Was the Blake's house party but a façade behind which dwelt jealousy and hate and envy? Had disappointment, disillusionment, sickening sycophancy and greed for fame created the murder lust and released it?

Oh yes, the case was well worth his attention and the sacrifice of his leave, which ought to have been spent on holiday with his wife. In a day or two he would go to town and call on Miss Nancy Chesterfield with Bagshott's letter of introduction. That would be an experience, and probably a pleasant one, but he would have to mind his p's and q's, and meanwhile study some of this Australian literature, and swot up a few quotations.

He stretched and sighed. Sleep would have been preferable to the study of literature, but the character he was gradually assuming was going to be difficult to maintain. He had pretended to be a swagman. He had pretended to be a wealthy cattleman. He had even set himself up as an opal buyer, an insurance agent, and a drummer, and had once pretended with fine success to be an Indian rajah. He felt, however, that to pretend to be a South African journalist was going to take a lot of effort to achieve even moderate success.

"Ah well, Mr Pickwick, let's look into these damn novels," he murmured to the cat, who had stretched full length at his feet. "I'm sure it will be quite a task on a day like this."

In under ten minutes he was finding it so. Wilcannia-Smythe was unfortunate, for the day was distinctly hostile to his work, despite the smooth and balanced prose, the clever simile, the brilliant paradox and the rest. With boredom not wholly generated by the book, Bony read for an hour before forming an opinion. Without doubt the author was a brilliant writer, and equally without doubt he was a poor story-teller. He was able to lay bricks with the tradesman's proficiency, but he lacked the architect's vision of the mansion to be built.

The Bachelor of Arts said to the cat, "If that is first-rate literature, Mr Pickwick, my education was faulty."

With grim determination Bony picked up Mervyn Blake's last novel, published ten years before. The temperature in the shade was now in the vicinity of ninety degrees, and this was emphatically unfair to the dead author. Judgment, however, was delayed when, with vast relief, Bony saw Miss Pinkney emerge from the house carrying a tray of morning tea.

"Now don't you get up," she cried a moment later. "I've brought you a pot of tea and a few scones I've just baked. Only just a smear of butter, mind you, to recall that we were once civilized and had plenty. Oh, Mr Pickwick! There you are! I hope he's no trouble to you, Mr Bonaparte."

"On the contrary, Miss Pinkney, we are on terms of great affection," he assured her, accepting the tray.

"Now do sit down," he was urged. "I must rush back to the house because I'm running late. It's your fault for keeping me so late at breakfast this morning."

Bony smiled into the warm grey eyes, and because he knew it would please her he sat down and rested the tray on his knees. The cat staggered to its feet and came to rub itself against a leg.

"A day for tea," Bony said lightly.

"It is so, indeed," Miss Pinkney agreed, and then watched her guest remove the cup from the saucer, fill the saucer with milk, and set it down before Mr Pickwick. "You love animals, don't you, Mr Bonaparte?" she said.

"I certainly do," he averred. "Why, if I saw anyone throw a stone at our Mr Pickwick, I'd—I'd probably punch him on the nose."

The grey eyes instantly hardened and the wide mouth tautened.

"I'd try to," she said, barely above a whisper, and then abruptly turned back to the house.

Bony watched the angular figure in the neat print house

dress, frowned, and sipped his tea. Other questions came crowding forward for attention. He recalled that Miss Pinkney herself had told him she once spoke to Mervyn Blake for throwing a stone at her cat, had "remonstrated with him somewhat after the fashion of my brother".

Almost idly he looked at the division fence, and then at the loosely hanging boards where he had slipped through into the adjacent garden. Had Miss Pinkney ever gone through that hole in the fence? She was undoubtedly resourceful; the manner in which she had followed Wilcannia-Smythe to the Rialto Hotel proved it.

Perish the thought! He picked up *D'Arcy Maddersleigh* by Mervyn Blake, flicked up the cover, noted the titles of five previous novels, and began to read. The style was pedantic, the subject matter presented as factual history. He read three chapters before putting it down. If the fire of inspiration had ever burnt in the mind of Mervyn Blake it had died before he wrote that book.

"Must be the heat," Bony murmured to Mr Pickwick. "We'll look into *Greystone Park* by I. R. Watts. Dear me, I haven't worked so hard for many a long day."

He was still reading *Greystone Park* when Miss Pinkney came to the kitchen door and tapped on a small bronze gong to call him for lunch. He used an old envelope for a bookmark, and, putting the book down on the others, stood up, stretched, and yawned. The next instant he trod on Mr Pickwick's ping-pong ball.

He set his foot squarely upon it, and instinctively stopped the downward pressure of his shoe before the ball could be squashed flat. For a moment he looked down on the wreck, vexed with himself, for it would never bounce again to give joy to Mr Pickwick.

Thinking to take the ruined ball to his hostess with the ready promise to purchase another, he picked up the wreckage. It was crushed and split almost in halves. Within was a greyish powder, some of which was spilled on the ground. Carefully he picked up the broken ball and emptied a little of the powder into the palm of his left hand. It was light in weight and rough in texture. The amount of powder still within the ball might have covered a two-shilling piece. He emptied it into the envelope he had used for a bookmark, and the envelope he twisted securely and slipped into an inside pocket.

Did the manufacturers of ping-pong balls place grey powder inside them?

Another question to confront him and scream for an answer.

If ping-pong ball manufacturers put powder into them, then why?

CHAPTER TWELVE

A Couple of Locals

AFTER lunch, Bony returned to the shade of the lilac-trees and *Greystone Park*. Despite the heat, I. R. Watts got it across, for Bony found this book emotionally powerful and soundly written, the characters being clear and strong in their presentation. Watts was a born story-teller, restrained and therefore dramatic, humorous and therefore human. When Bony had read a third of the book he was determined to get in touch with this writer, for he was sure that the author of such a story would also be indisposed to over-statement as well as under-statement.

He was engrossed by *Greystone Park* to the extent of becoming oblivious to heat and annoying flies, but the world of historical romance into which I. R. Watts had inducted him was not proof against a lazy voice saying, "Some people has all the ruddy luck."

Bony looked up from his book to see a man leaning on a hoe not four yards distant. He was large and disreputable. There were pouches under his filmy eyes and purple lines criss-crossing his shapeless nose.

"It would seem so from your point of view," Bony said. "Who are you?"

"I'm the casual gardener around here. You a friend of Miss Pinkney?"

"Yes," Bony confirmed, and then added as though by an afterthought, "Warm afternoon."

"'Tis so. Good day to drink beer, but there ain't none. Good day for a smoke, too, but there ain't no tobacco. Things is crook all right. How do you stand?"

"For beer, no good. For a pipe of tobacco, fairly good."

The gardener shuffled towards Bony and held forward a huge and grimy hand for Bony's proferred tobacco tin. He helped himself generously and stuffed the finely shredded weed into the bowl of a broken-stemmed pipe.

"Thanks," he said, without meaning it. "What this ruddy country is coming to beats me. No beer, no tobacco, no meat half the time, and work all the time. It's 'When are you coming to my place?' and 'You promised to give me a day last week', and so on until I gets giddy picking and choosing who I'll work for." He lit his pipe, from which, in spite of the eternal shortage, dangled streamers of Bony's precious tobacco. "Everythink's short," he went on, becoming fierce. "Couldn't be anything else but short when we gotta pay for the politicians, thousands of 'em having holiday tours all round the ruddy world. What do they care for the likes—"

"So you help to keep other people's gardens in order, do you?" Bony cut in. "Earning good money?"

The gardener pulled at his pipe, puffed his cheeks and emitted a cloud of smoke.

"Pretty good," he replied. "I don't work for less than thirty bob a day and no Sat'day work. But what's the ruddy use? Them dopes in the city goes on strike after strike for more money, and about a week after they get the rise the cost of everything catches up with 'em and then they're still behind. Any'ow, what's the use of money when you can't get enough beer and got to scrounge for a bit of tobacco? We was all better off on a quid a week and unlimited beer and unlimited tobacco. What I says is—"

"How often do you work for Miss Pinkney?" inquired Bony.

"Whenever she wants me to," with a leer. "I never says no to Miss Pinkney, and I never said no to Mr Blake next door, when he was alive and kicking. For why? I'll tell you. Miss Pinkney always gives me a reviver just before I goes, just a little taste, sort of. I likes working for her sort. There ain't many of them around here. The doctor's all right, but, ah"—

and a sigh floated into the still air—"that Mr Blake was a bonzer bloke. He'd never see a man dying of thirst."

"Generous, eh?"

"Never failed. My name's Sid Walsh. What's yours?"

Bony told him, and Sid Walsh repeated the name, and said, "Seems familiar to me. Musta met you somewhere before. Lemme think."

"Don't. It's too hot. Is the Mr Blake you spoke of the author?"

"Yes, that's 'im," Walsh replied, expectorating with remarkable accuracy at a waltzing butterfly. "One of the best, he was. He'd come along sometimes when I was working in there and he'd gimme a wink, and that was the office for me to foller him, sort of casual like, to his writing-room or the garage where he'd have a bottle planted nice and handy."

"H'm! In the garage as well as his writing-room?"

"Too right, he did. Always kept a bottle and a couple glasses in a cupboard inside the garage." Walsh winked, glanced nervously towards the near-by fence, and went on, "His missus uster go crook at 'im for drinking, especially when there was no one staying there, and he'd have plants all over the place. But he was cunning, though. He never left the garage unlocked while I was working for him."

"And you have a little luck with the doctor?" remarked Bony.

"Oh yes, the quack's all right in his way. He tells me I drinks too much, and then when I'm knocking off and I tells him I'm all a-tremble with exhaustion, he takes me into his surgery for what he calls a tonic. It's tonic all right. The real McKay from Scotland. Cripes! There's Miss Pinkney looking at me. I'd better get on with my slavery."

Sid Walsh drifted back to his hoeing, and Bony took up *Greystone Park*. He found it easier to read than to meditate and the next intrusion came when Mr Pickwick sprang up the back of his cane chair and settled himself comfortably on his right shoulder.

"If you continue to kiss me, you'll have to get down," Bony told him, and went on reading.

The shade cast by the lilac-trees lengthened. The flies continued faintly to irritate the reader of novels. The gardener proceeded with his hoeing, and the third intrusion came when Miss Pinkney said, "Well, I never. Dr. Nicola, I presume."

"You refer to Guy Boothby's famous character of thirty years ago," he murmured, and then was on his feet with Mr Pickwick clawing for support and the book in his hands. Miss Pinkney had brought him afternoon tea.

"The same. You are the image of him, and Mr Pickwick is the very identical cat. But please don't date Dr Nicola—and me."

Bony put the cat down and took the tray.

"The inference cannot possibly apply to you, Miss Pinkney," he told her gravely. "Thank you for the tea. I'll bring in the tray later; I have letters to write."

"The post closes at five o'clock, remember."

"I will."

Miss Pinkney departed and Bony sat down. He heard her call to the gardener, "Walsh! Your afternoon tea is in the kitchen waiting for you. You don't deserve it because you've done very little work so far."

And then Walsh, "Sorry, Miss Pinkney, but me rheumatism is crook today. This kinda weather always plays hell with me joints." He staggered after her as though one foot were in the grave and the other almost in.

Bony smiled, and Mr Pickwick lapped milk from the saucer.

After another hour with *Greystone Park* Bony took the tray to the house and there wrote a letter to Superintendent Bolt, saying that he was picking up one or two threads of the Blake case and asking that the Editor of the *Johannesburg Age* be primed to counter the chance that an inquiry might reach him concerning a member of his staff, to wit Napoleon Bonaparte, now on holiday in Australia.

Having posted the letter and noted that the time was half past four, he walked on down the street with the intention of calling on Constable Simes. Simes was in the narrow front garden of the police station disbudding dahlias and, on seeing Bony approaching, he stepped to his gate, smiled in his broad and open manner, and said, "Having a look round?"

"No, I am hoping to pay a call on Dr. Fleetwood. D'you think he would be at home now?"

"Yes, almost sure to be."

"I wish you'd go inside and ring him and tell him that an important friend of yours is about to pay him a visit. Nothing more than that. I'll go along. His house is just round the bend, isn't it?"

"Yes. Only house there." Simes regarded Bony steadily. "Any developments?"

"Nothing, so far. I've been reading novels all day. It's been too hot to engage in my profession. When there are developments, I'll tell you of them."

Arrived at Dr Fleetwood's house, he was conducted by a maid to the doctor's surgery where he was met by a tall, stoop-shouldered, ascetic-looking man bordering on sixty.

"Slight, dark, blue-eyed—that's the police description and it fits you," he said with a mere trace of Scotch accent. "Sit down. What can I do for you? You don't look ill."

"Thank you, doctor. I am, in fact, remarkably well," Bony said, accepting the invitation to be seated. "I have not come to you as a patient but as a police officer engaged upon the recent death of Mervyn Blake."

When the doctor again spoke, the accent was more pronounced.

"Indeed! Well?"

Bony told him who he was and who and what he was pretending to be, before saying, "Inspector Snook, who had charge of the inquiry, apparently became satisfied that Blake died from natural causes. Superintendent Bolt, Snook's superior, is not quite so satisfied, and he prevailed upon me to see what I could do to satisfy him completely that Blake died from natural causes—or—or unnatural causes. Er—I have succeeded in gaining Constable Simes's confidence. I'd like to have yours, doctor."

The grey eyes were steady.

"Well, go on."

"Simes has also consented to collaborate with me," Bony continued. "So has his sister, whose brother-in-law I am supposed to be. Inspector Snook is an efficient and somewhat ruthless policeman. I was associated with him once and he then incurred a little debt I wish to collect. Perhaps you feel the same way?"

"Perhaps I do," and the thin lips barely moved.

Bony felt he was making no progress. Still he persisted.

"Having read all the data collected by Inspector Snook, I find that I cannot be as satisfied as he that Blake died from natural causes. My opinion is based partly on the circumstances surrounding the discovery of the body, and the evidence that led both Simes and yourself to believe that someone entered the room after Blake died and before he was found the next morning. Now, doctor, I'll be blunt. I want your collaboration."

The grey eyes narrowed.

"Very well, inspector, I'll do what I can to assist you."

"Thank you," Bony said, making no effort to conceal the satisfaction he felt. From a pocket he took the crumpled envelope containing the powder from Mr Pickwick's ping-pong ball. "I have here a substance that mystifies me. I want it examined and identified. I don't want to send it to the Victorian C.I.B. Would you analyse it?"

"I'll do my best," assented Dr Fleetwood. "If I do not succeed, I could send it to the University for analysis."

Bony unscrewed the envelope and proferred it to the doctor. Fleetwood looked closely at the contents and then rolled it slightly from side to side. He sniffed at it, wetted the ball of his little finger and thus carried a grain, or flake, to his tongue. Finally he picked up a magnifying glass and used that to look upon the powder.

"Peculiar substance," he said. "All right! I'll do my best this evening, or as soon as possible. You have no suspicion of what it is?"

"None. I came upon it by chance, and that it has any bearing on the Blake case appears at the moment to be fantastic. It might be, let us say, chalk from the downs of England, or heather from the Highlands of Scotland. It might even be dust from the western plains of the United States. It might be—no matter. I want to know what it is."

"Very well. I'll see what I can do to name it. Where are you staying?"

"I am staying at Miss Pinkney's cottage."

Dr Fleetwood smiled for the first time. "I'll wager that you've gained her confidence at least," he said dryly.

"Yes. I like her very much. In her way she is quite a character." Bony rose, smiled and added, "Another character I've met here is Mr Pickwick. I understand that Miss Pinkney gave Blake a tongue-lashing when he threw a stone at Mr Pickwick, threatened to change the position of his face to his—ah—posterior."

"Miss Pinkney is downright in everything she does and thinks," Dr Fleetwood said, and laughed. "A good woman, though. Genuine and all that."

"Have you any opinion of what caused Blake's death?"

The smile vanished from the lean features.

"Yes, an opinion based on a probability. His death was not caused by stomach ulcers, from which he had suffered for some time. His heart was sound, meaning that its condition was normal for a man of his years and manner of living. It seems probable that he ate or drank something which of itself is harmless and yet becomes a virulent poison when in contact with something else. For instance, strawberries are harmless and yet in some people strawberries will produce a violent upsetting of their health."

"Thank you, doctor. Did you visit Blake, or his wife, at their home?"

"No. Blake came to me for an overhaul."

"Well, thank you for giving me so much of your time. Please let me know through Constable Simes the result of your work on that powder, will you? And you will treat the subject of our talk with strict confidence, I know. Thank you again. I must be off. Tomorrow I have to meet a cosmic blonde. Have you ever met a cosmic blonde?"

"Cosmic?"

"Yes, cosmic, doctor. I understand that they are more dangerous than the atomic genus of the species."

CHAPTER THIRTEEN

The Cosmic Blonde

AT half past seven the following morning Bony boarded the train for Melbourne, and as this modern railroad wonder took more than two hours to traverse the forty miles, he had plenty of time to prepare for the interview with Nancy Chesterfield.

Having dawdled through morning tea, he arrived at the offices of her newspaper at half past eleven. He expected to be shown into a cubby-hole of a room, or a vast space covered with reporters in shirt-sleeves either writing furiously or yelling for boys. He found Miss Chesterfield seated in a most luxurious chair on the far side of a magnificent writing desk littered with a hundred and one odds and ends. On the floor was a thick carpet. The room was a fit setting for the jewel of a woman occupying it.

"Good morning, Mr Bonaparte," she said, offering her hand as one accustomed to welcoming all who have, or may have, news value. The letter of introduction he had withheld in favour of his card, and his vanity was fed by the belief that his name had paved the way to her presence. She studied him for a fleeting instant before saying, "I've seen you before."

"Strangely enough, I have that same impression, Miss Chesterfield," he told her, making his famous bow. "I'll try to recall where whilst you're looking at this letter addressed to you by my friend, Clarence B. Bagshott. I trust I am not occupying your most busy minutes?"

"Of course not. Sit down. Cigarette?"

"Thank you."

"So you are a friend of Clarence B.," she said, accepting

the letter and smiling at him, clever enough to put the smile into her remarkably lovely eyes, but not to hide from him that her welcome was professionally cautious.

He refrained from looking at her as she read Bagshott's letter. She might be tough, as Bagshott had said, and he had most likely not exaggerated, but to Bony this morning she did not look tough or even brittle. He sensed a keen brain, and was confident he could match it with his gift of intuition and his mastery of guile. He felt her power, and judged that to be not only the power of sex but, in addition, the power of the successful in a chosen profession. That was akin to the power he himself possessed, and so he was not perturbed.

"Where, Mr Bonaparte, did we meet?" she asked, looking up from the letter. He brought his gaze from a picture of a saturnine man in a wing collar and a fearful-looking tie to rest upon her flawless face.

"It was at the Rialto Hotel last Thursday afternoon," he replied. "You were having afternoon tea with a man with snow-white hair, and I was in the company of a woman with jet-black hair. There were four tables between us."

"At Warburton! So it was. I remember seeing you. You reminded me of Basil Rathbone when he played in *The Lives of a Bengal Lancer*. Now tell me about yourself, Mr Bonaparte. I like your name."

"Permit me to assure you that it is not a fictitious name," Bony countered, chuckling. "Sometimes I find it a positive burden, but—I am ambitious, you know, and my name might very well assist me to fame. At the Rialto I was entertaining my sister-in-law. My brother would not carry our father's name and so adopted the name of Farn. He was lost in the fires of '38. As there is no extra accommodation at the house occupied by my sister-in-law and her brother at Yarrabo, I am staying near by. I visited Bagshott, with whom I have corresponded for several years. It was through him that I learnt a little about Australia, enough to make me want to visit your country. I'm so glad I came to see it for myself."

"And he suggested that you call on me?"

The dark-grey eyes were devoid of guile.

"No. I suggested to him that he give me a letter of introduction. It was a suggestion that came easily to mind immediately he mentioned your name. He gave me ample warning, however."

"Indeed, Mr Bonaparte!"

"He warned me that I should want frantically to cast off at least twenty years. I said that the warning was ample, but, Miss Chesterfield," and Bony bowed in deference, "in this particular instance Clarence B. made an under-statement."

Nancy Chesterfield felt rising annoyance, only to be banished by the smile on the dark face and the twinkle in the blue eyes.

"You remembered, of course, seeing me at the Rialto?" she shrugged.

"Oh no! I didn't know you when I saw you at the Rialto," came the statement without hesitation and with skilful assurance. "It came about like this. From time to time Bagshott sent me bundles of the *Recorder*. I understand that in his letter to you he mentioned that I am on the staff of the *Johannesburg Age*. I have always liked your section of the *Recorder*, and also your Personality Pars. We have tried to make our women's section conform to the standard you set. In addition, Bagshott has sent me copies of *Wyndham Nook* in which your articles on writers have been exceptionally interesting. Then, being a stranger in Australia, I thought perhaps you might have declined to see me. Hence the bludgeon of Bagshott's letter."

Nancy Chesterfield smiled.

"You needn't have been doubtful on that point, for I couldn't have declined to see a man with your name—after the commissionaire reported that you seemed quite sane." The grey eyes gleamed, and the impressionable Bony was delighted by her sense of humour. She asked, "What is your work on the *Johannesburg Age*?"

"I am a special writer," he replied, and did not feel quite so complete a liar since very often he wrote special articles, which were read with keen interest by Crown Prosecutors. What followed was more difficult. "I am able to get through an amount of free-lance work too. And I completed my first novel just before I left home."

"Good! What are you calling it?"

It was a question for which he was quite unprepared.

"The provisional title is *I Walk On My Toes*," Bony answered with creditable celerity. "However, my present ambition is to write a book about Australia, and I want to include a section on Australian literature. I've read many anthologies and several novels by leading Australian authors. I have been hoping for the opportunity of meeting several of them, and I did think that Bagshott would be able to help me. He's rather a peculiar fellow. He insisted that here in Australia authors are divided into two classes, one producing great literature, the other merely commercial fiction. Naturally my interest lies in literature, and he said that that being so he could not assist me save in sending me along to you."

About the beautifully moulded brows a frown was strangled at birth. Nancy Chesterfield inserted a cigarette in a long jade holder, and instantly Bony was on his feet holding a match in service. Whilst she drew at the cigarette she regarded him with a whimsical smile, and he knew he had baffled her regarding the degree of his sophistication.

"Tell me what Australian authors you've read, and then we may discover a starting point," she said, softly but distinctly.

Wisely he confined himself to the three novels he had read in Miss Pinkney's garden, devoting a full minute to each. He rhapsodized over Wilcannia-Smythe's *The Vine of Abundance*. He praised Mervyn Blake's *D'Arcy Maddersleigh*, and then went on, "One doesn't come across their work in South Africa, nor in England, where I was two years ago. On the other hand, the books of I. R. Watts are widely read outside Australia. I like his novels. He holds his readers with fine suspense."

Nancy Chesterfield listened attentively, sitting almost motionless and keeping her gaze on a pile of manuscripts on her desk. Bony liked her more and more. She was certainly very clever. She had watched his face and his eyes to get inside his mind, and now she listened to his voice in her search for the door. He was baffling her, and intuition, upon which he often relied with implicit faith, was informing him that the experience for Nancy Chesterfield was both rare and pleasing. When he had finished, she said, "When discussing Australian literature in your book-to-be, you should, I think, soft pedal on I. R. Watts. I agree that Watts writes excellent romances. When in need of light reading I go to him, but—er—he is not a creative artist like Mervyn Blake or Wilcannia-Smythe."

For the moment Bony was baffled. But only for the moment. A woman in the position occupied by Nancy Chesterfield should most certainly have a higher appreciation of literature. Here once again was the invisible object he sought to uncover.

"Well, no, perhaps not," he agreed reluctantly. "Still, I. R. Watts—well, well! By the way, I cannot find I. R. Watts in the local *Who's Who*. I suppose he *is* an Australian writer?"

"Oh yes, he's an Australian. He's something of a mystery, I understand. He's not a member of any literary society of national importance." Nancy Chesterfield tapped the ash from her cigarette and Bony sensed that she was gathering her forces to attack. "You see, Mr Bonaparte, our national literature is fast growing up, and it is vitally important that the work of our authors should be judged with extreme care, that the grain should be winnowed from the chaff, so that the authors of the future will be influenced by the masters of the present. If you give your attention to the work of Mervyn Blake and Wilcannia-Smythe, and Ella Montrose and others of their standard, you cannot go wrong in an appraisement of Australian literature today. A critical survey you should also study is that made by Dr Dario Chaparral, of Colombia, South America. He visited Australia twelve months ago and has just published in English the result of his study of our literature. I haven't a copy here, but you can obtain one at most booksellers, I think."

"Dr Chaparral!" Bony echoed. Screwing his eyes into

blue points, he went on, "No, I haven't met him, but I've heard of him. Did you meet him?"

"Yes. When in Victoria he stayed with Mr and Mrs Blake. Do you know their house at Yarrabo?"

"Oh yes, it's next door to the cottage where I am lodging. Blake died suddenly, did he not?"

"That is so," Nancy Chesterfield replied. "If you stay long you will doubtless learn as much about that unfortunate event as anyone. Australian literature suffered severe loss in Blake's demise. Still," and she brightened with astonishing swiftness, "there are others to carry on the leadership and continue directing our young authors in the way they should go. I do hope your book is successful, Mr Bonaparte, and I'm really delighted that you came to see me. I like talking to important oversea people, especially literary people, and I am going to give you an introduction to Mr Wilcannia-Smythe, who is staying at the Rialto. In fact, he is the man I was having afternoon tea with. You'll like him, I'm sure. He's a Sydney man, and is here gathering material for a new book."

"You are most kind, Miss Chesterfield. I shall be delighted to meet Mr Wilcannia-Smythe. You place me in your debt."

"Not at all, Mr Bonaparte. You must also meet Mrs Blake and Mrs Montrose before you leave us. It's a pity we didn't know you were coming to Australia. We like to entertain men like you and Dr Chaparral and Marshall Ellis of London."

Bony bowed from his chair.

"It's most charming of you," he said. "I feel sure I shall like them."

"Well, I do want you to return to South Africa with a balanced opinion of us," she went on. "So many visitors to Australia leave with a distorted view of us simply because they haven't been able to meet the right people." She smiled at him and added, "My job here is to publicize anyone with news value, as of course you know. After you've gone I shall write a happy little paragraph about you. You'll find it in tomorrow morning's paper. I hope you will come and see me again."

"I am daring to hope that you would lunch with me," Bony said, having risen.

"I'd love to—but remember what Clarence B. said about me."

"I shall never forget it, Miss Chesterfield. Could we arrange a day?"

A well-manicured hand was put forward to turn the leaves of an engagement book.

"Would Friday suit you?"

"Of course."

"Then you may call for me here at one. Don't bother with a taxi. I have my own car. I'll post the letter of introduction for friend Wilcannia-Smythe to the Yarrabo Post Office. You'll get it tomorrow."

He thanked her, and she shook hands in a manner he liked. She was entirely outside all his previous experience, but he felt he was parting from her on equal grounds. Impressionable as when an undergraduate, he walked out of the building feeling pleasurably excited, believing that he had detected a façade behind which dwelt the real Nancy Chesterfield.

CHAPTER FOURTEEN

Wilcannia-Smythe's Adventure

BONY arrived back at Yarrabo shortly after half past three, and near Miss Pinkney's gate a little girl stopped him, saying nervously, "Please, sir, my father wants to see you at the police station."

Having given the message, the child instantly left him to cross the road and enter the store. Hot, thirsty, and fatigued by the journey from the city, Bony hesitated whether to obey the summons or first find out if Miss Pinkney's kettle was boiling. He decided to go to the police station.

There was no one in the office with Constable Simes, who at once crossed to the door and closed and locked it.

"So's we won't be interrupted," he said. "I'm glad you returned by that train or I'd have had to play off my own bat and that mightn't have suited you."

"I hope it's important," Bony said, seating himself. "I was looking forward to Miss Pinkney's afternoon tea."

"My sister's taking care of that," Simes hastened to say. "I saw you turn into the main road from the station, and I sent my girl after you in preference to bailing you up. Something has happened that may bear importantly on the Blake case."

"So! Go on."

"At eight five this morning an old car stopped here and two men came in. I had just begun my office work. One of these men was Wilcannia-Smythe and the other was a forestry man named Jenks. At this time Jenks is camped about three miles from the junction of the Old Warburton Road with the main highway. At half past seven this morning he left his camp in his old car and came this way down the Old Warburton Road to his work. He was about half a mile from his camp when he saw a man tied to a tree. This man, Wilcannia-Smythe, was in full view, although the tree to which he was tied is about eighty yards up the side of a foothill. Jenks left his car and walked up to the tree, released Wilcannia-Smythe, and brought him here.

"Smythe—blast his silly hyphen—looked all right, though his hair was dishevelled and his clothes were creased and slightly stained. He said he felt all right, except for a stiff jaw, wanted his breakfast, and wished to return to his hotel. He said he had been grossly assaulted, but for what reason he didn't know because he hadn't been robbed. And he didn't want to lay a complaint, let alone make a statement."

"Did he say why?" asked Bony.

"Yes. He said that as he hadn't been robbed he didn't want the matter to go further and get into the newspapers. He liked publicity, being an author, but not publicity of that kind. I told him I could not have that sort of thing going on in my district, and that he must give me all the details.

"He said he was out last evening walking along the highway towards Yarrabo when a car overtook him, stopped, and two men jumped out. He was able to see that both had handkerchiefs draped under their eyes. One was a large man, the other was tall and lean. The large man pointed a pistol at him and ordered him to get into the car. Smythe said he couldn't do anything else but obey, and he got into the back seat where he was followed by the big man. The other got into the driving seat.

"The car was driven through Yarrabo and then turned off the highway on to what we know as the Old Warburton Road. This road is now in disuse after the first half-mile, where there is a house. The car passed the house, and then began to climb the track, which passes a stone-crusher and then winds up and round, past the quarry and on for some distance.

"Then the car was stopped and Smythe was forced out and made to walk up off the road to the tree. He was lashed to the tree and gagged with his own handkerchief. That was about nine last night and he was there until found by Jenks shortly after half past seven this morning. Luckily for him, it was a warm night."

"What was he tied to the tree with?"

"Old, but still good, half-inch rope," replied Simes. "The gag was kept in position with ordinary parcel string."

"Wilcannia-Smythe did not even suggest a motive for the assault?"

"No. He was angry all right, but not angry enough, in my opinion. If anyone had tied me to a tree and left me there all night, I'd be fighting mad. The explanation he thought might hold water was that he had been mistaken for someone else."

"H'm! Interesting. Did you visit the scene?"

"Yes. I went out there with Jenks. It just happens that everything I know about the bush old Jenks taught me. It happened, too, that Jenks stopped his car yards away from the place where the kidnappers stopped their car, and he was careful not to overrun that car's tracks. When I went back with him, both of us avoided spoiling the tracks from the kidnappers' car to the trees and down again, for I knew you'd want to look at them, too."

"Good man!" murmured Bony.

"Jenks and I agreed that one man was wearing a size seven boot or shoe, and that the other man was wearing the same size in shoe-leather."

"But you said—"

"I know. Wilcannia-Smythe said that one man was big and the other tall and lean. He gave me the impression that the big man would wear a bigger size in boots than a seven."

"Even a big man may have comparatively small feet, and wear a seven boot," Bony pointed out.

"Those tracks still prove that Smythe is a liar."

"Indeed. How so?"

"Smythe said that one man was large and the other man was tall," Simes said with slow deliberation. "Jenks and I first saw the tracks of the three men where the car stopped. Then we followed the three sets of tracks up to the tree, being careful not to overstep 'em. We agreed that one man was lean, but not taller than five feet ten, and that the other man was about as tall and slightly heavier. Our agreement was based on the length of stride taken by both men."

"Ah!" murmured Bony. "Good work, Simes, good work. Mr Wilcannia-Smythe's inaccuracies do not confirm the theory that he was mistakenly kidnapped for someone else. What d'you think?"

"The tracks don't fit into his statement, and his demeanour doesn't fit in, either," Simes said with conviction. "It's likely that he knew who kidnapped him, and why. I think that the reason was not revenge so much as to get him away from his hotel or some place for the night."

"It's feasible, Simes. Do you think that the kidnappers intended to return to release Wilcannia-Smythe, or let him stay there to rot? What's the position of the tree in relation to the road?"

"I'm inclined to think that the tree was very well chosen, because no one coming down the road or going up the road could fail to see Smythe lashed to it."

"Would there be many people likely to use the road at that place?"

"Yes. Beyond the camp occupied by Jenks there is another occupied by a dozen men who are at work cutting a firebreak. They have a truck there, and that truck is driven to Yarrabo every day. Why?"

"It would seem that the kidnappers knew that road intimately, and were aware of the use made of it by forestry workers. Unless, of course, they intended to return there tonight to make sure that Wilcannia-Smythe had been released. It would hardly be their intention to leave him there to die. I'd like you to take me out there."

"All right! I'll see how that tea's coming along. Like to read my report?"

Simes was back again within the minute, carrying the tea-tray with the skill of a club steward.

"I forgot to tell you," he said. "Dr Fleetwood wants to see you."

"Please ring him and ascertain if six o'clock this evening will suit him."

Bony poured tea into two cups, and sipped from his own with genuine relish. Simes replaced the telephone saying that the doctor would be at home that evening at six, and he drank his tea without apparent consciousness of its temperature, regarding Bony like a man who has many questions to ask.

Bony said, almost languidly, "Life is like a moving picture that can't be stopped. There would be few successful investigations into homicide if murders would, or could, suspend their own animation for a few months. In very many cases it is what they do after the crime that brings them to face the judge, not what they did before it. I am going to accept the responsibility of asking you to retain your report on this Wilcannia-Smythe incident. I agree with you that this Wilcannia-Smythe affair may have an important bearing on the Blake case, and the Blake case, my dear Simes, belongs to you and me. Have you ever been inside Mrs Blake's garage?"

"Yes, I was in there the day after the discovery of Blake's body," Simes answered. "I helped Sub-Inspector Martin to examine the place for—anything unusual. Nothing unusual was found."

"Did you come across any spirits—whisky or brandy?"

"No."

"There is a cupboard in the garage. What did that contain, d'you remember?"

"Yes. Battery acid and distilled water. Cleaning rags and tins of polish."

"No spirits?"

Simes shook his head.

"Any drinking glasses?"

"No."

"How long have you known Sid Walsh?"

"Why, ever since I took up duty here."

"H'm! Let us go along to examine those tracks. Thanks for not asking pertinent questions. When I establish anything of value, I'll let you have it."

The policeman's car was standing at the rear of the station, and at the end of ten minutes they had passed the stone-crusher on the Old Warburton Road. Swinging round a bend, they saw the road running almost straight for two hundred yards when it was thrust to the right by the hill-slope. At that right turn the slope above the road was denuded of trees save one growing eighty or ninety yards up the slope, and on reaching the turn it could be seen that the road ran again straight for almost a hundred yards. Thus anyone approaching that bend from either direction would be bound to note the tree growing in solitary state.

Simes pointed it out as the tree used to secure Wilcannia-Smythe, and then braked his car to a halt.

"The car that brought him here stopped half a dozen yards farther on," the constable said. "It was turned round half-way along that stretch of road where gravel was once dug out of the hill-side for the track. Jenks had to turn there, too. As I told you, his camp is half a mile up along the road."

"Let us relax," Bony said, and it was a command.

This was a page of the Book of the Bush with which he was unfamiliar, and it occurred to him that Constable Simes and Jenks might prove to be better trackers than himself in this class of country. Accustomed to the interior and its limitless plains and mulga belts, its gibber deserts and sandy wastes, here Bony was in an entirely different country and might have been on a different planet.

Requesting Simes to remain in the car, he alighted and went forward to examine the place where the abductors' car had stopped and they with their victim had alighted. From this point to the tree high on the slope, human feet had laid ribbons of darker green on the floor of closely-growing bracken, and presently Simes watched Bony zig-zagging to and fro across these ribbons as he mounted the slope. Then, having arrived at the solitary tree, Bony circled it several times, finally leaning with his back against the great trunk.

So clear was the air, Simes could observe Bony roll a cigarette and then, having lit the weed and pocketed the spent match, move out of sight behind the tree, remaining hidden for almost a minute. On reappearing, he came striding down the slope, the bracken to his waist so that he might have been wading in green dye. On reaching the car, he got in and slammed the door.

"You were right," he said. "Both men wore size seven boots or shoes. Neither was a big man and neither was a tall man. The left leg of one man is slightly shorter than his right, and he is not a bushman because he places both heels as one used to walking on hard pavements. The other man is stouter, for his stride is a fraction shorter. He is slightly pigeon-toed and he has a corn on the fore-part of his right foot. Also, the lace of the right shoe or boot was undone."

"Gosh!" Simes exclaimed. "Dinkum?"

"I might have read more clearly had it not been for the bracken," Bony said. "Your friend Jenks is at least six feet tall, weighs something like sixteen stone, chews tobacco, has grey hair and has done a great deal of riding."

"The exact picture," the astonished Simes admitted.

"By the way, you had an accident when your right ankle was injured."

"No, never. You're mistaken there."

"Am I? You astonish me. Alas, I am growing old and my sight is failing. I hope my brain is not failing, too. Let us return. My dear man, a really gifted aboriginal tracker could have added much to what I've been able to read. In comparison, I am a novice. Quite sure you never hurt your right ankle—say when you were a lad?"

"Yes, quite sure," Simes answered, now frowning. "Would you recognize those tracks if you came across them tomorrow or next week?"

"I would know them if I saw them again next year. You see, Simes, no two men walk alike. The Law says 'by their deeds shall criminals be known'. I say, by their foot-marks shall I know them. Do you think you could obtain some plaster of paris?"

"I could."

"Then you drive back and get it. We'll make casts of those human tracks and the tracks made by the car tyres. Judges and juries are Doubting Thomases. I'll wait here."

Simes was back within twenty minutes, and then watched Bony make plaster casts, watched him lift them when dry and pencil data upon each.

"I have quite a collection at home," Bony said, and then added after one of his little dramatic pauses, "made by the boots and shoes of men who have hanged or gone to prison for many years."

On arriving back at Yarrabo, Bony suggested that Simes should drive direct into the open garage behind the police station, and they were about to emerge when Mrs Farn appeared, carrying a watering can.

"Thank you for that delightful afternoon tea," Bony said to her. "I find your Victorian summer very humid and mind-dulling. I have been reading tracks, and then I discovered that your tea stimulated my brain to the extent that I misread only once—according to your brother."

Simes chuckled, saying, "Read mine and said I had had an accident once to my ankle."

"And so you did," snapped Mrs Farn. "You were playing football when it happened. It was five years ago when Yarrabo was playing Yarra Junction. You were laid up for a week."

"Well, by gosh, so I did!" Simes almost shouted.

"The effect of your afternoon tea was even better than I was led to think, Mrs Farn," said the delighted Bony, and left them to call on Dr Fleetwood.

CHAPTER FIFTEEN

Ping-pong Balls

DR FLEETWOOD himself answered Bony's knock, conducting him this time to his den and inviting him to be seated before a single-paned window overlooking a well-kept garden. The doctor at once concentrated on the subject of the grey powder with which, it was evident, he was deeply concerned.

"I am regretting that I'm not a toxicologist," he said. "I got so far as proving that the powder you left with me is animal residue. I thought at first it was chalk, which is compact limestone composed chiefly of the shells of rhizopods. I might be able to tell you more if you gave me details of its history, where you found it and under what circumstances."

"Then it is not poisonous?"

The thin lips were compressed into a faint line. Then, "I placed a little of the powder on a lettuce leaf and gave it to a rabbit. The animal shows no signs of distress or even discomfort. This morning I prepared an alcoholic extract which I injected into another rabbit. That rabbit died within half an hour."

Bony's gaze was removed from the thin, pale face of the speaker to the garden beyond the window. The silence within the room was emphasized by the ticking of a small clock somewhere behind him.

"How much of the powder did you use in the extract?" he asked.

"Slightly more than half of the quantity in the envelope."

"Of itself, therefore, the powder is non-poisonous?"

"It has produced no signs of poison in the rabbit that ate it."

"Might it be poisonous to human beings?"

"In the form of alcoholic extract, probably."

"Pardon me if I appear unduly persistent," Bony said. "You are sure that the powder is neither mineral nor vegetable in origin?"

"I am sure on that point, yes."

"Do you think a toxicologist could determine what it is?"

"I believe he could," replied the doctor. "Anyway, if you permitted me to send the remainder of the powder to Professor Ericson, of the University, he would inform us. Ericson is a personal friend of mine. He has command of laboratory equipment far beyond the means of the ordinary medical practitioner."

"H'm!" Bony pondered. "I would not like to place you in the position of wasting the professor's time with a common and innocuous substance."

"I think it is neither common nor innocuous," asserted the doctor.

"Very well, doctor. Please send the remainder of the substance to the Professor. It will be interesting to know what it is, and when we do know I will tell you where I found it. It's likely that we'll have a good hearty laugh over it, and then apologize to Professor Ericson for wasting his time." He rose to his feet, and said, "I'm sorry I cannot take you fully into my confidence about the Blake case. The autopsy revealed a foreign substance in the dead man's viscera, but the substance is not stated in the report and therefore could not have been considered toxic. If, let us assume, Mervyn Blake had consumed some of that powder just before he died, would the autopsy reveal it as a foreign substance?"

"I don't think so. Being animal residue, it would be digested as is meat." The doctor paused, before adding, "I do not believe that the foreign substance reported by the toxicologist is the same as the powder you brought to me."

"Thank you." Bony turned to the door and the doctor stepped past him to open it. "I would be glad if you would answer a straight question," he said. "Do you believe that Mervyn Blake was murdered?"

"Yes."

"On what do you base your opinion?"

"Mainly upon the rapid onslaught of his illness, and that in relation to his general health, which was reasonably good for a man of his age and habits—and also on my belief that someone entered the room after he died and left it before day broke the following morning."

"Thank you again, doctor." Bony glanced into the grey eyes of this studious-looking medico, and suddenly smiled. "Inspector Snook has a habit of putting people's backs up," he said. "Once he raised the hackles on my neck. I'd be delighted if we made a fool of him. Good-bye! I'll be glad to have Professor Ericson's report when it reaches you. Ah! I hear the evening train coming in. I must get along or Miss Pinkney will wonder where I've been in Yarrabo."

"Good night, and all the best," Fleetwood said from his doorstep, and Bony made his way to the front gate and set off up the long road gradient. On rounding the turn, he met Constable Simes.

"Been waiting for you," Simes said. "Wilcannia-Smythe has cleared out. I was down at the station when the five forty to the city came in, and there in a window seat was our friend, and on the rack above him several of his suitcases. When I asked him if he was leaving us for good, he said he was, and if I wanted his address in Sydney it could be found in any *Who's Who*."

"Well, well, well!" Bony exclaimed. "And I've been promised a letter of introduction to him. Too bad. Never mind, Simes. We can lay him by the heels should it ever be necessary. Do your best to trace the car in spite of the fact that Wilcannia-Smythe was unable to tell us anything but that it was, to use his own words, a dark-looking sedan. The more I think about it, the more I'm inclined to the thought that he was abducted to get him out of the way for the night. If I hadn't the evidence of those tracks I might think he had put over a tale of woe, or got himself tied up in order to gain a little publicity."

Simes grinned in his peculiar manner, and asked, "Get along all right with the doctor?"

Bony nodded. "Very well. I like him. I think he will cure me." Then came the sudden flashing smile. "Don't be impatient, Simes. I promise you you shall know everything long before Inspector Snook does."

Five minutes later, he was met by Miss Pinkney in the hall of her cottage, a smile of welcome banishing the years from her unadorned face.

"You poor man!" she exclaimed. "You must be hot and tired after your day in the city. When I heard the train come in, I made a pot of tea and I've put it on the table in your room. Dinner will be ready in half an hour, so there's really no need to hurry."

"I thank you," he said in a manner conveying how touched he was by her kindness. "Oh! I did manage to buy Mr Pickwick a few ping-pong balls."

He gave her three celluloid spheres, and she asserted that Mr Pickwick could play with only one, and flushed prettily as though the gift was to herself. While standing by the little table and sipping the tea she had provided, he thought of her, and the tragedy that had blighted her life. The reflected sunset tints from Donna Buang filled the room with colour, dyeing the bed sheets and pillows, and the cloth upon the table, laying upon his dark hands a purple mist.

"Now the day is ending and night is drawing nigh, with all the glory of the earth enthroned against the sky," he parodied and then, softly chuckling, he went on, "Not bad, that. I must practise. I may even become a poet."

He opened the subject of the ping-pong ball shortly after he sat down to dinner with his hostess.

"How long ago was it that Mr Pickwick found that ball?" he asked.

"Oh, he's had it for months. I forget just when he found it."

"Was it before Mr Blake died?"

"Yes. Oh yes, months before then. Sometimes he lost it and then would come and tell me so. I'd forget about it and, suddenly, he would bring it to lay at my feet to toss for him."

"Were the Blakes keen players?"

"She was. I never once saw Mr Blake playing."

"Did Mr Pickwick have his ball when the Spanish gentleman was staying there?" pressed Bony, in an effort to establish about when the cat had found that particular ball.

Miss Pinkney pleaded for time to think. Presently she said, "It was a long time after he was there. The Spanish gentleman was staying there last summer. Mr Pickwick found the ball—oh, damn it, why can't I remember? Yes, I do. He found the ball round about Easter time."

"He's had it a long time, hasn't he? Did you ever hear the Spanish gentleman's name?"

"No. They used to call him 'doctor'." Miss Pinkney laughed. "He was a funny little man," she cried. "He would dance up and down when he played, and blow out his cheeks and make faces. But my word, he could play! So could Miss Chesterfield and Mr Wilcannia-Smythe, and several other people they had staying with them."

"No one inquired about the ball Mr Pickwick brought home?"

"Oh no."

"You didn't happen to see anyone making determined efforts to find it, I suppose?"

"Of course not, Mr Bonaparte," she replied, colour mounting into her face. "If anyone had hunted for it, I should have returned it. They often lost one, I think, and never bothered to look carefully for it."

"Hardly worth the trouble. They are not expensive and appear to be plentiful."

"But they weren't plentiful last year, and for years before last year," asserted Miss Pinkney. "I know, because I tried to buy ping-pong balls for our young men's club at the church. You see, when my brother developed thrombosis, I gave our table to the vicar. Poor man, ping-pong was my brother's favourite form of exercise. I used to play with him quite a lot, especially after he retired." Miss Pinkney laughed again, and the swift change from sadness to gaiety was startling. "He would get so angry if he mis-hit a ball that he would pick it up and smash it against a wall or something, and rant and rave about getting old. You would have liked him, Mr Bonaparte. So downright in his opinions. So able at expressing himself."

"H'm! Such an illness must have been a great trial for him."

"Oh yes, it was, poor man. It was a trial for me, too."

"When did he retire from the sea?"

"In 1938. He went down in 1941 to thrombosis—and a broken heart. He wanted to go back to sea, and no one would give him a command. Some men are like that, you know. They won't grow old gracefully. A war or something happens, and they think they can go to it as though they were twenty. I believe in being one's age, don't you?"

"Up to a point, yes," Bony admitted. "Your brother must have missed his ping-pong."

"Oh yes, he did. He ranted and raved at me for giving the table away, but I told him he couldn't play and I couldn't play by myself. And he said he wouldn't have let thrombosis stop him, and all that kind of nonsense. Anyway, we had come down to our last ball, and there was no hope of getting new ones. Then, when I gave the table to the vicar, I couldn't find that last ball, though I hunted high and low for it."

"It wasn't the ball found by Mr Pickwick?"

"No. He didn't find that one. I got rid of the table early in '42, and my brother died late that year. Besides," Miss Pinkney added triumphantly, "all the balls we had were marked. My brother marked the balls with an ink-spot immediately he received them. He always bought them from Lavrette Frères, in Marseilles. He said they were the only balls that could stand up to his play. Do offer me a cigarette."

Bony presented his own case, in which he kept cigarettes for very special occasions.

"Try one of these," he urged, his eyes twinkling. "They are supplied to me by my pet black marketeer. I understand that he obtains them from Parliament House. Naturally they are very good."

"What lovely fat ones!" Miss Pinkney cooed, and Bony

held a match in service. He continued to press his questions, having no particular object in mind.

"It didn't occur to me that the strength of ping-pong balls varied so much," he said. "Where did the Blakes purchase their balls, I wonder, when it was so hard to procure them in Australia?"

"I don't know, Mr Bonaparte. I think the Spanish gentleman brought some with him. I know he brought his own bats because I saw and heard him speaking about them. Such a funny little man. My! This is a lovely cigarette."

They went on to talk of the unwarranted shortage of tobacco, and to laugh good-humouredly at the naive excuses put over by statesmen who seem to think their victims have no intelligence. Miss Pinkney became a vocal butterfly flying from one flower-subject to another, and for an hour Bony listened and enjoyed it.

On rising from the table, he begged to be excused to write letters. In his cool and quiet bedroom, he took from his suitcase the crushed ping-pong ball and held it close to the table lamp. There was no ink-spot on it, no evidence to his sharp eyes that there had ever been one. There was neither maker's name nor mark.

CHAPTER SIXTEEN

Checkmated

DURING the night it rained heavily, and when Bony left the house to saunter in Miss Pinkney's garden after breakfast, he was welcomed by a revivified world. The wind coming from the south was cool and tempering to the sun. The birds were active and happy. And D.I. Napoleon Bonaparte was thoroughly enjoying his holiday.

Admiring Miss Pinkney's flowers and shrubs and vegetables, he arrived eventually at the far end of the garden where he had sat to read novels in the shadow provided by the lilac-trees. Beyond them, and obviously in the next garden, a woman was talking and a man was making short comments. Bony could not resist taking a peep over the fence.

Standing on the middle of the lawn, Mrs Blake was giving orders to Walsh, the casual gardener. He could not hear what she was saying, but she was pointing to various sections of the garden, and Walsh was nodding either in assent or understanding. Then, when he attempted to argue, she silenced him with a command of her hand, and spoke sharply and loudly enough to reach Bony.

"That will do, Walsh. I will not be dictated to," she said, and left the man to gaze after her with the ghost of a leer on his dissipated face.

The newspapers arrived by bus at half past nine, and shortly afterwards Bony called at the shop to buy the *Recorder*, in which should be Nancy Chesterfield's promised paragraph.

Having purchased a copy of the paper, he stood on the footpath to search for the paragraph, eventually finding it and reading:

Who should call on me today but an old friend who bears the distinguished name of Napoleon Bonaparte. Mr Bonaparte is an author and journalist of Johannesburg, South Africa, and he is visiting Australia to strengthen his impressions of us and further his knowledge of our literature. The last occasion I met Mr Bonaparte was before the war at a little Queensland village called Banyo, a few miles from Brisbane, and I recall the many stories he had to tell of Queensland, where he seems more at home than we do in Melbourne. I hope to meet him again before he leaves Victoria for Queensland which is, I think, to be his next port o'call.

Bonaparte raised his head and broke into delighted laughter.

"Morning! Happy about something?"

He turned to meet the inquiring eyes of Constable Simes. "Very," he admitted. "It's a great day after the rain."

"Do the gardens a lot of good," Simes asserted. "I have a message for you. Er—Mrs Farn presents her compliments to Mr Bonaparte, of South Africa, and desires to invite the said Bona—sorry, invite Mr Bonaparte to supper this evening in order to meet Miss Ethel Lacy, one time maid to Mrs Mervyn Blake."

"The said Bonaparte—no, sorry, Mr Bonaparte presents his compliments to Mrs Farn. He will be delighted to accept her very kind invitation—say about eight o'clock."

"You made a note about who owned the Blakes' house," Simes said. "I found out that Mrs Blake purchased the property two years ago for cash. Paid £2,250 for it."

"Indeed! She must be in the money. Well, I mustn't linger, Simes. See you later."

With the folded newspaper under an arm and his hands clasped behind him, Bony paused before a bed of Miss Pinkney's gladioli, seeing in the depths of their colours the face of Nancy Chesterfield. She had caught him out, and now he was interested by his own reactions, finding that he was not mortified but amused.

A man less balanced might have felt horribly annoyed,

especially a man as vain as Napoleon Bonaparte. It was his sense of humour that saved him on this occasion from temporarily abnormal blood-pressure, as so many times in his life it had helped to maintain that imperturbable suavity.

He had made, and admitted, the common error of underestimation. He had found what seemed to be a small clique hedging about the death of one of its members, and he had found a possible means of inserting himself into that clique. With all the confidence in the world, he had begun to go for his objective through Nancy Chesterfield, and he had failed by not giving due weight to her intelligence. He had talked to her in her office on the basis of his estimate of her formulated when observing her on the terrace of the Rialto Hotel, whereas, immediately he saw the appointments of her office he should have revised that estimate. A woman occupying such an office must be an important member of the newspaper staff, a position to which no one rises without intelligence far above the average.

The lesson was salutary, and he enjoyed it. He carried the chair from the veranda to the shade of the lilac-trees, and there reread the paragraph three times. Thereafter he lounged deep into the chair, his hands behind his head, unaware that Mr Pickwick was pouncing upon the paper sheets being stirred by the wind.

He thought he had captured the spirit of the paragraph writer when she was composing the item for publication. Through some channel or other, she had ascertained what he was. She was not angered by the deception he had practised, but could not refrain from punishing him for it. Had she been angry, she would have published his profession and probable interest in the Blake case, but she was content to slap him with the reference to his stories of Queensland. She wanted him to know that she knew he was a liar, and had then expressed the hope that they would meet again before he left the State. Why? To have the opportunity of slapping him again? The paragraph did not give him that impression.

Hang it! He had blamed Clarence B. Bagshott for exaggerating, and he had sinned as badly.

Slightly vexed with himself, he took up *The Literature of the Western Pacific Peoples* by Dr Dario Chaparral. The copy in his hands had been issued by a London publishing house, and it contained a portrait of the author. Without doubt, he was Miss Pinkney's "Spanish gentleman".

Dr Chaparral had devoted some sixty pages of his book to the history of Australian literature. He wrote lucidly and it was apparent that he treated his subject with respectful earnestness. When he came to his review of the works of the moderns, Bony noted the names, and finally totalled seven. Mervyn Blake's work was given priority in importance. In receding order were the names of Wilcannia-Smythe, Ella Montrose, and Twyford Arundal. Janet Blake was acclaimed as Australia's most noted short-story writer, and the remaining two were beyond his knowledge.

On putting down the book, Bony was inclined to agree with Bagshott that Dr Chaparral had been carefuly shepherded in Australia, for the names of several Australian authors and poets that had become household words were not included in the doctor's survey.

Bony was, indeed, finding this an absorbing investigation, and was tasting it with the pleasure of a gourmet at a banquet. Here were eight people drawn together with one unifying interest. One of the eight could be safely eliminated—Marshall Ellis, the Englishman, who had apparently been led along the same path as Dr Chaparral. With the exception of Wilcannia-Smythe, they all drank, Blake and Arundal to excess. Of the seven, all played ping-pong but Mervyn Blake.

If, as Bagshott had said, these seven comprised a clique that arrogated to itself the leadership of literary criticism, there would seem to be no grounds for thinking that one of its members killed Blake. Also, as Bagshott had said, it seemed most unlikely that one of the "outsiders" or the "unmentionables" would be aroused, either by adverse criticism, or by being ignored, to the point of committing murder, that is, assuming that writing people are as sane as any other cross-section of humanity.

If Blake had been murdered, then it was probable that one of the seven people, or one of the domestics, had slain him. As he had so often thought, the killer would most likely be uncovered once the motive for Blake's murder was uncovered.

Of the guests, who might have a motive sufficiently strong to kill Blake? According to Dr Chaparral, Blake was the leader of modern literature, with Wilcannia-Smythe second. But quite a long way second. Supposing that Wilcannia-Smythe disliked the position assigned to him? Supposing that Wilcannia-Smythe was jealous, and foresaw that with the death of Blake he would be first? The fellow's actions since Bony's arrival on the scene were extraordinary, to say the least. Did the papers and the note-book he stole from the dead man's writing-room have any bearing on Blake's death? Had he been lashed to a tree all night so that those papers might be taken back from his hotel room? Bony thought it quite likely because, having lost them again, Wilcannia-Smythe decided to return to Sydney.

Martin Lubers, the wireless man, appeared to have a will of his own, and a feeling of hostility towards Mervyn Blake. He could not be jealous of Blake professionally, but there could be another cause for murder. He was a member of the staff of the Australian Broadcasting Commission, but despite that organization's importance and respectability, it was not beyond the bounds of possibility that a member of its staff could have and had committed murder.

Murder! A beautiful word to Napoleon Bonaparte, because here and there a murderer became his adversary, and he had marked respect for those who were intelligent enough to provide exercise for his mind, and his patience—especially his patience. People who killed on impulse were mere children and unworthy of his attention; it was those who planned before the act who captured his interest and his respect—until they made a stupid mistake.

He did not observe Miss Pinkney until she spoke.

"Day-dreaming, Mr Bonaparte?" she asked, and came very close to giggling. "I've brought you some letters. Oh, look what Mr Pickwick has done to your paper! He's utterly ruined it."

On his feet, Bony accepted the small batch of letters.

"There's nothing much in the paper, anyway," he said. "They are still wrangling about the atom bomb, and they are going to raise the price of cigarettes."

"What a frightful government!" exclaimed Miss Pinkney. "My brother used to say that it's a pity a Guy Fawkes wasn't born every other month. One in every generation would surely succeed. Now I must run to get lunch."

She departed and Bony examined his mail. There was a letter from his wife, bearing the Banyo postmark, and another from the chief of his own department. Its large and sprawling caligraphy he recognized as belonging to Superintendent Bolt. The handwriting on the third letter was strange to him, but on the left-hand corner were the printed words, the *Recorder*.

"Dear Mr Bonaparte," wrote Nancy Chesterfield. "Shortly after you left today, Mr Wilcannia-Smythe rang me to say he was leaving Warburton by the next train, and hoped to catch the evening express to Sydney. I am therefore enclosing a letter of introduction to Mrs Blake. You don't deserve it, you know, after telling me all those fibs about Johannesburg. Do call in for a chat when you are again in Melbourne."

Miss Pinkney had twice to sound the gong for lunch.

CHAPTER SEVENTEEN

Bony Makes a Call

AT half past three Bony knocked upon the fly-wire door protecting the front entrance to Mrs Blake's house. A woman he guessed was Mrs Salter, the cook, answered his summons and, having tendered his private card, he was invited to be seated in the hall. Three minutes later he rose to meet Mrs Blake.

She was dressed in a linen house frock not unlike a hospital nurse's uniform. The dark eyes examined the visitor with steady appraisal. Her voice, when she spoke, was low and modulated.

"You wish to see me, Mr—er—Bonaparte, is it not?"

Bony bowed as though to vice-royalty, and when his head was low her eyes narrowed and then opened with an expression of gratitfication.

"I do hope that the hour is not inconvenient," he said in his grand manner. "I received by this morning's mail a letter of introduction from Miss Nancy Chesterfield. It will explain the reason for my visit."

Without comment, Mrs Blake accepted the envelope and read the contents, at first hurriedly, and then again with greater care. When again her eyes met Bony's, the welcoming smile barely managed to creep into them.

"I am, Mr Bonaparte, a very busy woman," she said. "However, I'm glad you have called to see me. Pray sit down. Anyone from another country interests me, and I am always glad to welcome a writer to Australia. Nancy says that you are the author of at least one novel."

"My novel hasn't been published," he said depreciatingly.

"I sent it off to the London publishers just before I left South Africa."

"Indeed! What is the title?"

"I have called it *I Walk On My Toes.*"

Mrs Blake repeated it, then saying, "Titles are important. They should be arresting, and should not contain a word about the pronunciation of which anyone could be doubtful. What is the story about?"

There was a trace of eagerness in her voice that gave him courage to proceed. Only now was he beginning to gain confidence that Nancy Chesterfield's character was not such as to betray him thus early. Mrs Blake's eyes were empty of suspicion or hostility. They were alive with genuine interest. The liar went on with his lying—to amaze himself.

"The story concerns the life of a man of the little-known people called the N'gomo, who inhabit a corner of the country, formerly German South-west Africa. The action begins when the young man is persuaded to leave his tribe to become the personal servant of a hunter. On the death of the hunter he becomes the servant of a ne'er-do-well, who deserts him in Cape Town. Eventually he is taken into the service of a rascally fortune-teller with whom he remains for three years.

"Following the arrest of the fortune-teller in Johannesburg, he makes his way with much adventuring back to his own country, taking with him knowledge of the gullibility of human beings, and many of his last master's tricks. Having returned to his tribe, he rises swiftly to become its witch doctor and autocratic ruler. They called him Lu-mo-lam Aye-glomph-ah-ee, which, translated, is "I Walk on my Toes." Thereafter the story relates his rule and subsequent fall, and his influence upon the lives of a small community of white people living on the borders of his country. I have tried to portray the evil influence of white civilization on the savage mind, and how through that savage mind the evil is passed back to the members of that small white community."

Bony could have counted slowly up to six before Mrs Blake spoke.

"The plot of your novel is certainly original, Mr Bonaparte," she said thoughtfully. "You know, I—I rather like it. I do hope it is successful. You have studied the natives of your country?"

It was less a question than a statement, and Bony hoped that she knew little, if anything, about the natives of South Africa.

"I have always been interested in them," he said, "chiefly, I think, for their diversity of customs and their wide range of intellectual powers."

"You have delved a little into voodooism and that kind of thing?"

"I have merely skated over the surface," Bony replied, adding with a smile, "The more one skates the more one is conscious of the deeps below."

"Yes, that is so, Mr Bonaparte. Have you met Professor Armberg?"

Luck favoured Bony, for only recently had he read an anthropological work by Professor Armberg.

"Unfortunately, I have never met the professor," he said. "I have, of course, heard a great deal about him, and my paper has published a number of his articles."

"A learned man, Mr Bonaparte, and a charming correspondent. We have been writing to each other for some considerable time. He can have no equal in knowledge of the savage superstitions and of the practice of black magic. Are you staying long in Australia?"

"No. My return passage is timed for the end of February. By then I hope to have gathered sufficient material for a travel book about Australia. It can, of course, be only superficial. I have in mind a section devoted to the growth and status of Australian literature, and thus it was that during my conversation with Miss Chesterfield she said I must meet you. I am indebted to Miss Chesterfield."

Mrs Blake caught the gleam in his eyes and smiled.

"Nancy Chesterfield wrote that you are staying in Yarrabo."

"For a few days, yes," he said, a trifle relieved that he

123

could speak the truth—partially. "My brother was Mrs Farn's husband, who changed his name by deed poll, and when I came to see her, I was so struck by the beauty of the locality I decided to stay for a week at least. She couldn't put me up, and so she persuaded Miss Pinkney to take me in. A charming lady."

The dark eyes momentarily hardened. Then, "As you say, Mr Bonaparte, Miss Pinkney is a charming woman. She is, however, a little inclined to gossip, and you will know what that means in a small place like Yarrabo."

"I do suspect her, just a little," Bony admitted, lightly. "I've had, now and then, to be a little cautious."

Mrs Blake smiled for the first time with frankness.

"Wise man," she said. "Well, now that we have met, I'd like you to meet a friend who has come from the city to see me. Would you care for a cup of tea?"

"I do not remember ever declining the offer of a cup of tea, Mrs Blake."

"Then come along," Mrs Blake urged him, rising. "We'll go to my writing-room."

Bony was conducted along a passage to a room that widened his eyes. It was a spacious room dominated by pale yellow and white and gleaming walnut. He received the impression of many eyes watching him, and of one pair of eyes, dark and sombre, set in the tragic face of a tall woman standing with her back to a service trolley.

"Ella, this gentleman is a novelist and journalist from South Africa. Nancy persuaded him to call. Meet Mr Napoleon Bonaparte. My friend, Mrs Ella Montrose, Mr Bonaparte."

For the second time within the hour, Bony bowed low.

"Mrs Montrose is an established novelist, Mr Bonaparte, and so you two should have much in common," Mrs Blake proceeded. "Poor me, I am merely a short-story writer."

Only in colouring was Ella Montrose akin to Mrs Blake. Her eyes were softer and set in a pale and slightly over-long face. She had the figure of a young woman, though her age was probably verging on fifty. Her clothes were expensive, but a little bizarre. Her voice when she spoke was low and rich in tone.

"Welcome to Australia, Mr Bonaparte," she murmured. "I am not going to be so silly as to ask what you think of Australia, but I do hope you like the country and will like us."

Bony was induced to sit down and Mrs Blake served tea, at the same time telling Mrs Montrose what the visitor had related about his novel *I Walk On My Toes*. Mrs Montrose evinced keen interest, and her interest was not assuaged until she had gained the answers to several questions. He talked easily of cabbages and kings against the background of literature, mentioned the titles of Ella Montrose's two novels which, regretfully, he admitted he had not read, and was cautious in his praise of the work of the late Mervyn Blake and Mr Wilcannia-Smythe. After his interview with Nancy Chesterfield, he dared not mention I. R. Watts.

He hoped he was acquitting himself well, because his mind was unsettled by the framed portraits that covered the whole of one wall of this luxurious room.

Mrs Blake evidently noted this distraction, for she said, "I see you are interested in my friends, Mr Bonaparte. Let me introduce them to you."

They rose, and she led him to the end of the gallery nearest the door. Ella Montrose wheeled the trolley out of the room, closing the door after her, and Mrs Blake continued talking, more vivacious in manner and warmer in voice.

The pictures were not of the same size, but the frames were uniform in size and of the same wood. They were spaced along three rows, and there must have been more than forty.

"I am, Mr Bonaparte, more liberal in my views than was my late husband and Mrs Montrose," Mrs Blake told him. "That man, for instance, had published nine novels and two volumes of verse when he died a few years ago. His name was Edwardes. He wrote very well, but just failed to make the grade. Actually, he wrote better novels than Mr Wilcannia-Smythe is doing, but it is said of Mr Wilcannia-Smythe that his prose is exquisite in balance and rhythm. The next portrait is of Mrs Ella Montrose. Her work is much appreciated by the discerning, and we are still expecting her to produce the Great Australian Novel."

Bony was introduced to Professor Zadee and Mr Xavior Pond as "powerful friends of Australian literature". Mrs Blake discoursed on several others, men and women who were revealing "great promise". Then he was looking at a picture of the late Mervyn Blake, whom he recognized from the pictures of the man contained in the official file.

There was something about this picture that disturbed him. Mrs Blake spoke of her husband's novels and literary work in general. "He was the acknowledged premier critic in Australia," she told him, and still the picture disturbed him. For one thing it appeared to be in the wrong position in this gallery, and the thought occurred that Blake should have the place beside Wilcannia-Smythe and Mrs Montrose.

Then he was being introduced to Dr Dario Chaparral, and the Blake picture passed from his mind.

"Dr Chaparral visited this country early last year," Mrs Blake said. "He stayed with us for a little while. A charming man, he spoke English fluently—which was fortunate for us, as he is a Colombian."

"I have read his book, *The Literature of the Western Pacific Peoples,*" Bony confessed, for the first time feeling himself on firm ground. "I thought it a very sound piece of work. Miss Chesterfield commended it to me."

"Indeed! Yes, Dr Chaparral's study was well done, although perhaps he might have been a little less conservative in his final judgments. He could well have been more generous to little Twyford Arundal here. If it were not for a slight weakness, I could confidently predict that Twyford Arundal will become Australia's greatest poet of all time.

"There is Mr Martin Lubers," Mrs Blake went on. "He is a great friend, and he has done a very great deal in his own sphere to assist the growth of public appreciation of our literature. Often we need a check upon our vanities, and Mr Lubers provides the check. A country's literature, you will agree, is a plant that must feed on the spirit of its people, and become deep-rooted in the generations of its writers.

We in Australia have been inclined to force the plant to grow in accordance with our pet ideas, and therefore it tends to become a hybrid. Mr Lubers, being a Director of Wireless Talks, is distinctly valuable to the growth of our literature."

They went on from picture to picture, every one of which was autographed. There were forty-three altogether. They came to the picture of a man who was a poor imitation of the late G. K. Chesterton, even to the black ribbon attached to the pince-nez. He was introduced as Mr Marshall Ellis, and passed by to come to Nancy Chesterfield.

"Miss Chesterfield is a beautiful woman," Bony commented.

"And a very talented one, Mr Bonaparte," supplemented Mrs Blake. "Nancy has always been a powerful supporter of Australian writers. She has done more, perhaps, than anyone else to bring our writers to the notice of the public."

They were coming to the end of the gallery, and Bony thought it strange that literary people did not possess a particular cast of countenance like army officers, naval men, and churchmen. Those before whom he had passed had no common denominator. The pictured Americans, Europeans, South Americans, and Australians would have been of interest to any criminologist had they been included in a Rogue's Gallery. Standing a little back, he wondered which of them had murdered Mervyn Blake.

Mrs Montrose came in, and he sensed a subtle change in his hostess. Mrs Blake reverted to that shade of stiffness he had felt on first meeting her, and the absurd thought entered his mind that she had revealed to him a side of her character never revealed to her friends. Mrs Montrose once again examined him with her fine eyes, seemingly trying to probe into the inner recesses of his mind.

"I do wish you would come to our next literary meeting on the twenty-fifth of the month, Mr Bonaparte," she said. "So many people would like to meet you. May I send you a little note of reminder?"

"The twenty-fifth!" he murmured. "I'm not sure, but it is

unlikely that I shall be in Victoria on that date. However, if I should be, I'd be delighted."

As they gravitated towards the door, Bony made another comprehensive examination of the picture gallery. The feeling that there was something not quite in order returned strongly to him.

In the hall, he said, "Permit me to offer my sympathy in your bereavement, Mrs Blake. There are other novels by your late husband I have not yet read. It will be a pleasure tinged with sadness. If it is at all possible, I'd very much like to have a portrait of him for inclusion in my book."

Mrs Blake smiled wanly.

"I appreciate your kindness, Mr Bonaparte, as my husband would certainly have done. I'll try to find a picture for you. The last time he sat for his portrait must have been at least ten years ago."

They accompanied him to the shaded porch and appeared reluctant to let him go, these two handsome women with their dark eyes and positive personalities. They shook hands with him, and smilingly bade him *au revoir*, and he heard them speaking of flowering shrubs as he walked along the well-kept driveway to the front gate.

Sid Walsh reached it first, opened it, and they passed out together.

CHAPTER EIGHTEEN

Further Donations

SMILING oilily, Mr Sidney Walsh closed the gate after Bony and proceeded to walk with him to the corner and the main road.

"Bit cooler today," he observed, the watery brown eyes craftily assessing. "Good day, any'ow, for a guts-shudderer."

"Meaning?"

"A drop of the doings, a deep noser, a snifter, a Jack London, a gargle, a lady's waist, a corpse reviver, and so on and so on," replied the casual gardener. "I am myself partial to guts-shudderer, meaning what used to be called whisky but what's coloured metho."

"Ah! But I understood that one of your complaints against the Government is the limited output of beer."

"Beer's easier to say than guts-shudderer."

"I incline to agreement," Bony said, finding the change from one strata of society to another somewhat jarring. "Have you finished work for the day?"

Walsh changed the old suitcase he carried from his left to his right hand. He dragged his left foot just a fraction, making a soft noise as the boot scraped over the loose surface of the sanded footpath.

"I've finished work for a long time," he said, slowly. "Made up me mind about it today. I've got a bit sunk here and there and I'm now going to retire, sort of. One thing, I won't have to pay no ruddy income tax."

"For most people that will happen to them only in the next world."

"I mean to make it happen in this one." Walsh spat and did not miss the fly on the fence of the vacant allotment.

They turned left at the corner and proceeded down the main road, Bony's destination being Miss Pinkney's garden gate. Never could the charge of snobbery be levelled against him, but he hoped that Miss Pinkney would not see him in the company of his derelict. There was neither the superiority nor the inferiority complex in Sid Walsh's make-up.

"What about a drink?" he said.

Against his inclination, Bony accepted the suggestion and five minutes later they were occupying a quiet lounge. With Bony's money, Walsh went away to the bar, and Bony gazed with idle curiosity at the old suitcase that had so often necessitated a change of hands. Picking it up, he found it quite heavy. Walsh returned, wiping his lips with the tip of his tongue, indicating that he had got in ahead of his fellow debauchee.

They wished each other luck, without meaning it, and Bony suggested refills, the suggestion being accepted with an eagerness a trifle pathetic. Seated in an old chair, Bony's mind travelled erratically until it alighted on the long wall upon which hung three rows of portraits. What was wrong with that picture of Mervyn Blake?

Walsh returned with the filled glasses, and sat down.

"Been living here long?" Bony inquired.

"Twenty odd years."

"Did you work for the people who lived in Mrs Blake's house before she took it?"

"Too right, I did. Old Ben Thornton owned that place. You interested in the property?"

"I'd like to buy it if I could," replied Bony.

Walsh regarded Bony with distinct respect.

"You couldn't," he said. "The Blakes had a lot done to it. Still, you don't know what Mrs Blake might do about it. You asked her?"

"Oh no," Bony said quickly. "Don't you mention it, either."

"Me! I'm the most secret bloke in the 'ole of Orstralia. 'Ave another?"

"At my expense."

When Walsh was again absent, Bony leaned back and closed his eyes to recreate the picture of the portraits on the daffodil-tinted wall. They were arranged so symmetrically, and there was something wrong with them.

He was finding the problem tantalizing when Walsh returned, to sit down and look intently over his glass, and to say, "That Mervyn Blake was a funny sorta bloke. Up today and down termorrer. Some days he wouldn't say good day, and the other days he was all over a bloke—when he wanted me to buy an extra bottle for him."

"That bad, eh?"

"Ya. Mrs Blake uster scream at him for drinkin'. He'd go off the guts-shudderer for weeks at a time, and when he was on it he was on it and made no bones about it, if you know what I mean. Then he'd get me to buy a few extras on the quiet. Brandy it was, and it would be me to get rid of the bottles so's she wouldn't know about 'em."

"She wore the trousers?"

Walsh shook his head and gazed into his empty glass.

"No, she didn't wear the trousers," he said, without looking up. "He was man enough to stand up to her. The drunker he was the calmer he was. Without raisin' his voice he'd tongue-lash her from here to Young and Jackson's. Ever been in there? Grand pub and all. He'd use words I never even heard of, tellin' her she was makin' herself cheap and lowerin' herself to be popular, just to feed her un'oly vanity.

"Any'ow—pity they uses such small glasses these days. Good, hefty pint-pots is one of the four 'undred freedoms we been robbed of."

With renewed interest in life, he left Bony for the bar, and on his return took up the conversation where he had broken it off.

"Any'ow, he took pretty good care to plant his empties for me to collect and dump in an old gravel pit back of my place. A few times he forgot where he did plant 'em, and the last time he forgot was just before he rattled the pan. Once I found three of 'is bottles under a japonica. Another time I found a bottle and a glass, and a—no, that wasn't it.

It was two bottles and a glass. I found 'em buried near the front gate."

Mr Walsh wiped his eyes with what once might have been a handkerchief. He looked at Bony suspiciously, and Bony suggested a refill.

When again he came shuffling in, Bony said, "He must have been drunk to bury a glass with his empties."

"Blind all right," Walsh agreed. "In all me days I never seen a bloke stand up to it like he did. If you seen him coming like a parson to a funeral you could bet he was as drunk as Chloe."

"When was it he buried the glass?"

"When was it? Lemme think. The Melbun Cup was run on the Toosdee. It was on the Fridee before. No, it wasn't. It was the Fridee after, because there was a policeman in plain clothes muckin' around the place tryin' to prove that Mervyn Blake was short circuited, sort of. He was short circuited, all right."

"How do you know?"

"Poison."

"Oh! Sure?"

"Too true. Poison outa a bottle, a brandy bottle, dozens of brandy bottles. Hundreds. Boy, oh boy! What a death! And here's me can't even get a bit giddy on this guts-shudderer."

"Better try again," urged Bony, and for the seventh time, Walsh tried again. When he had lowered the tide once more, Bony yawned and said without interest in his voice, "You didn't throw the glass into the gravel pit, did you?"

"I did not," Walsh replied with indignant emphasis. "It was a real cut-glass tumbler. Throw that away! I got it home right now."

"That was a find, all right. Use the glass at all?"

"Ya. I puts me false teeth in it at night. Never use a glass for drinkin' except in a pub."

"One way of employing a find. How did you get on when Blake wanted to give you a drink?"

Without any fault in articulation, Walsh said, blinking at

his interrogator, "He was a card, that Blake bloke. I'd be doin' a bit of weedin' or a bit of diggin', and he'd come along and sort of pass me casual like, and say in a whisper, 'In me writin'-room, Sid.' Or it might be, 'In the garridge.' And then I'd let him get well ahead and sorta follow him careless like after I takes a decko to see where his old woman was. When I caught up to him, he was all set and we'd have a couple of drainers."

"Drainers!" echoed Bony, and Mr Walsh grinned.

"Ya. Drinks what goes down without swallerin'."

Bony chuckled. "Two more drainers," he said. "And then I'm going home."

"Pretty good 'ome, too," remarked Mr Walsh, standing at the door, the glasses in his shaking hands. He winked, evilly, and added, "When you gets the chance, you have a look round for Miss P's little store. She's got some whisky there somewheres what was never bottled in Orstralia. Musta been some what her brother brought ashore."

Mr Napoleon Bonaparte was determined that the next drink was to be the last, and so far he had not arrived at his objective.

"They used to have plenty of company, didn't they?" he asked over the last glass.

"Ya, plenty," replied Walsh. "All sorts. All la-de-da stuck-ups, too."

"They tell me they often played ping-pong."

"When they 'ad guests, most of the time. Blake, he never played. Reckoned he couldn't see the ball."

"What did you have to do? Pick up the balls?" Bony asked lightly.

"I'd have to find 'em," replied Walsh. "I was always 'untin' for ping-pong balls. Why, I remember about a year ago spending all of three days doing nothink else. They had a champeen stayin' there. Brought his own balls. Thought they was made of gold or somethink by the way Mrs Blake made me hunt for 'em. I seen Mr Pickwick playing with one, but I didn't say anythink about it. They could afford to lose a ball now and then. 'Ave another?"

"No, thanks. I'm finished. You ought to be, too."

"I am," Walsh agreed with astonishing alacrity. "It's me for a hard-earned feed. I'm goin' your way."

It was unfortunate for Bony that Mrs Blake was accompanying Ella Montrose to the railway station, and that they passed them before he could part from the friendly Mr Walsh. Both ladies recognized his salutation with frigid smiles which did not include the said Mr Walsh, who eventually parted from Bony at Miss Pinkney's gate with a loud, "Hooroo! See you again some time."

Throughout dinner, and afterwards, Bony's mind constantly reverted to the little problem concerning Mrs Blake's picture gallery, and he was still thinking about it when he entered the police station at half past eight that evening.

Mrs Farn might have climbed high had she married a Napoleon Bonaparte, or an author with social ambitions. She welcomed Bony with smiling eyes and the confidence of a woman able to live outside herself, and at once took him to her small lounge and there introduced him with formality to Miss Ethel Lacy.

"I'm pleased to meet you," the girl said, and Bony still liked her voice. "Mrs Farn's been telling me all about you, and I'm just thrilled to bits at meeting an author."

"I hope that Mrs Farn hasn't been giving away too many of my secrets, Miss Lacy," Bony said over their clasped hands. "As a sister-in-law, she is sometimes a little trying. She has been telling me about you, too, so we may have to join forces in mutual defence." He sat down and leant forward to gaze at Red-head as though all the thrills were his. "I'm not a famous author, you know, and you have met a number of really famous writers. I do wish you would tell us something about them, what they are like, what they talked about and what they ate. What did you think of poor Mervyn Blake?"

"He reminded me of the feeling I had when I saw a fat spider inside a daffodil," Red-head asserted, giving a very prettily excited shrug. "He was all right, you know. Nothing sexual, or anything like that. Always a thorough gentleman. But the spider had a horrid look of being satisfied with itself, and Blake had a look like that. He was clever all right. Could talk about anything under the sun."

"You've read his books, I suppose?"

"Several. They're very high-brow, and all that."

"Did you like them?"

"Ye—es," she replied with the air of one who must not admit dislike of a book without a story and music without a tune. Then suddenly she smiled straight into his eyes and said, "No. I only read bits of them. You see, I never had a good education."

"Neither did I," Bony told her with charming assurance. "Please go on. What did you think of Mrs Blake and Mr Wilcannia-Smythe and the others?"

"Yes, do tell, Ethel," urged the supporting Mrs Farn. "That Miss Chesterfield now. She was there, wasn't she, the night Mervyn Blake died?"

A shadow passed across the green eyes.

"She isn't so extra specially friendly with Mrs Blake as she made out to the police," Ethel said in dramatically lowered tones. "In their different ways they were a funny lot. They had only one thing in common."

"What was that?" pressed Mrs Farn.

"A good opinion of themselves. The worst of the lot was Mr Wilcannia-Smythe. I hope, Mr Bonaparte, that you don't get as conceited as he is after you've had a few novels published."

"If he does, we'll have to take the conceit out of him," threatened Mrs Farn, and Red-head laughed at Bony who was pretending, successfully, to be self-conscious.

He said, "I hope that no amount of success will make me conceited. How did you get along with Mrs Blake?"

"Mrs Blake is very nice and very kind to everyone. She puts herself out no end. When I first went there, she took me to my room, and asked me if it was to my liking, and said I was to say so about anything that wasn't. There was no key to the door, and so I asked for one, telling her that men had been known to walk in their sleep after telling me what lovely hair I had, and the rest. She found a key all right. Then, after dinner, when they had several guests, she'd come out to the kitchen and help cook and me to clean up."

"That was considerate of her," Bony murmured. "She writes, too, doesn't she?"

"A lot," replied Red-head. Her eyes became wistful, and she clasped her hands before continuing, "Mrs Blake's got a peach of a writing-room. Primrose walls and a primrose carpet. There's a big walnut writing desk with silver ornaments, and a tall ebony statuette of Venus and—and a man riding a great horse with wings. Oh, I wish I had a room like that. Nothing frilly, you know. And all one wall covered with pictures of her friends. They are all there except—except her husband. But then—" and the girl laughed, softly —"I wouldn't want to have a husband like that in my room."

"Marry an author and have such a room," advised Bony. "I'd ask you to marry me—if I could, Miss Lacy. I suppose Mervyn Blake's room was almost as luxurious?"

"No, it wasn't," she said. "He had his room built in the garden. It's just plainly furnished with a bed couch, an arm chair, a felt carpet, and a writing desk. There's hundreds of books in cases and a big typewriter on its special table. In a cupboard he kept brandy and dry ginger and a glass. A great man for his drink. He even had a cupboard in the garage."

"In the garage!" exclaimed Bony.

"In the garage," she repeated. "I never knew a man like him. The more he drank the plainer he spoke and the steadier he walked."

"Did he keep drink in the garage as well as in his writing-room?" persisted Bony, and the green eyes smouldered. She spoke slowly to emphasize the truth of her words.

"I saw him at the cupboard in the garage that night he brought Miss Chesterfield from the city. I had a headache and took a couple of aspirins, and cook advised me to get out in the cool of the evening for a little while before dinner was served. It happened I was at the side of the house when I saw him drive the car into the garage. He went to the cupboard in the far corner, and he took out a glass and a bottle, and he poured himself a drink and dashed it down. A sneaker, I called it. And then he hurried outside and shut and locked the doors.

"And Mrs Montrose waiting on him hand and foot," Ethel went on. "Came into the kitchen herself for his jug of milk and glass, and took them to his writing-room, saying he'd have had a tiring afternoon in the city and the milk would steady his poor stomach. A slinky, scheming woman, that. Making eyes at him all the time and Mrs Blake laughing up her sleeve at her. Not that he took any notice of the Montrose woman. Not a bit. I reckon he had used her up long ago."

"He always drank milk before dinner, didn't he?"

"Yes. Cook said it was to settle the booze in him he'd had in the afternoon so's he could begin again sober in the evening."

"Mrs Montrose is a well-known writer, too, isn't she?"

"Oh yes, written a lot of books, I think. She was telling the Pommy writer about them for hours, and he was putting it all into a large note-book. Insulting, filthy beast."

"Mrs Montrose, or the—"

"The Pommy writer. Man by the name of Marshall Ellis," Red-head said aggressively. "Thought it was clever to be rude. Food stains on all his waistcoats. Little piggy eyes, and picked his teeth after eating. But his voice! Oh, his voice, when you weren't looking at him! If they pushed a voice like his into a fillum star, there'd be a screaming riot with all the bobby socksers in the world."

"A peculiar man, Miss Lacy. Please go on. What of the others?"

"The others? Oh! Well, there was Twyford Arundal. He was lovely. Give him two gins and squash and he'd recite poetry. Give him four and he'd compose it, and Ella Montrose would take it down. They had to be careful with him after the sixth, because when he'd had about six, he'd still go on composing poetry but nothing would come out of his mouth.

"Then there was Martin Lubers. He's in the wireless, you know. More than once he'd say something that would rile them, but they crawfished to him no end. I was telling cook about it one day and she said it was because he had a high job in the wireless, and got them all a lot of publicity. It's all wheels within wheels, she said, and I think there's a deal of truth in that."

"H'm! Well, that's all most interesting," Bony said. "Er, they often had people from overseas staying with them, Mrs Farn tells me. Were you there this time last year when Dr Dario Chaparral was visiting the Blakes?"

"Yes, I was. There was the same crowd almost. Wilcannia-Smythe, Ella Montrose, Twyford Arundal, and Martin Lubers, and Miss Chesterfield some evenings. The doctor was a character, if ever there was one. I just used to like waiting at table when he was there. The stories he told! Ooh! Tales about the people in his country. All sorts of tales, and about the natives who cut off the heads of dead people and reduced them to the size of an orange, and that kind of thing. Mrs Montrose would write them down sometimes, even at dinner. And all the time, the little doctor would laugh and smile and look as though he was telling smutty stories."

"He brought his own ping-pong balls with him, didn't he, Miss Lacy?"

"Yes, he did. Before he came the Blakes didn't have one and they couldn't be bought, either. He gave a whole box of them to Mrs Blake. My! Could he play! He was like lightning."

Bony thoroughly enjoyed the evening, though it cost him an effort to tell of his own activities in the newspaper world of Johannesburg. Mrs Farn provided a light supper of tea and sandwiches and her brother came in in time to join them.

At half past ten the party broke up, Bony gallantly escorting Ethel to her parents' home. He was her very first escort who did not evince a passionate desire to kiss her good night, and for several days she was unable to make up her mind whether she was pleased about that or not.

He reached Rose Cottage at eleven. Miss Pinkney had retired, leaving in his room a bottle of whisky and a barrel of biscuits. He spent two hours going through the official file again, and when eventually he poured himself a drink and munched a biscuit, he was frowning.

CHAPTER NINETEEN

An Unexpected Ally

It was Friday morning, and Napoleon Bonaparte strolled along the shady side of Swanston Street, pleased with the world in general and with the prospect of meeting Nancy Chesterfield in particular. He had dawdled over morning tea and the newspapers, and now intended interviewing the Australian publishers of the internationally known I. R. Watts.

Arrived at the offices of the Monarch Publishing Company, he asked to see someone in authority.

"My name is Napoleon Bonaparte," he said bluntly to a large man behind a resplendent desk. "I am a visitor to this country from South Africa, where I am known as an author and journalist. I am a strong admirer of the works of I. R. Watts. You publish his books, and you would be bestowing a great favour on me if you gave me his address."

"That, I regret, I cannot do, Mr—er—Bonaparte," stated the large man. "It would be against the fixed policy of this firm to give to anyone the address of its authors. However, if you care to write to I. R. Watts, I'll have the letter forwarded."

"I thank you. Yes, perhaps that will be the best way," Bony agreed. "Could you relent so far as to inform me if I. R. Watts is living in this State?"

"Oh yes, that is so."

"Thank you. Forgive me for presuming once more. Can you tell me exactly what is commercial fiction?"

The publisher smiled as he might at a harmless lunatic.

"Commercial fiction is any piece of fiction that will sell."

"Oh! What, then, is literature?"

"Same thing, with the addition of non-fictional writings up to standard for offering for sale."

"Ah! The same thing!" Bony murmured. "Thank you. I have been given to understand that in this country there is a distinct difference between literature and commercial fiction."

The publisher smiled, saying, "The distinction doesn't exist in any publishing house anywhere in the world."

"Again I thank you, sir," Bony said. "I haven't read any Australian authors other than I. R. Watts. May I assume that there are other masters of Australian literature?"

"Thousands of 'em, Mr Bonaparte, tens of thousands of them. A master of literature is the man, or the woman, who enters a bookshop or a library with money to spend on books."

"Just so! Very neat indeed," Bony exclaimed. "I thank you. Good morning. I'll write to I. R. through this address."

Still pleased with the world, Bony walked down Swanston Street, strolled in and out of several book shops, filling in time until he came to stand outside the main entrance of the newspaper building where Nancy Chesterfield marketed vanity. He continued to stand there until three minutes past one o'clock, the time set for his luncheon appointment. When he went up in the lift it was four minutes past one, and when he entered Nancy Chesterfield's office he was exactly five minutes late.

"Why, it's Inspector Bonaparte!" she exclaimed.

"My apologies for being late, Miss Chesterfield. I was detained on a quest for information. There is no need to ask after your health."

"Neither is there need to ask after your own," she countered, her brows arched.

"My health concerns me less than my appetite. I could eat—anything."

She was putting on her gloves, and she looked up from them to say, "You have no regrets for having deceived a poor female?"

"I am the gayest deceiver in the country."

The blue eyes clouded. "What is it you want from me?" she asked, her voice brittle.

"Table companionship, the envy of other men, and to be informed on the difference between literature and commercial fiction. In return, I am able to give—well, very little. You see, I am a person of no importance in the political, the social, or the literary world. How did you unmask me?"

The cloud vanished from her eyes, and her voice shed its brittleness.

"That was easy," she said. "After you left the other day I rang through to the morgue—that's our Records Room, you know. They found your name easily enough, your profession, all about you, even that you caught a swordfish weighing over four hundred pounds."

Bony laughed without restraint, and she laughed with him.

"And I went to no end of trouble in having the editor of the *Johannesburg Age* prepared to receive an inquiry about me. Alas, I am becoming too famous. Well, do we go along?"

"Of course, Mr Bonaparte. I would have been disappointed had your courage failed you."

He opened the door and she passed into the corridor. He said, before they reached the lift, "My courage often fails, Miss Chesterfield, but my will to succeed, never."

"To succeed in what?"

"In what I set out to accomplish."

They talked of nothing as they descended to the street level, and he accompanied her to her car parked outside the building. They continued to talk of nothing as they drove to a women's club in Spencer Street.

"Being a foreigner in Victoria, Mr Bonaparte, you are lunching with me," she explained. "You want to talk to me, don't you? Cross-examine me, and the rest of it? As a matter of fact, I want to talk to you. Here we may talk."

"You are being exceedingly generous," he said, quietly.

She examined him with thoughtful appraisement, liking the cut of his light-grey suit, the expensive shirt, the tasteful tie. She liked his face and the shape of his head, and the way he did his hair. He was a new experience to her, and she was liking that, too.

Herself smartly tailored in a blue-grey suit, with a suggestion of flame in the soft red of her blouse, and wearing a small black hat that threw into relief the tint of her perfectly coiffured hair, Nancy Chesterfield was an experience quite new to Napoleon Bonaparte. As they faced each other across the white and silver table, the eyes of two fencing masters clashed, held firmly. She was the first to speak, and she astonished him.

"If you want any assistance in this Mervyn Blake business, I'll give you all I can."

"Mervyn Blake business!" he echoed.

"It is why you are staying with Miss Pinkney. It is why—and she smiled—"you are pursuing me."

"It is admitted, Miss Chesterfield."

"I have a friend in the C.I.B. who knows something of you," she told him. "He said that in certain circles you are known as the man who never fails."

"Partially true, only partially, Miss Chesterfield. I have failed to instil into my eldest son's mind the necessity for conservative spending. I have failed my long-suffering wife. I have—"

"Never failed to—the word is finalize, and I like it—never failed to finalize an investigation."

"I have certainly been fortunate in my professional career," he said, unsmilingly.

"To what do you owe your uninterrupted successes? It sounds as though I were interviewing you, doesn't it?"

"I think I owe it to patience, to a disregard of inconvenient orders from superiors, and to a slight knowledge of human psychology."

"And," she took him up, "to an extraordinary mixture of pride and humility. You had a lot of hurdles to get over, didn't you? Almost as many as confronted me. We have the same type of mind, Mr Bonaparte. We started, I imagine, from the same scratch line. Mervyn Blake was like us, but he failed. We have been successful because we love our work.

He failed because he wanted the rewards with all his passionate heart, without having to work too hard for them. For him, writing was a means to an end, and the end was fame. With us, were we creative writers, the end would be the joy in creative writing and the fame to go to hell. I liked Mervyn Blake. He had many fine qualities. I want to help you unearth his murderer." Her mouth tightened, and then she asked, "May I call you Nap?"

It brought the flashing smile.

"If it pleases you," he told her. "If you want to please me, call me Bony."

"Bony it shall be, and you shall call me Nan. Don't think me swift, because I'm not really. I want you to treat me as an ally, not a suspect, and I want you to accept the relationship without any waste of time. Don't let us fence any longer. We both know that Mervyn Blake didn't just die."

His gaze dropped to his food. Of what he was thinking she could not guess, but she was sure he was not seeking an advantage. For a full minute neither spoke. Then he was looking at her as no man ever had regarded her. In another it would have been an insult. His bright blue eyes began with an examination of her clothes, and continued with an examination of feature by feature until finally they gazed with penetrating steadiness into her own eyes.

He said, "Are you prepared to give me your full confidence and be satisfied with only a portion of mine?"

She nodded, and he asked, "When shall we begin?"

"Now, if you like."

"Very well. Why are you so sure that Mervyn Blake was murdered?"

"I don't know why. I can't tell you."

"Do you know of a probable motive for killing him?"

She shook her head.

"You must not be offended if I throw your words back to you," he warned. "You said just now that Blake wanted the rewards but did not like the work that earned them. Will you enlarge on that?"

"I didn't say that he disliked the work of writing," Nancy

asserted. "He liked it well enough, but it took second place to the ambition to be famous. He wasn't the great man a number of people thought he was, and he knew it. He had in high degree the gift of word painting, and in low degree the gift of telling a story. The division of those two gifts is even greater in Wilcannia-Smythe, but he is more accomplished in deluding himself."

"I confess that I don't see where this affair begins and where it ends," Bony said. "I find myself unable to make a reasonably accurate assessment of the importance of these people. I am very feminine in my gift of intuition, and I have felt, and still do, that the motive for killing Blake, if he was murdered, lies somewhere in a distinction between what is termed literature and commercial fiction. Bagshott may have thrown me out of gear. On the other hand, he might very well have pointed out the track for me to follow. Am I right in assuming that a great novelist has in high degree the gift of story-telling added to the gift of word painting?"

"Yes—and the gift of taking pains."

"Apply your measure to I. R. Watts."

"He can paint word pictures and tell a story, but he lacks the gift of taking pains."

"And Clarence B. Bagshot?"

"Bagshott is a born story-teller, but he lacks the gift of taking pains with his word painting. He is too slipshod ever to become a great novelist. But a story teller—he is certainly that."

"Was Blake conscious of his own limitations?"

"I think he was. You see, he must have realized that when his books were refused publication in London and America they were not—well, good enough."

"Go on, please."

"I know this much about Mervyn Blake," she said. "When he could not publish overseas, he strove to exert his influence on Australian literature so that he would secure an undying place in it. Long ago he and Wilcannia-Smythe planned it all. Fitted only to be flunkeys at the Court of World Literature, they decided it would be preferable to be joint dictators of the local Court of Literature."

"What influence did they exert on Australian literature?"

"Actually very little. They tried to lead it. No one can do that. A nation's literature goes on and up or on and down in accordance with the mental virility of its writers."

"Was there, or rather, is there a great deal of what is termed back-slapping going on among author-critics?"

"Quite a lot, but, as Abe Lincoln said, you can't fool all the people all the time, and in the long run it doesn't do them any good. They have news value, not because they are authors but because they succeed in having themselves elected office bearers in literary societies. They don't influence the unbiased critic."

"Thank you, Nan. We are getting along very nicely."

"I thought we could move once we got started, Bony."

"Of course. Let's attack the problem from a different angle. Was there any other woman in love with Mervyn Blake?"

"Ella Montrose was very fond of him. But—"

"Don't think it. Was any other man in love with Mrs Blake?"

"Little Twyford Arundal worshipped her from a distance," Nancy replied. "I think that Martin Lubers liked her."

"Only liked her?"

"That is all, I think."

"I have read the record of what occurred that last afternoon and evening of Blake's life as set down by you. Did you forget anything when you made your statement?"

"No. Inspector Snooks saw to that."

"Was Blake interested in women?"

"I don't think so. He liked me. Liked me; no passion."

"What about his private life? His relations with his wife?"

"Quite normal, I believe. She scolded him sometimes for drinking too much. I fancy they got along very well. They lived to a great extent independently, and they worked independently, though for the same end."

"In their objective, therefore, they were united?"

"Yes, they were."

"Tired of being questioned?"

"No, Bony, I'm not."

"I would like to ask more personal questions."

"Do so. Have you a cigarette?"

"Of course. Forgive me, please." Having held a match to her cigarette, he said, "What was your interpretation of the meeting of Wilcannia-Smythe and Mrs Blake at the Rialto Hotel?"

"I don't know what to think about that," she confessed. "It seems that Mrs Blake found Wilcannia-Smythe's handkerchief and accused him of leaving it somewhere or other. I don't understand it at all."

"Why did you leave without speaking to Mrs Blake?"

Nancy Chesterfield hesitated, and Bony was sure she was marshalling her facts.

"In the first place, I was furiously angry when Wilcannia-Smythe did not return to me, and in the second place, I felt that Mrs Blake was in such an emotional state that she would not appreciate it if I spoke to her."

"She has a temper?"

"Yes. Also she has a forceful personality."

"That night you spent with the Blakes, you slept in Mrs Blake's room. Where did she sleep?"

"In the dressing-room, next to it."

"And where did Mrs Montrose sleep?"

"In the room beyond the dressing-room. The dressing-room served both bedrooms."

"You met other oversea visitors at the Blake's beside the man Marshall Ellis, did you not?"

"How did you know that? Yes, I did. Janet Blake has always been keen to entertain foreign literary people. Her correspondence with literary people in other countries is very large."

"What was your impression of Dr Chaparral?"

"Good! I liked him. He could talk well and always interestingly."

"He played ping-pong exceptionally well, I understand."

"He held the South American Championship for three years running."

"And he was almost an expert on the customs and superstitions of the backward peoples of his country, was he not?"

"Yes, he knew a great deal about them."

"And as he told his stories, Ella Montrose jotted them down?"

Nancy Chesterfield frowned and regarded Bony with narrowed eyes. She nodded, and Bony pressed on, "What did she write on, do you remember?"

"Yes," she said. "Ella started off by making memos of the doctor's stories on pieces of paper and then either rewrote them in a note-book, or left it to Blake to do. Some of them were extraordinary stories, and terribly gruesome."

"Did the note-book have a black cover?"

"It certainly did. How do you know all this?"

"Intuition."

"Fibber."

"You are correct. Thank you very much for taking me to lunch. It has been much better than if I had taken you. May I call on you at your office—when I want to?"

"Of course. And I hope you will want to soon and often."

CHAPTER TWENTY

Report on Powder

BEFORE leaving for Yarrabo by the afternoon train, Bony purchased writing materials and, in the G.P.O., wrote a letter to I. R. Watts, asking for the favour of an interview. Since lunching with Nancy Chesterfield, his desire to interview Watts for a check-up on Bagshott's statements had increased because of his own liking for the man's books. Bony felt that I. R. Watts would be able to give him an accurate and impartial opinion of the Blake-Smythes.

When he alighted from the train at Yarrabo, he was for the second time accosted by Constable Simes's little girl, who told him that her father would like him to call at the police station.

"It looks as though it's not possible for you to go to town without something happening," Simes said. "A couple of hours ago, old Sid Walsh was found dead in his hut. Died some time during the night, according to Dr Fleetwood. The doctor rang up this morning asking for you, so that that can have nothing to do with Walsh's death."

"Where is the body?"

"Still in the old hut. Walsh lived on a half-acre block up the hill behind the church."

"Did Fleetwood say what he died of?" asked Bony.

"Alcoholic poisoning."

"Oh! Relatives taken charge?"

"Walsh hadn't any relations—as far as we know."

"I'll go and have a look at him. You come, too."

"All right! What about the doctor?"

"Ring him. If he's disengaged, ask him to come along to

149

Walsh's hut. He and I may as well discuss there the matter he wishes to see me about."

Simes regarded Bony with thoughtful eyes, and then turned to the telephone on his desk. The doctor said he would join them at Walsh's hut. The constable and the inspector left the police station and walked up the road.

"You don't think there's anything underneath this death, do you?" asked Simes.

"N—no, nothing concrete."

They walked a hundred yards in silence before Simes again put a question.

"You are not quite sure it's natural causes, eh?"

"As an ordinary layman, Simes, I should have no opinion," Bony replied. "Being a layman, and having conversed, and even boozed, with Walsh, I must think that the doctor's diagnosis is correct. However, through the chances of birth, there is another facet to my mental make-up—or should I say spiritual make-up? That other facet could be called intuition, and intuition causes me to think that Sid Walsh did not die from alcoholic poisoning. Stupid of me, isn't it?"

Having passed the church they came to an unmade road, overgrown with grass and bracken, and Simes and Bony took the path that curved to and fro along this unmade road. The path was of native earth, and the surface was only now beginning to dust after the rain of two nights before.

As they stepped on to the path Bony paused for a moment, then stepped off it again and proceeded along its grassy edge. Simes copied him, and thus they went on, flanking the church property on their left and a private house and grounds on their right. Well beyond the church they came to a fenced half-acre of land on which was built a small hut. A branch path led to a ricketty gate.

The gate was open. Once more Bony paused to examine the bare earth about the gateway before entering and continuing along the path to the hut.

It was a two-roomed structure in fair condition. About it the dead man had planted flowers and shrubs. They passed round to the back and found the open space that served as a back yard, clean and swept. In spite of his love for "guts-shudderers" and "drainers", Sid Walsh had taken pride in his bachelor quarters.

"He had a dog," Simes said. "I let a neighbour take it away."

"A neighbour!" Bony echoed, looking about the landscape.

"Yes. A quarter of a mile away beyond those trees. Did you see any suspicious tracks?"

"How could I?" Bony demanded, brows knit. "Since Walsh came home last evening from a session at the hotel with me, you have tramped up and down that path, the doctor has done so, and at least two other persons have also done so. Still—I don't know what you Victorian Police would do without me. Do you remember those two sets of tracks left by the men who abducted Wilcannia-Smythe?"

"Yes."

"One of those men came here last night—and after Walsh got home. The one who is slightly pigeon-toed and has a corn on the fore-part of his foot. I could not see enough of any one of the tracks he left on the path from the highway to the gate to enable me to be sure about him. But his tracks are on the path from the gate to this back door. In fact, you are standing beside a clear specimen imprint of his right boot."

Simes stiffened before bending to gaze at the ground. After a few seconds, during which his attitude did not change, Bony also stooped and pointed out the track.

"Size seven boot or shoe," said the constable. "But—but how the devil d'you know he's got a corn on his right foot, and that the corn is on the front part of it? That's what gets me. Yes, that's the track of one of the men who tied up Smythe. Yes, that's the track all right—now that you've pointed it out." He straightened and said, "It connects the Smythe hold-up with Walsh's death, doesn't it?"

"It would *seem* to, Simes," Bony said reprovingly. "You have not, of course, come across the tracks of the abductors' car, or either of the men's tracks anywhere in the township?"

"No! Oh, no."

"The footpaths are excellent registers of pedestrians. Those two men and the car must have come from beyond the limits of the township, at the very shortest. We might see the car's tracks again at the junction of the path with the highway. We'll have a look round here presently. It's singular that I've detected the tracks of only one of those two men."

"You're telling me," Simes agreed. "Here comes the doctor."

"Crime and criminals provide an absorbing study, Simes. You see, crime works out, broadly, along the same pattern. I am reminded of what Creon wrote—'Man's crimes are his worst enemies, following, like shadows, till they drive his steps into the pit he dug'. The steps part of it interests me more than the shadows. Ah! Afternoon, doctor!"

"Good afternoon, Inspector Bonaparte. Why did you want me here?"

"Merely to get you out into the fresh air," Bony replied, smilingly. "Actually, of course, because I think it possible that Walsh's death may be connected with the Blake case. Has the body been moved since it was discovered?"

"Yes," Simes replied. "Walsh was lying on the floor of the living-room."

"Let us enter."

The doctor frowned at Bony, saying, "You don't suspect foul play, do you?"

"It's possible."

"It's fantastic—if it is foul play."

They entered, and Simes produced a stick of chalk from his pocket and drew on the bare boards of the floor the outline of a human figure.

"That's about where he lay, doctor, wasn't it?" he asked.

"Yes. About there," Fleetwood agreed. "There, you see, is where he was slightly sick. He drank two bottles of whisky."

"Two bottles, eh? Where?" asked Bony.

"In the bedroom. Let's go in there."

The sinister figure on the old bed was covered with a

blanket. Beside the window was a small deal table. Upon it stood a hurricane lamp, boxes of matches, several cheap reprints of racing stories, a glass and two whisky bottles, a corkscrew and a bottle opener. One of the bottles was empty. About a noggin of spirit remained in the other.

"Have these bottles been touched by either of you, or by anyone else in your presence?" asked Bony.

Simes said he didn't think so. The doctor said he had not touched the bottles or the glass.

Bony said, "Both these bottles were opened quite recently. There is still distinct moisture in the empty bottle. On what do you base your opinion that he died of alcholic poisoning?"

"On my knowledge of the man's habits over a long period," Fleetwood replied. "And also upon the outward evidence of death on the features. There is a ghastly, vacant expression on the face, which is suffused and bloated. The lips are livid, and the pupils of the eyes are much dilated. That Walsh died in convulsion is also evident. All are the outward signs of death by alcoholic poisoning."

"He and I were drinking at half past five yesterday afternoon," Bony said. "He appeared to be much more sober than I felt when we parted."

"That's not significant. However, I am not sure of my diagnosis. A post mortem would prove or disprove it."

"Would you mind conducting the examination?"

"No. But the situation is involved because the man has no known relations from whom permission could be obtained."

"A Justice of the Peace, acting as Coroner, could give the authority," Simes advised.

"In that case—"

"Thank you, doctor, we'll have the examination done."

"I shall be interested in view of what Professor Ericson said about the powder you handed to me."

"Ah! You have his report! Let us go outside to hear it. Bony led the exodus, and they walked across Walsh's tidy back yard to sit in the shade cast by several gum-trees. "You may speak freely before Simes, doctor. He is collaborating with me."

"Wish you'd tell me where you obtained that powder," Fleetwood said, his grey eyes hard. "I'll read Professor Ericson's letter. Here goes: 'Dear Fleetwood. I am glad to hear from you and to know that all is well with you and yours. Thank you for the little task concerning the packet you sent along. It was quickly apparent that it is neither mineral nor vegetable, and that, as you thought, it is animal matter. What animal, however, it was difficult to prove. Even now friend Mathers, who assisted me, and I am not in complete agreement.

"'We are agreed that the dust is the residuum of a long-dead animal body. We are agreed also that the ptomaines have survived the decomposition of the body and are still unimpaired in the residuum. In Mathers's opinion, the dust is of the body of one of the canine species. In mine, it is that of the body of any primate excepting man, but in my mind exists the thought that it may be the residuum of a human body.'"

Dr Fleetwood looked up from the letter and regarded Bony with the frown even deeper between his eyes.

"Pardon my ignorance," Bony said. "What are ptomaines?"

"Basic organic chemical compound which is derived from the decomposing animal or vegetable protein. It bears a resemblance to an alkaloid."

"And is, therefore, poisonous?"

"I said it bears a resemblance, not that it is an alkaloid."

"This particular protein could possibly be poisonous?"

"Oh yes, not only possibly but probably. When injected in the form of an alcoholic extract the rabbit died, remember."

"But the rabbit that ate the powder on a leaf did not die."

"That is so."

"H'm!" Bony gazed downward at his dusty shoes. Then, "So far so good. In layman's phraseology, if the stuff is eaten it is not poisonous, if it is injected it is. Might not the powder be poisonous if eaten by a body saturated with alcohol?"

"It might, inspector. I will not commit myself. It would have to be proved by experiment. Is it in your mind that some of that powder was taken by old Walsh—probably in his whisky?"

"It is, doctor. It is also in my mind that the putting of any powder similar to that examination by Professor Ericson in Walsh's food or drink is an extremely remote possibility. But because of that possibility, I should like you to conduct a post mortem. You might then be able to determine if Walsh drank two bottles of whisky. If, say, you determined that he drank, or could have drunk, no more than one bottle of whisky, then I should be disinclined to believe that he died from alcoholic poisoning, because a large number of men in any given community can drink a bottle of whisky in an hour or two without noticeably ill effects."

"I'll do the P.M.," Fleetwood said. "And if I find that death was not due to alcoholic poisoning, that it was caused by another poison, an alkaloid, for instance?"

"It will strengthen a theory in my mind that this death is connected with the death of Mervyn Blake. It will compel an inquest, and in that both Superintendent Bolt and Inspector Snooks will take exceptional interest—long before I am ready to permit their interest to be roused. Is Professor Ericson in a position to assist you with the post mortem?"

"Yes, and I feel sure he would be very willing," replied the doctor. "That's an idea. Ericson could go very much farther than I could to establish the poison, if there is poison."

Bony rose to his feet and loosened his shoulders.

"Assuming that the professor assented, when would you make the examination?"

"Tonight, if the professor is agreeable. If not tonight, then first thing tomorrow. I could do the preliminaries this evening."

"Could you delay your findings, assuming you found poison?"

"For two days, perhaps, before reporting to the Coroner. We could find excuses."

"Good. I am placed, doctor, in the position of fighting for time." Bony reached forward and touched Fleetwood upon the label of his coat to emphasize his words. "Cicero said, 'Certain signs precede certain events'! I am now threatened by certain events preceding me, and that is a situation I find irksome."

CHAPTER TWENTY-ONE

Points of Interest

HAVING assured Bony of future co-operation, Dr Fleetwood departed, and before his shadow had passed over the old front gate, Bony and Constable Simes were inside Sid Walsh's bedroom.

"We must preserve these bottles," Bony said. "Wrap them in newspaper. Perhaps there's an old case handy."

Without commenting, Simes went to work salving the two whisky bottles.

"When found, did Walsh have his false teeth in his mouth?" Bony asked.

"I didn't notice," replied Simes.

"All right. Don't touch that glass yet. Deal with the bottles by pushing your little finger into the top of them."

Bony caught his breath, hating what he had to do. He pulled the blanket down from the face of the dead man, forcing himself to look upon it and mentally shrinking from the awful picture it presented. Simes heard him say, "You didn't lead a good life, Walsh, did you? Your liking, or weakness, for what you termed guts-shudderer, was your ruin. But you loved flowers, and that must be credited to you. You died with your teeth in your mouth and with your boots on your feet, and you died before you could go to bed. Just too bad. Well, we'll find out all about it."

Covering the face, Bony made a superficial examination of the bedroom, and then looked over the living-room. He went outside and found a lean-to wash-house, and there he poked about for several minutes.

"Looking for anything in particular?" asked Simes.

"Yes, a cut-glass tumbler in which Walsh put his false teeth."

"Haven't seen such a tumbler. Only glass in the place is that one on the table in the bedroom. That's plain and cheap."

"Be extra careful of that glass, Simes. No, I don't think Walsh would tell a lie about the cut-glass tumbler he found buried just inside the Blakes' gate. There is an old quarry where he used to dump his empties. How far is it from here?"

"Just outside his eastern fence—about a hundred yards."

Bony returned to the bedroom, and examined it more carefully. With the same care he went through the living-room, and on emerging into the glare of the westering sun, confessed that he had learnt nothing from the interior of the hut, save that a cut-glass tumbler was not there, and that a plain glass tumbler was.

Simes, having packed the whisky bottles and the glass into a wooden case, proceeded to load his pipe whilst he watched Bony walking round and round the hut, shoulders stooped, head bent down. He noted that Bony was moving on his toes, and he received the impression that even the report of a gun would not disturb a mind so completely concentrated on reading tracks. Every time Bony completed a circle, he began another and wider, until eventually he had covered all the ground to the distance of fifty feet about the hut.

Abruptly the concentration disappeared from the shambling figure, and Bony came walking with his usual smart step to join Simes.

"That pigeon-toed man who wears a seven in shoes or boots did not immediately knock on Walsh's door, Bony said. "Before he knocked on the door, he passed on round the house to stand and look in through Walsh's bedroom window, probably for several minutes. The dog, now—was it found tied up?"

"Yes, over there. That old barrel was its kennel."

"What kind of a dog?"

"Water spaniel."

"Friendly?"

"Very. Not much of a watch dog, I should think."

"Well, we find that the pigeon-toed man came and looked at Walsh through his bedroom window and then went to the back door," Bony asserted. "I can find no evidence that he entered, because, for one thing, the floor is of boards and was kept reasonably well swept. I wonder why Walsh's visitor took a cut-glass tumbler and left a plain tumbler in its place? There was the smell of whisky in it, too. Strange that. Walsh told me he never drank from a glass except in a hotel."

The patience of the policeman gave out.

"What the hell are you talking about?" he almost shouted.

"About drinking glasses, cut and plain, expensive and cheap."

"Oh, damn!"

"No, quarry. Come on."

Bony was not satisfied with looking down upon a litter of rusted iron, pots and pans, and broken glass reflecting the sunlight. He walked round the quarry to its entrance and proceeded to poke about among the glass, asking Simes to look for pieces of a cut-glass tumbler.

At the end of half an hour he gave up, and suggested they sit on a boulder and smoke, and the now desperate constable silently reloaded his pipe and glowered at Bony's long, brown fingers engaged with making a cigarette.

Then Bony said, "You've been very patient with me, Simes, and in reward I will tell about a ping-pong ball and a cut-glass drinking tumbler." Ten minutes later, he asked, "Well, what d'you make of it all?"

"Nothing without the key," replied Simes. "The toxicologist said he found no poison when he looked at the insides of Mervyn Blake. That dust might be an unknown poison."

"Perhaps not unknown. Perhaps the toxicologist looked for a stomach powder when Blake died of a blood poison. I don't know that I am expressing my ideas intelligently. I often wish I had studied medicine. What Professor Ericson reported was exceedingly interesting, and he certainly exercises one's imagination."

"I read a book once—now let me think—where—wait a minute."

Simes blew a cloud of smoke, which for a moment hung above his head like a crown. "It was a heck of a good book. The feller in it poisoned his wife's lover with coffin dust. The doctor saying that Professor Ericson thinks that powder is the residuum of a—what kind of animal body was it? Why, what's the matter?"

Bony's blue eyes were blazing and big, and Simes blinked and held suspended a mouthful of smoke.

"Did you say coffin dust?" Bony asked.

"Yes, in the book the feller put coffin dust in his wife's tucker. Bit far-fetched, I thought. I might be wrong, and it might have been the wife's lover who got it. Anyway, it was a good yarn. My sister got hold of it from somewhere."

"Is the book still in your house?"

"Couldn't say. You don't think that that powder could be coffin dust?"

"What is coffin dust?" Bony demanded. "Did the book tell you that?"

"Yes," replied Simes, continuing to be astonished by Bony's intensity of mind. "In the book, the husband went into an ancient churchyard in the dead of night, opened up a vault, opened a coffin and scooped up the dust that was lying underneath the skeleton. The dust was the—what was the word Fleetwood said? Yes, I remember—the residuum. Think we've hit on something?"

"So much so, my dear Simes, that I am very glad you lost your temper just now and so persuaded me to tell you about Mr Pickwick's ping-pong ball. We must find that book. You go back and bring some plaster of paris. You could return in your car to pick up the case of bottles. I'll wait for you. We shall want the casts to add to our little collection."

When Simes had departed, Bony entered the hut and carried out a further examination of the two rooms. Again he found nothing out of place, but one slight oddity. Where the ends of two floorboards came together, the end of one had recently been re-nailed with two new nails. At first, he thought nothing of it, as the boards were much worn and the age of the hut was, at the shortest, thirty years.

Subsequently he admitted that had he not had to wait for Constable Simes he would not have investigated further. For a moment he listened for the sound of Simes's car and, not hearing it, he went to the lean-to wash-house in which, he remembered, there were several tools. Selecting a crowbar he prized up the newly nailed board, and beneath found a glass jar containing a heavy roll of one-pound notes. There were exactly one hundred.

When Simes returned with the plaster of paris, he was given the money in the jar to lock away in the police station safe, and Bony proceeded to make casts of the significant tracks. The casts having hardened and the date being written upon them, Simes was instructed to take them also to the station, and then try to find the book containing the story about the coffin dust.

Bony waited for five minutes before leaving the hut and walking slowly along the unmade road to its junction with the highway. There, instead of turning down the hill to Yarrabo, he turned up the highway, keeping to the gravelled footpath and behaving as though he had time to spend admiring the beauties of nature. Not until he had walked a quarter of a mile did he turn about.

Between the wide strip of macadamed road and the flanking water-gutter there were lesser strips averaging two feet in width, ground comparatively impressionable. Since turning up the road, he had examined the narrow strip between macadam and gutter, as well as examining every inch of the footpath. He had seen tracks of human shoe leather, the tracks left by dogs and by a horse, but among them were not the tracks of either of the men who had abducted Wilcannia-Smythe, or of their car. Crossing the road, he made the same examination of that side as he walked downhill towards the little township. He arrived presently at the side street down which was Mrs Blake's house. Crossing that, he proceeded until he had gone several yards beyond Miss Pinkney's gate, and there he paused and stood as though admiring the church on the opposite corner. Then, crossing the macadam again, he sauntered up the road, passing the church, in which he evinced great interest, and so completed the full cycle since parting from Constable Simes. He had found neither the tracks of the car nor of either of the two men who had assaulted Wilcannia-Smythe. And yet the part-prints of the pigeon-toed man on the path from the highway to the gate proved that he had walked from the highway to visit Walsh and had returned to the highway.

On his way to the Police Station, Bony deliberated on having Wilcannia-Smythe "pulled in" for examination. He could be held on an information, but not for long, and if Mrs Blake did not prosecute, the fellow would have to be freed. As Wilcannia-Smythe could not be made to talk, it would be better to leave him in cold storage a little longer.

The sun was dipping behind a distant mountain, and the evening train for the city had left Yarrabo, when he reached the police station and called in through the open front door of the house. Simes came along the passage, inviting him to enter and saying that his sister must be at the store, and would certainly soon be back. He conducted Bony into the dining-room, offered him an easy chair beside the open window, and told him that as the kettle was boiling he would have a cup of tea ready "in two ups". He had not recalled the title of the book, and expressed the hope that his sister would do so.

Bony could not but like Constable Simes.

When Simes returned with the tea, Bony asked, "Did you know Captain Pinkney very well?"

"Oh yes. He was a peppery man and, I'll bet, a nark at sea," replied Simes. "After he went to bed I used often to run over there and sit with him. Sometimes his language would be so bad that if he had used it on the street I'd have run him in."

"He used to play ping-pong a great deal, according to Miss Pinkney," Bony stated.

"Yes, and a heck of a good player, too."

"I am going to tell you something else of interest. After

her brother became an invalid, Miss Pinkney gave their ping-pong table to the vicar. There was then only one ball of the last batch obtained by the captain from a French firm. Miss Pinkney assures me that the ball found by Mr Pickwick was not that last ball, which could not be found when the table was given to the vicar. Further, she said that her brother always marked the balls he bought with a small ink-spot. There was no ink-spot on the ball Mr Pickwick played with, and so we can assume that that ball was not the last one of the captain's store. Assume it, I say, because, Simes, the ink mark could have been washed off, or sucked or licked off by the cat, in the course of weeks, if not days."

"Ye—es," Simes agreed, wonderment in his eyes.

"Miss Pinkney had, at the time Blake died, access to his garden," Bony went on. "She hated Blake for throwing stones at her Mr Pickwick."

"I'm not sure of your drift," Simes said.

"Captain Pinkney sailed his ship into all the little-known ports of the world, according to his sister, who often sailed with him. When he retired he had a collection of all kinds of curios and odds and ends, and after he died, she dispatched most of it to a city auctioneer. One of the items he had collected could have been a set of ping-pong balls containing that sinister powder."

"But why put the stuff into ping-pong balls, in the first place?"

"To get it past the customs."

"You don't think that Miss—"

"I think nothing about it—yet," Bony said, so seriously that Simes almost believed him. "I have outlined what is a little lesson in deduction. There is the motive. There is access to the scene of the crime. There is the poison—if that powder is a poison—on Miss Pinkney's premises. And there was the chance to put the powder into Blake's brandy, and the chance, after he died, to replace the bottle and glass with another bottle and glass."

"But could Miss Pinkney replace the glass with a similar one?" asked Simes.

"That small point reduces probability to possibility," Bony conceded smilingly. "Having access to the next-door garden, she could previously have burgled Blake's writing-room for a glass, and Blake might not have noticed the loss, and would not have cared twopence if he had. Remember, we think that the bottle and glass were changed because the person who changed them thought of fingerprints after the poison had been put into the bottle. It would not have mattered so very much if the bottle containing the powder had contained the prints of Mrs Montrose, Mrs Blake, Ethel Lacy, or any one of the guests. But if Miss Pinkney's prints had been found on a bottle in Blake's writing-room—what then?"

"Ah! But it's impossible! Why, Miss Pinkney would never have done such a thing. No—by heck, Bony, you'd make a man believe anything."

"Please don't mention what I've said to Mrs Farn," Bony pleaded. "I could shoot holes through it as big as the Melbourne Cricket Ground. To be a successful investigator, one must be as cautious as a pawnbroker being offered the Crown Jewels as security. I think this is your sister."

"Hullo!" Mrs Farn exclaimed. "Having a little tea party all on your own?"

"And thoroughly enjoying it," Bony asserted.

"Say, sis," cut in Simes, "d'you remember that yarn we read some time ago in which the hero poisoned his wife's lover with coffin dust?"

"Yes. Why?"

"Do you remember what book it's in?"

"Yes. It's on the shelf behind you. That blue one next to the gardening book. See it? *The Vengeance of Master Atherton*, by I. R. Watts."

[NOTE—The authority for "Coffin Dust" as a poison is taken from Taylor's *Principles and Practice of Medical Jurisprudence*.]

CHAPTER TWENTY-TWO

R Ine I. R. Watts

THE following morning, at half past ten, Bony rang Nancy Chesterfield from a public telephone in Flinders Street. It was a hot and sultry day, and inside the box the heat was unbearable.

"Good morning, Nan," he said, in greeting. "Can you come out for morning tea with me?"

"I could, but I won't, Bony," she replied. "It's far too hot and my office is ever so much cooler."

"Then could I call on you? It would not be time wasting."

"By all means. I'll order a second cup of tea and biscuits," she said. "Honestly though. I couldn't possibly get away this morning. I've got a big news story to deal with. But if you will come up to me, I can spare you half an hour."

Five minutes later he was seated beside her desk, and thanking a young lady who had poured tea for them.

When the girl had gone, he said briskly, "I am not going to detain you very long. This is a busy day for me, too," and she sensed the earnestness beneath the smile he gave her. "I'm getting warm. Metaphorically, of course. In temperature, I have long since passed the 'getting' stage. This tea is delicious. What a train journey, to be sure! Cast your mind back to your visit to the Blakes when Dr Dario Chaparral was staying there. Ready?"

Nancy Chesterfield laughed delightedly.

"What a volcano you can be," she said, mockingly. "D'you know that when we lunched the other day, you didn't tell me what you thought of Janet Blake and Ella Montrose?"

"And forgot to thank you for the introduction you posted to me," he hastily supplemented. "I thank you now—for being a downright good sportswoman. I found both the ladies very charming. How did you know I called on Mrs Blake?"

"Ella wrote from Melbourne that same night. She said, *inter alia*, that she could not approve of the company you keep at Yarrabo."

"She need not be further concerned. The company is dead. They are conducting a post mortem on the body this morning."

"Oh!" The exclamation came slowly, and the grey eyes contracted.

"Died the night before last. Alcoholic poisoning. Well now, about this Dr Chaparral. Will you go back in mind to that evening, or evenings, when you dined with him at the Blakes' table?"

"Very well."

"You will remember that he told many stories which were so interesting to Ella Montrose that she noted them on slips of paper."

"Yes. I can even recall some of the stories he related."

"Good! Can you remember if he related the queer story that in certain districts of his country it is believed that the dust of a long-buried human body, if mixed with food, will poison the eater?"

"How horrible! No, I can't remember anything like that. He told stories of the customs of primitive peoples, and of their practices and beliefs. But not such a story as you have mentioned, Bony. Tell me more about it."

"There isn't much more to tell. I don't know much more than that, and what I do know is based chiefly on an incident in one of I. R. Watts's novels, *The Vengeance of Master Atherton*. Have you read it?"

Nancy Chesterfield replied in the negative as she shook her head.

"I have it with me," Bony said, indicating the small case at his feet. "Unfortunately, nowhere in the book is the year of publication stated. As I have already applied to his publishers for his address, and was refused it, I am diffident about approaching them. But I must know. And I must know where Watts obtained the data concerning what he calls 'coffin dust' in his novel."

"I'll ring them, shall I?"

"If you would."

Whilst waiting for the connection, Bony said, "I wrote to I. R. Watts a few days ago asking for an interview. The publishers did tell me that he lives in Victoria. I could get the address out of them through police pressure, but that would not, I think, be diplomatic just now."

The bell shrilled and Nancy picked up the instrument. She announced her name and said she was writing a literary article and wanted the year of publication of Watt's particular novel. Then, having put down the instrument, she said, "It was published in Australia in 1942."

And Dr Chaparral visited the Blakes in 1945. It disproves a theory that someone heard Dr Chaparral at the Blakes' table relate a story about coffin dust, and passed it to I. R. Watts, who, however, knew the story in 1942 or previously."

"Do you think—"

Bony held one hand.

"Please," he pleaded. "I do not think anything just now. You must not, either. Nor mention this matter to anyone. Cross your fingers and promise."

Attempting a smile, she obeyed.

"I believe you could tell stories far more bizarre than Dr Chaparral even imagined," she said.

"Do you think he drew upon his imagination?"

"He must have."

"You have played ping-pong at the Blakes' house, have you not?"

"Often. I have never seen anyone play better than Dr Chaparral. He is a wizard."

"Do you remember if he made any differentiation with the balls? Did he favour one kind and reject another?"

"No, I don't remember that he did. He brought the balls with him from overseas. The Blakes had none left, and they could not be bought anywhere in Melbourne at the time. You know, you are making me as confused as a rabbit in a car's headlights."

Bony suddenly smiled, and abruptly rose to his feet taking up his case and his hat.

"I am just as confused as you are. I don't know whether I'm coming or going. Will you dine with me this evening and then do a show?"

Nancy hesitated, decided to sacrifice an important engagement, and consented.

"Make the reservation, will you?" he implored, worry written plainly on his face. "Choose a dinner with an orchestra and a show with bright music. I am more grateful to you than I can express. I'll ring you about four o'clock to arrange where to meet you. Some day I'll tell you a story that will make a newspaper scoop, if you would like to use it."

"I hope it will be soon," she said. "Curiosity is suffocating me. And thank you so very much for wanting to take me out tonight."

Bony bowed and departed.

Once in the street his face no longer registered worry. He was actually smiling as he walked up Collins Place to Collins Street, and then down along that thoroughfare to a café that had become a favourite with him.

Before ordering more morning tea he rang up Police Headquarters, and asked for Superintendent Bolt.

"Good morning, super! Great day for the blacks," he said in greeting.

"Good morning. Rotten day—even for the blacks. Where are you?" came the loud and distinct voice.

"At the Café Italiano, which I estimate is five hundred and seventy yards from your palatial office. Care for a cup of tea, or an ice-cream or something?"

"I'd like the something with ice in it. How's the work going?"

"Work, did you say? I'm on holiday. You coming along?"

"Can't. I'm up to my eyes. But I'm open to see you here to talk business. Any progress?"

"Very tenuous. Can you spare your delightful Inspector Snook?"

"Yes. The milk in my tea was sour. He looked at it, so the clerk says. What you want him for?"

"To chaperon me round Melbourne. I want to make a few calls, and I haven't the authority."

"You could name someone more pleasant as a companion," Bolt said.

"Impossible. I'd like the companionship of the officer mentioned, super."

"Righto! I'll send him to you. Cough it up, Bony. You doing any good?"

"I think I am," Bony replied. "I've waded into a flood, and now I can see my way to wading out of it. You know the usual run of these investigations. I'll hand it to you on a lettuce leaf one of these days—with very many thanks for a most engrossing holiday. Well, tell Snook his morning tea will be waiting."

Three minutes later Detective-Inspector Snook alighted from a police car and entered the café.

"Do you want the car for the sightseeing?" he asked, and when Bony said it was an excellent idea, he sat down and regarded the Queenslander with cold, granite-grey eyes. The short-cropped grey hair added to the deathlike pallor of his square face gave the impression that he was bloodless.

"It's a fine day for tea," Bony observed. "Milk and sugar?"

"You mucking about on that Blake case?" Snook asked, and Bony admitted it. "Have you found who shot Blake, or was it a knifing?"

"It was coffin dust."

Snook grunted. The significance passed over him.

"What was the foreign matter found by the toxicologist in Blake's stomach?"

"Been worrying you, eh?" and Snook almost leered. "Blake must have accidentally swallowed a lump of chewing gum after he ate his last dinner. Nothing poisonous in that."

Bony, smiling affably, sipped his tea. He said, "I want to make several calls in this city, and as I've no official authority,

I am glad you consented to come along. The first call I want to make is on the Income Tax people. Happen to know anyone there, so that our time would be saved?"

"Yes. What do we go there for?"

"To locate the address of a gentleman whose work I admire. Ready? The idea of a police car is excellent."

Arrived at the offices of the Income Taxation Commission, Inspector Snook asked for a Mr Trilby, and without having to wait they were shown into a single office inhabited by a man who looked like a bookmaker. Bony having been presented, they were asked to be seated.

"I want the address of a taxpayer named I. R. Watts," Bony said. "Because I do not want Watts to learn that I am making inquiries through the Investigation Branch, I cannot compel his publishers to give me the address. And that they decline to do."

The imitation bookmaker raised a switch, lifted a telephone and requested the address of a taxpayer named I. R. Watts. Then he began a conversation with Snook on the recent form of Test cricketers, and this subject occupied the time until a buzzer sounded and the telephone again came into use.

"H'm! All right! Thanks," murmured the expert extortionist. Replacing the instrument, he grinned at the visitors, and said that in the State of Victoria there was no taxpayer by the name of I. R. Watts. He would contact the publishers, if Bony desired.

Bony decided against getting in touch with the publishers, because there was yet reasonable time for I. R. Watts to answer his letter, and when again in the street, he asked to be driven to the Colombian Consulate.

CHAPTER TWENTY-THREE

Killing with Kindness

THEY arrived at the Colombian Consulate a few minutes before noon, and were admitted to the presence of a man not unlike but less well dressed than Bony. Having introduced themselves, the Consul expressed eagerness to be of all possible assistance, backing his words with constant movements of hands and eyes. Snook sourly resigned the talking.

"You have been the Colombian Consul for how long, sir?" Bony began.

"Three years, yes."

"Did your countryman, Dr Dario Chaparral, pay his respects when he visited Victoria at the beginning of last year?"

"It is so, yes."

"Was that his first visit to Australia?"

"His first visit, no, gentlemen," replied the Consul. He slapped his forehead and implored them to be patient with him whilst he thought. Then, "Ah! I recall. Dr Dario Chaparral first paid a visit to Australia in 1936. I was then not the Consul for my country, you understand? Yes? I was then in business in Sydney."

"You could not tell me, I suppose, if Dr Chaparral visited Victoria on his first visit to Australia?"

"But I could, gentlemen. Dr Chaparral himself informed me that during his first visit to Australia he was unable to come to Melbourne."

"Did he visit you on his first visit—when you lived in Sydney?"

"Yes. Yes, that is so. On several occasions he dined with me and my wife at my home there."

"Where did he stay?"

"At Petty's Hotel, most of the time," replied the Consul. "During his visit to Sydney he stayed over the week-end with literary friends. You understand? Yes? Dr Chaparral is a literary personage."

"Could you tell me who these literary people were? I should be grateful if you could."

"But of course I could. Dr Chaparral when in Sydney stayed for several days with Mr and Mrs Alverstoke of Ryde, and he stayed also with Mr Wilcannia-Smythe, who had a house on the Hawkesbury River."

"H'm! I thank you, sir," Bony said, smilingly.

"Can you tell us anything more of Dr Chaparral?"

"Perhaps, what is it, ah, yes, but little. Yes!" The bold black eyes in the lean face passed their gaze swiftly from one to the other of his callers. "Dr Chaparral is a doctor of medicine. He is famous in Bogota, where he is in residence. He has written several novels and other works on the aboriginal inhabitants of my country."

"Thank you, sir. You have placed me in your debt," Bony said, to which the Consul countered with, "It is but a pleasure, Mistaire Bonaparte."

"What are the Doctor's hobbies?" pressed Bony, and Snook revealed signs of impatience.

"His—his—what do you say?"

"Hobbies, games, collections?"

"Ah, but yes! He is a philatelist. And I remember also that he told me he was beginning to play golf. That was in Sydney. The last time he came here to Melbourne, he said golf was too much walking and he had played very hard the table game, what was called ping-pong."

Bony rose smilingly to his feet, and with a cluck of impatience Snook got to his. The Consul rose with alacrity, as though glad that this police inquisition was nearing its end. Bony regarded him with his strangely deceptive blue eyes, which now were softly beaming. The Consul, however, was not deceived. He sensed that the most vital question of all was to be put.

"Have you heard of the practice in parts of your country of taking the dust from a long-buried coffin for the purpose of poisoning an enemy?"

Despite his preparedness, the Consul failed to maintain the open frankness with which he had met Bony's previous questions. Although his hesitation was but for a second, both policemen noted it, and he knew they had noted it.

"A silly superstition, Mistaire Bonaparte," he said, his hands fluttering like the wings of a moth. "In the far interior of Colombia there is a belief that the remains of a long-dead body can poison the living and leave no trace. Me, I cannot believe it. It is what the English say an old wives' tale."

"When or where did you hear of that superstition? From Dr Chaparral?"

"Ah, no, no, no!" replied the Consul. "I heard about it when I was going to school. Everyone knows about it in my country. The mass believe it to be true. There have even been cases when the law has punished personages for robbing old graves of coffin dust, as it is called."

Snook spoke for the first time; in his voice was contempt.

"Must be a pleasant occupation," he said.

Bony took up his hat, and the Consul revealed relief.

"Thank you, sir, for your kindness in receiving us," Bony said and shook hands. "By the way, does your country manufacture ping-pong balls?"

"Yes, but of course," replied the Consul. "My country exported in 1945 more than a hundred thousand gross. There are two firms in Bogota making them."

"Thank you again, sir," and this time Bony bowed and walked out, followed by the mystified and therefore angry Inspector Snook.

"What's this coffin dust racket?" he demanded when they were again in the police car. "You're not going to put it over that Mervyn Blake was poisoned with coffin dust, are you?"

"Now do I look like a fool?" Bony mildly inquired. "Years ago I heard about coffin dust being used to murder a man in

173

France, and I have often wondered if there was anything in it."

"Then what connection has it with the death of Mervyn Blake?"

"So tenuous as not to be seriously considered, my dear Snook. Naturally, I have been interested in the Blake case, but I am on leave, and when on leave I permit myself many interests. Ask the driver to take us to the Chief Customs Officer, Marine Division."

The Supervisor of Customs called up his henchmen. The date on which Dr Chaparral landed at Melbourne was dug out of the files, and the man who had examined his luggage was summoned.

"Do you remember checking through the luggage of a Dr Dario Chaparral who landed here from South America on 10th February last year?" Bony asked him.

"It's a long time ago," the customs officer replied doubtfully.

"He is a native of Colombia, South America. He brought with him at least one box of ping-pong balls."

"Yes, I remember him now. The ping-pong balls does it. He had four boxes, each containing two dozen balls. The boxes were still sealed as when sold by the manufacturers in Colombia. I broke open the boxes to make sure of the contents, and the passenger paid the duty on the goods. The passenger also had in his effects a complete ping-pong set."

"Were there any balls with the set?" pressed Bony.

"Yes, several. As they had been in use, the passenger was not asked to pay duty on them, or on the set."

"You noticed nothing peculiar about the balls, I suppose?"

"If I had done so, I'd have passed the goods to the Research Group for X-ray examination. I hope I didn't miss anything?"

"No, I don't think so," replied Bony. "Thank you very much."

Again in the police car, the two officers sat in silence, Bony cogitating on what he had been told, Snook two degrees further infuriated.

At last he said, "You not going to play ball?"

"Not when I am unable to see the ball."

"All right! What do we do next? Instead of sitting here like a couple of lovers, what about suggesting where we go from here? The driver and I are entirely at your highness's service."

"Well, I suggest we go somewhere for lunch," Bony said, mildly. "After lunch, I'd like to visit a doctor at Essendon, and an undertaker in that same suburb. Let's lunch well. I'll be the host."

"I always lunch at the office," snapped Snook. "I'll drop you at Menzies, as you want to be flash, and pick you up later."

"As you like," Bony said quietly. When the car was in motion, he asked, "Was any brandy found in Blake's garage?"

"What was found was listed in the official file."

"In the official file there is no mention of brandy being found in the garage. Neither is there any mention by any member of the household that Mervyn Blake kept brandy in the garage, and that there was brandy in the garage that last evening of his life."

"So what?" sneered Snook.

"The bottle of brandy in the garage was taken to the writing-room and the bottle then on the desk was removed —some time after the man expired and before the rain stopped at half past four in the morning.

"Which means?" snarled Snooks, the sneer no longer in his voice.

"A slight point of interest. Ah! Menzies Hotel! Who, in all Australia, hasn't heard of it?"

"I think I will lunch with you," Snook said, glaring at Bony.

"Not now, my dear Snook. I have decided against any further calls today. Au revoir!"

Bony smiled, quietly closed the door and strolled into the hotel. Snook bit his lip and snapped at the driver to take him back to Headquarters.

Bony sought a telephone compartment and raised Superintendent Bolt.

"Had a pleasant morning?" Bolt asked, and chuckled.

"Very. Poor Snook is heading for a nervous breakdown. You should look after him better. Can you get me a reservation on a plane for Sydney this afternoon?"

"For social calls or business, you tantalizing swab?"

"You wouldn't interfere now in this Blake case, would you?"

"Of course not. As I told you, it's all yours."

"Get the reservation for this afternoon. And come along to Menzies and lunch with me. I may confide."

"Good-oh! If you don't 'toik', you'll be for it."

The enormous Chief of the C.I.B. thoroughly enjoyed his lunch. For one thing, Menzies is a place where one can enjoy lunch, and for another Napoleon Bonaparte could be a charming host. Bolt was told just as much as Bony thought was good for him, and that much was a great deal for Bony to bring himself to tell anyone. No mention was made of the adventure of Wilcannia-Smythe, of the novels of I. R. Watts, of the death of Sid Walsh.

The story of Mr Pickwick's ping-pong ball gave Bolt food for thought, and the fact provided by Ethel Lacy, that there was brandy kept in the garage, and the bottle possibly exchanged for that on Blake's writing table after he died, brought forth the remark, "I felt it in my bones that there was something screwy about that bloke's death. Snook assured me he had experimented with the ruddy door, and that the experiment proved his theory that the wind had closed it. The meteorological people supported it with a report that that night the wind did blow in gusts of up to twenty miles an hour. Then, of course, there was the toxicologist's negative report. How do you get over that last?"

"No man is infallible, super," replied Bony. "I wonder if his mind was predisposed to the thought that Blake died through what is termed alcoholic poisoning. If it was, then he might have been content to seek only for one of the common poisons. The other point, the weather, is more clear. Evidence of several people goes to prove that at Yarrabo—at Yarrabo, mind you—there was hardly any wind throughout the night."

"You getting warm?"

"Yes. You know how it is. In the beginning one has to test doors. None of them will budge. One goes on testing doors, and then, unexpectedly, a door will open, and beyond that door there are the keys to unlock several of those doors that wouldn't budge."

"That's how it moves," Bolt agreed. "You haven't told me about all the doors you've opened, have you?"

"No." Bony smiled into the shrewd, brown eyes of his enormous guest. "I shall, eventually, finalize this case to my satisfaction, and therefore to your own. I'll hand it over to you, tied up neatly, and append to it my grateful thanks for having made my leave very enjoyable. I shall look for no credit but I want payment."

"That's not like you, Bony. All your exes will be refunded, of course."

"The payment I desire is recognition of Constable Simes, who is being unprofitably used up at Yarrabo. He has revealed marked intelligence, and his collaboration has been invaluable. I'll give you the ammunition with which to urge his promotion. You'll find it in my report. It is little for me to ask for in view of the sacrifices my unfortunate wife has to make, and the sacrifice I have now to make by cancelling an evening's engagement with the most vital woman I've ever met. My plane leaves at three, I think you said. Where do I pick up a transport car?"

"Take the police car—outside. I can walk back. I'll fix the payment for you. I know a thing or two about Simes that you don't know. Wouldn't care to tell your old pal why you are toddling off to Sydney, I suppose?"

"Of course. I'm going to run the rule over Wilcannia-Smythe. Be a good fellow, super, and telephone the Sydney Branch to have him in the ice-box when I arrive."

CHAPTER TWENTY-FOUR

A Stubborn Subject

Bony's plane touched down at Sydney shortly after 5.30 p.m., and on reaching ground he was accosted by a man who was evidently a plain-clothes policeman.

"Inspector Bonaparte?" he said, softly. When Bony nodded assent, he took over the suitcase, and announced that a police car was waiting. Twenty minutes later, Bony was shaking hands with the Chief of the New South Wales Criminal Investigation Branch.

"Sit down, Bony, you old scoundrel," the Chief urged, and almost pushed Bony into a chair beside his desk. "Good trip?"

"I prefer travelling by car, via Bermagui where the sword-fishing is particularly good just now," Bony replied. "Bolt evidently rang you up."

"Oh yes! Said you were interested in a writin' bloke named Wilcannia-Smythe. We contacted him and he promised to be here at six. Do you want him taken up?"

"No. Not at present, anyway. I would like to interview him in a comfortable office, with a stenographer unobtrusively in a corner. The interview may take some time, possibly all night. And possibly all day tomorrow, too."

The New South Wales Superintendent raised his bushy black brows and pursed his thin lips.

"You may have this office for the time being," he said. "I won't be here, D.V., until about eight tomorrow. I'll get you a man to record the words. You eaten? What about grub before you start in on this bird?"

"H'm! Three minutes to six," murmured Bony. "Thanks for the suggestion. Do my man good to be kept biting his nails for half an hour. Give instructions that once he is here he is not to be allowed to leave."

"That goes. Come on. I know a place."

It was fifteen minutes to seven when Mr Wilcannia-Smythe, who was seated in a waiting-room, was approached by a uniformed constable and told that "the Inspector is disengaged now". He was conducted into a large, severely-furnished office where Inspector Bonaparte was standing behind the file-littered desk.

"Good evening, Mr Wilcannia-Smythe. Please be seated," Bony greeted him, and the constable indicated a chair on the opposite side of the desk, and then seated himself at a small table.

"Good evening," countered Wilcannia-Smythe, and sat down. "I hope you are not going to take too much of my time. I have an important literary gathering to address at eight."

Bony regarded the clock fixed to the wall above the constable's table, and then sat down and lit one of a respectable pile of cigarettes he had made.

"Our little business can be accomplished within fifteen minutes," he said briskly. "It was good of you to oblige by coming to see me. I, too, am a busy man, and so we both can appreciate the value of time."

The evening sunlight slanted across Bony's shoulders to fall upon the desk and to illumine the face of the man whose hair was snowy white and over-long, to be reflected by the hazel eyes, now wide and inquiring, to harden the lines about the sensitive mouth.

"You were recently in Victoria, Mr Wilcannia-Smythe," Bony proceeded. "Whilst there you stayed at the Rialto Hotel, Warburton. Am I correct?"

"You are. What of it?"

"I am given to understand that when walking alone one night you were waylaid by two men who took you in their car to a lonely place and there tied you to a tree. In that predicament you were found the next morning. I want you to tell me all you can about those two men."

179

"I'm afraid I am unable to tell you anything about them."

"Why not?"

"It was a dark night, and both men had handkerchiefs drawn across their faces under their eyes."

"Indeed! Well, that's a beginning. You noted their physique?"

"Yes, I did that, of course. One of the men was a very large person, and the other was as tall but thin."

"Let us deal first with the large man," Bony said, pleasantly. "How large would he be? As large as my secretary? Please stand, Hawkins."

That, most likely, was not the constable's name, but he did as suggested and Wilcannia-Smythe turned to look at him. He was six feet tall if an inch, and he must have weighed over fourteen stone of bone and muscle.

"Yes, I should think that the larger of the two men would be as big," conceded Wilcannia-Smythe.

"What size boots do you wear, Hawkins?"

"Size nine, sir."

The constable sat down. Not a sign of perturbation did Bony detect in the hazel eyes or about the mouth of the white-haired, youngish man.

"The other man, Mr Wilcannia-Smythe. You say he was tall and thin. Was he as tall as Hawkins, d'you think?"

"Yes, I think he would be. You see, it was very dark that night. They didn't waste much time in getting me into the car, or when they ordered me out and made me walk up the hill to the tree. Anyway, I don't know what this is all about. I suffered no hurt. As I told the Yarrabo policeman, I think it was a case of mistaken identity. I don't think there's any more I can tell you. I'm terribly sorry, you know, but that's how it is."

"Would you prefer a charge against those two men?"

"I don't want to, really." Wilcannia-Smythe smiled, and added, "You see, Inspector, actually I owe them something. They presented me with a rather thrilling experience. Being a novelist, that is of value to me. I can make use of it in a future work."

"Yes, of course," Bony agreed. "H'm! There's that to be said about it. Still, we cannot allow desperate men like that to waylay peaceful citizens and leave them tied to a tree all night. Your experience would have been less thrilling perhaps had the night been bitterly cold, or had your situation not been discovered by the workman for, let us assume, two days. Frankly, I think it odd that you don't wish to charge them."

"It is not at all odd," Wilcannia-Smythe said, still with perfect calm. "I am a public figure. A fact worth mentioning, I think, is that this evening—at eight o'clock—I am to address a literary gathering of distinguished people. In view of what I have said, you will agree that I would not like that little experience of mine to be published in the press, made a feature by the lurid weekly journals. I have most certainly no desire for such publicity. Hence my refusal to prefer a charge."

"Would you, Mr Wilcannia-Smythe, be surprised were I to tell you that neither of those men was large—as large as Hawkins—and that neither was as tall as Hawkins?"

"I would, even although I would have to agree, if you proved it, because, as I have repeatedly said, the night was dark."

"Well, Mr Wilcannia-Smythe, I can prove it. Both those men wore shoes or boots size seven. We have just heard Hawkins say that he wears size nine. In addition to the known size of the boots, or shoes, worn by those men, is the length of their stride, and the weight of their bodies. You did not know those men?"

"Know them! Of course not. What is all this about anyway?"

Bony smiled, but Wilcannia-Smythe could not see his eyes as the sunlight was behind the inquisitor's head.

"Well, Mr Wilcannia-Smythe, it's like this. I am inclined to believe that you did know those men. In fact, I am so strongly inclined to believe it that I want you to tell me who they are. Wait one moment. Telling me who they are does not mean that you would have to lay a charge against them.

Those two men are suspected of being concerned in another and much more serious crime."

"I am sorry I cannot oblige you," Wilcannia-Smythe said, and sighed with vexed impatience. "In view of your assurance that I would not be legally associated with them, I would name them if I could."

"H'm! Just too bad." Bony lifted another cigarette from the pile. Wilcannia-Smythe stood up.

"I shall have to go, Inspector," he said. "As it is, I must rush. I have to dress and then be at the Town Hall by three minutes to eight."

"I must know the names of those two men," Bony said, slowly, distinctly, and coldly.

The hazel eyes suddenly blazed, but the face remained passive and the voice was without a tremor.

"I cannot assist you. I am very sorry, but I cannot assist you, Inspector."

Wilcannia-Smythe turned away from the desk towards the door.

"Please sit down," came the quiet voice, and the constable looked round.

"But, my dear man, I must go! Look at the time! Those people cannot be kept waiting."

"Please sit down."

Wilcannia-Smythe shrugged his elegant shoulders and sat down.

"I am not greatly concerned, Mr Wilcannia-Smythe, to disappoint a number of people interested in books," went on the quiet voice. "As you cannot recall the names of those two men who abducted you that night, and as you made such a gross mistake about their physique, let us pass to another subject. Do you know Clarence B. Bagshott?"

"No, I don't know the fellow."

"Do you know I. R. Watts?"

"Neither do I know I. R. Watts. If you cannot let me leave to attend my important function, I shall refuse to speak any more. You cannot compel me to stay, and I refuse to stay a moment longer."

"What were you doing in Mervyn Blake's writing-room on the night of 3rd January?"

Mr Wilcannia-Smythe was superb. Not a hair came out of place. Not an eye-muscle twitched. He resumed his seat and leant forward and tapped a manicured finger upon the edge of the desk. He did not speak. His hazel eyes regarded the blue eyes beyond the desk litter. Bony did not speak. The clock ticked away its seconds. The light waned, and the light within the office began to soften. Still neither man spoke. The wall clock struck eight.

"Ring for my supper, please, Hawkins," Bony said. "You could order something for yourself."

"Very well, sir. Thank you."

The constable got up, crossed to the desk, pressed a button and lifted a speaking tube.

"Supper for the Inspector, please, and a tray for the stenographer," he ordered, and returned to his table.

Bony picked up a file and began to read a report on the theft of a motor boat. Wilcannia-Smythe continued his silence.

Having read about the stolen motor boat, Bony yawned, tossed the file back on the desk, and said, "I think you are being very foolish, Mr Wilcannia-Smythe."

"May I use your telephone?"

"No, I regret I must refuse your request. You see, my superiors thought fit to issue a regulation that our office telephones must not be used for private calls. On the ground of economy, you know. They often have a fit of that kind. What did you say you were doing in Mervyn Blake's writing-room on the night of 3rd January? Mrs Blake did not arrive home until about ten o'clock, remember. Without meeting her, you slipped over Miss Pinkney's fence, and then walked down the road to your hotel."

"All that, Inspector, is an untruth."

"On leaving Mervyn Blake's writing-room, Mr Wilcannia-Smythe, you forgot to pick up your handkerchief. Mrs Blake subsequently found it and, the next afternoon on the Rialto terrace, she gave it back to you—as proof that you entered her husband's writing-room."

"The handkerchief Mrs Blake gave me at the Rialto was one I left behind at her house when spending a week with them."

"That conflicts with Mrs Blake's story."

"I am not aware of the story alleged to have been told by Mrs Blake. I say that the handkerchief she gave me at the Rialto was one which I left behind at her house."

"Miss Pinkney—" Bony craftily began when his victim cut him off.

"Miss Pinkney is a half-witted, gossiping old bitch," Wilcannia-Smythe stated matter-of-factly, and without emotion. "I'm astonished that you should take the slightest notice of what she has been saying. She's the most dangerous woman in Australia. The Blakes were always complaining about her."

"I was about to say," Bony murmured, "that Miss Pinkney has a very remarkable cat to whom she has given the name of Mr Pickwick."

No additional statement was added to that one. Bony regarded Wilcannia-Smythe with guileless eyes, picked up another cigarette, and would have lit it had not a constable entered with two trays. The stenographer took them from him, placed the larger before Bony, and carried the other to his table.

An appetizing odour arose from the covered dish. Bony poured himself a cup of tea. It was then that he lit the cigarette. Wilcannia-Smythe rose once more and walked to the door.

The door was locked, and he turned to say, "I am not conversant with the law, but I do know that you haven't any right or any justification for keeping me here against my will."

"Hawkins! Did you lock that door?"

"No, sir."

"See what's the matter with the lock. Mr Wilcannia-Smythe! As you say, I cannot detain you here against your

184

will. I can, however, have you arrested and charged with entering and stealing."

"With entering and stealing!" repeated Wilcannia-Smythe. "Entering where and stealing what?"

"I will leave that to your intelligence," Bony said and, lifting the cover, helped himself to a hot sausage roll. The stenographer, observing the action, left the door wide open and returned to his table where he made a few swift notes and then proceeded with his supper.

Wilcannia-Smythe advanced from the door. Behind him the door closed with a faint click, and he swung round quickly to look at it. Bony lifted his foot from the mechanism beneath the desk, and went on eating his roll, although he was far from being hungry. Wilcannia-Smythe advanced again, to sit down in the chair he had vacated. There were several tiny glass-like beads adhering to his noble forehead. Munching his roll, Bony asked, "Did you ever hear the story about coffin dust?"

CHAPTER TWENTY-FIVE

Concerning Cabbages

"Coffin dust!"

In the quiet of the room the words sounded like ivy leaves coldly caressing the door of a vault. Wilcannia-Smythe sat utterly still, his eyes seemingly frozen into immobility. Through bloodless lips he said, "No. I have not heard such a story."

"Have you read any of I. R. Watts's novels?"

"You mean I. R. Watts's romantic tales? No, I have not read them."

"You should, Mr Wilcannia-Smythe," Bony said pleasantly. "I commend his *The Vengeance of Master Atherton.* Sound story, well constructed. In that novel the author relates how a man poisoned his wife's lover with the dust he gathered from a coffin long occupied. You have met Mr Watts?"

"I have not." Wilcannia-Smythe had returned to animation. As though talking to a child, he implored, "Please tell me what all this about coffin dust and Watts's alleged novels have to do with me. Are you mad, or am I?"

"We will leave the coffin dust for the present," Bony said, sipping his tea. "Do you know where I. R. Watts lives?"

"I do not, Inspector. As one who has devoted his life to Australian literature, I would not know anything of any writer producing less."

"Was it literature that interested you in Mervyn Blake's writing-room that evening when Mrs Blake was away until a late hour, and her cook had gone to the pictures?"

For a moment the hazel eyes widened, but the mouth became firm. The man was the victim of vanity, and to break a way into the real spirit Bony must needs use sharp implements.

"The fact, Mr Wilcannia-Smythe, that you are an eminent littérateur who would naturally shrink from reading a Charles Dickens serial story, becomes quite insignificant when placed beside the fact that I am a detective-inspector. You are interested in what is loosely termed by people of your description, literature. I am interested in crime. Kings and statesmen, ministers of religion, tradesmen and barons of commerce, wharf labourers, and, Mr Wilcannia-Smythe, authors, have been known to commit serious crimes. You don't interest me as an author; you do interest me as a possible criminal."

"You are an insulting cad," whispered Mr Wilcannia-Smythe.

"On the night of 3rd January you were on enclosed premises, Mr Wilcannia-Smythe," went on the calmly in-exorable Bony. "Further, you were seen to put in your pocket certain documents that you found in the writing-room of the late Mr Mervyn Blake. When you left the writing-room, you were observed to escape over a near fence into property owned by a Miss Pinkney. And you made your escape after Mrs Blake arrived at her home in her car. I think that the lurid weekly journals, as you call them, will not have the slightest consideration for an author, even so eminent an author as yourself."

Wilcannia-Smythe did not relax. He remained silent. Bony tried again.

"It is possible, Mr Wilcannia-Smythe, that you have a very good answer to the charge of being on enclosed premises and of having removed documents from the writing-room owned by the late Mr Mervyn Blake. But assuming—and the assumption is possibly not so far-fetched as one might think—assuming that Mr Mervyn Blake was foully murdered, your subsequent actions in his writing-room would have a peculiar significance to a jury.

"I don't want to detain you, Mr Wilcannia-Smythe, because I am after much bigger game," Bony went on. "I am inclined to think that your actions were not particularly serious. Actually, I am not greatly concerned in you, but I am concerned by the contents of the documents you removed from the writing-room, and which subsequently were removed from your baggage at the Rialto Hotel."

The tip of Wilcannia-Smythe's tongue passed to and fro between his lips. He brought his gaze to rest upon the clear blue eyes now revealed to him by the electric light overhead. He changed the position of his slim body. When he spoke his voice was low and as controlled as formerly.

"I'll tell you everything," he said. "When you put forward the assumption that Mervyn Blake was murdered, I think your assumption may be one day proved fact. I've always thought that Blake might have been murdered, though I've had absolutely nothing on which to base the belief.

"Mervyn Blake was my friend. We had been friends for many years. What I took from his writing-room he gave to me some considerable time before he died. I took only what was mine, and I took it because Mrs Blake refused to give me what was mine. Mrs Blake never liked me. After her husband died, she never troubled to conceal her dislike.

"The Blakes, you will know, often entertained oversea authors. Some of them were widely travelled. The great majority were excellent raconteurs. At the end of an evening in the company of one of these visitors, Blake would record in a note-book the gist of the stories they told. In the course of years there were a great many anecdotes and queer stories entered into that note-book. Sometimes Mrs Montrose would record the stories and Blake would subsequently enter them in his book. On other occasions I would make the notes and afterwards give them to him.

"Not being a writer yourself, Inspector, you would not appreciate the great store of plots contained between the covers of that note-book. Blake at first intended to use them for short stories. Mrs Blake, in fact, did use a number of them. As I said just now, Blake gave them to me by promise. He did so repeatedly, and also he said he had bequeathed them to me in his will. Poor fellow, he put it off and put it off. I took what was my own."

"Is there anyone who would support that contention?" asked Bony.

"Yes. Mrs Ella Montrose would support it. And so would Twyford Arundal, the Adelaide poet."

"And you went to stay at the Rialto Hotel to seize the opportunity of taking those notes without the widow's permission?"

"When I learnt that the note-book was not mentioned in Blake's will, I wrote to Mrs Blake stating the facts," Wilcannia-Smythe said. "She wrote in reply, saying that she knew nothing of any such intended bequest, and that she would not part with anything belonging to her husband. I went down to Warburton, put up at the hotel, and then travelled to Melbourne one day to visit Mrs Blake, who was staying with Ella Montrose. Mrs Blake was adamant. I returned by the evening train, alighting at Yarrabo. I saw the cook board the bus for Warburton, and knew she would be off to the cinema. So I went to the house, sat on the back veranda and waited until it was dark. One moment, I'm a little out of order. I committed an additional crime. I entered the house through the rear door, which the cook had left unlocked, and knowing where the spare key of the writing-room was kept, I took it, intending to replace it before the cook returned from the cinema."

Bony eased himself in his chair.

"And the two men who tied you to a tree, who were they?" he asked.

"I don't know."

"They did remove the note-book and typescript from your effects at the Rialto Hotel, did they not?"

"Yes."

"What was the typescript matter?"

"Notes intended for transference to the note-book."

"Who else, do you think, might be interested in that note-book, other than yourself and Mervyn Blake's widow?"

"A considerable number of people," replied Wilcannia-

189

Smythe. "In its way, the note-book housed quite a famous collection of anecdotes. It represented a gold mine for any writer."

"And you think it probable that Mrs Blake persuaded a friend or two to get it back for her?"

"Yes. But who, I cannot tell you. I did not recognize the voice of the one man who spoke. I did not recognize either of them by their physical appearance. And I did not recognize the car."

"Was there anyone staying at the Rialto who was well known to you?"

"No."

"And you left the note-book—where?"

"In the larger of my suitcases."

"Thank you. Now let us discuss another matter—the contents of the note-book. How much were you conversant with the contents?"

"Very little. The note-book contained a large number of stories told when I was not present."

"So that the note-book could contain a story of coffin dust and you not know of it?"

"Undoubtedly."

"Would Mrs Montrose be more familiar with the contents of the book?"

"Yes. And so would Mrs Blake. Ella Montrose was closer to Blake than I was. She was always with the Blakes when they had important people staying with them." Wilcannia-Smythe frowned for an instant, and then added with greater warmth than hitherto displayed, "I believe I am not exaggerating when I say that all told there were close upon a thousand excellent stories in that book. Blake's writing was exceedingly small. As I said just now, the book was a gold mine, more valuable as a gift to a writer than a thousand pounds. Blake intended giving it to me. I think I can find one or two of his letters in which he states that intention."

"H'm! Still, Mr Wilcannia-Smythe, your actions in gaining possession of it were most reprehensible," Bony said severely. "If Mrs Blake should prosecute, or report the loss, you will certainly find yourself in an unpleasant situation. However, I appreciate your candour. Now kindly assist me in another matter by throwing light upon several people well known to you. Dr Dario Chaparral visited Australia for the first time in 1936. He stayed with you for several days. Was he then interested in ping-pong?"

"No, not nearly to the extent that he was on his last visit."

"How long prior to his first visit to Australia did you know him?"

"I heard of him about a year before," Wilcannia-Smythe replied, "through the Blakes. They were corresponding with him for several years before 1936, and when he came to Australia on that occasion, they came to Sydney especially to meet him. Ella Montrose also came up from Melbourne."

"Was the note-book employed at that time?"

Wilcannia-Smythe hesitated before answering.

"I'm not sure. I am inclined to think that it was."

"Thank you," Bony said. "Although you feel you cannot admit any knowledge of I. R. Watts—er—professionally, you must know, privately, something about him—where he lives, what he has done, other than his novels."

The left extremity of Wilcannia-Smythe's upper lip lifted in a sneer.

"When Watts first began to issue his tales, we examined them as a matter of course," he said. "On finding that they could not be considered as a serious contribution to Australian literature, no one troubled about the fellow. He kept himself to himself. He made no advances, nor did he attempt to enter any literary circle. For years I have held the opinion that I. R. Watts is a pen-name of someone very well known in Australia, possibly someone in the political or religious spheres. We made no attempt to find out as we were never concerned with his work."

"H'm! That's a point of interest, Mr Wilcannia-Smythe," Bony said, rising to his feet. "Why do you think that Mervyn Blake was murdered?"

"Why?" The grey eyes gleamed but the face remained calm, and almost expressionless. "I believe he was murdered because he was perfectly well when he went off to bed that night, and because of the way he looked when we discovered him the next morning. He had been in the hands of doctors for several years, and not long before he died he was overhauled by the Yarrabo doctor who found nothing wrong with his heart, and that even his ulcers were drying up."

"Have you any thoughts of a motive for murdering him?"

"None. I've no doubt that Blake was heartily disliked by those who turn out commercial fiction and whom we could never recognize. He had no personal enemies that I knew of."

"Do you think it probable that Mrs Blake instigated the successful attempt of getting back the note-book you—er—purloined?"

"No, I do not. And yet no one else knew I had taken it—excepting, perhaps, the Pinkney woman, or the person who seems to have informed you. Which reminds me, Miss Pinkney hated Blake for having tossed a stone at her cat."

"I heard of that episode," Bony said, and began to walk to the door with Wilcannia-Smythe. Opening the door for the distinguished novelist, Bony gave the merest hint of a bow, and Wilcannia-Smythe passed out without speaking. Back again at the desk, Bony said, "Constable! Try to get on to Superintendent Jacks."

Five minutes later, Bony heard the voice of the Chief of the C.I.B. speaking from his own bedroom.

"A hundred hours of sleep are due to me, and you—Never mind, Bony. What can I do?"

"Contact someone here who will despatch a cablegram to the police at Bogota, Colombia, South America."

"All right. Tell the constable to ask Inspector Inns to ring me. What d'you want from Bogota? Postage stamps?"

"No. Coffin dust."

CHAPTER TWENTY-SIX

The Way of an Alkaloid

BONY returned to Melbourne by the first plane leaving Sydney the following morning, and reaching Yarrabo at a quarter to one, he walked direct to his lodging, where Miss Pinkney awaited him with lunch. On the table in his pleasant room were several letters.

Nancy Chesterfield wrote expressing regret that he had been obliged to cancel the proposed dinner and show, and hope that he would be able to make it another time. There was a note from Dr Fleetwood asking him to call as soon as he returned to Yarrabo. And there was a short letter from I. R. Watts.

Watts gave his publisher's address, and he used his typewriter to inform Mr Napoleon Bonaparte from South Africa that he much regretted his inability to meet him as he was that day leaving on a visit to Adelaide. However, on returning to Melbourne, which he hoped to do late the following week, he would write again and arrange a meeting. The signature was barely decipherable. The letter had been posted in the city.

I. R. Watts was becoming something of a mystery, and without doubt he would have to be unearthed to provide much in addition to an opinion of the influence exerted by the Blake-Smythe clique on local literature. He was a piece of the puzzle that would have to be fitted into place, and any opinion he might have would be of lesser importance than the answer to the question, where did he get the story of the coffin dust he used in his novel *The Vengeance of Master Atherton*?

Having enjoyed Miss Pinkney's lunch, Bony left the cottage and strolled down the highway to the doctor's house. The sun's rays were hot. There was no breeze to temper the heat, and no trees to give shade until he was almost at the doctor's open drive gate, and therefore he was able to appreciate the dimmed and cool interior of the doctor's study.

"We finished the P.M. yesterday morning," Fleetwood said. "I have the result in this report. Perhaps you would rather I told you in layman's language than read the report to you."

"Yes. I am concerned only with bald facts," Bony assented.

"Good! Professor Ericson came here and after a preliminary examination of the dead man's heart and stomach, we took certain organs to Melbourne, where a more extensive examination was undertaken. That examination convinced both of us that Walsh died from failure of the heart brought about by the action of an alkaloid similar to that contained in the powder you gave me to analyse, and which I passed to Professor Ericson."

Bony had been watching the lean lips forming the words, and now he moved his gaze to encounter the grey eyes.

"Does the fact that Walsh drank spirits to excess have any significance?" he asked. "The rabbit to which you gave some of that powder on a lettuce leaf did not die, remember."

"The rabbit died some time last night."

"Oh!"

"We may assume, we think, that the alkaloid does act more swiftly when brought in contact with alcohol," Dr Fleetwood proceeded. "Walsh was a man whose body was saturated with alcohol. The alkaloid in the stomach was thus able to pass into the blood stream very swiftly. With a non-drinking man the poison would be very much slower in action, and possibly non-effective unless administered in doses given over a considerable period."

"The joint opinion of yourself and Professor Ericson would not be contested by opposing medical opinion?"

"It might," replied Dr Fleetwood. "In fact, if there were a trial the defence would almost surely raise an objection—unless the prosecution could produce more of the powder, or name it, and prove its origin. However, in view of what the examination has revealed, I could not certify that Walsh died from prolonged alcoholic poisoning self-administered. I am afraid the case will have to go to the Coroner."

"There is none of the powder left?"

"None. The remainder was used by Professor Ericson."

"What, do you think, would be the Coroner's finding?"

"On the evidence put forward by Ericson and myself, the finding would be, probably, that Walsh died of virulent ptomaine poisoning. Nothing more than that, unless, of course, it was stated that Walsh had been given some of that powder in his drink, and some of the powder was produced. Have you any more of it?"

"No, unfortunately," Bony replied. "If the body of Mervyn Blake was exhumed, could it be established that he had or had not died of that particular alkaloidal poison?"

Fleetwood bit hard upon his nether lip. "That particular poison is not common, nor as well known in its effect as, say strychnine. I fear that medical opinion would inevitably differ widely—if there were no evidence supporting the suggestion of homicide."

"How much longer can the report be kept back from the authorities, do you think?"

"Another day, perhaps."

"Very well. Please delay as long as possible. I am expecting information cabled from Colombia, South America, where it is an old belief that the residuum of a long-buried human body will kill without leaving any trace. The substance is known as coffin dust."

The doctor breathed an exclamation. Softly he repeated the words, his professional equanimity shaken.

Bony said, "May I use your telephone?"

He sat at the table waiting to be connected with Superintendent Bolt. The doctor stood before the semi-masked window, his hands clasped beneath his straight back. He had often been able to make death gentle in its touch, but for the first time he was confronted by death introduced by murder.

He heard Bony's voice, "Yes, Bony here, super. Speaking

from Yarrabo. Oh yes, I got along very well with friend W.-S. I am now interested in another man who writes novels. Name is I. R. Watts. Yesterday Snook and I called on the Income Tax people to find out his address, as I understand he lives in Victoria. We interviewed a man named Trilby, and he had their files searched and said there was no taxpayer of that name. I have now the thought that I. R. Watts might be the pen-name of the taxpayer who collects royalties paid to I. R. Watts. Will you put that to Trilby, and let me know if I. R. Watts can be traced by them? Yes, I know, super. Yes, but I don't want Watts to be told we are interested in him, and if we approach his publishers, they will surely tell him the police are looking him up. Good! And not a word to friend Snook, mind you. Yes, I agree. He's got a lot coming to him. Let me know about Watts as soon as you can. Ring Constable Simes. He'll fetch me to the telephone. What's that? Oh! Yes! Yes, of course! I never fail—you know that. Good-bye!"

Fleetwood turned and regarded Bony who, having replaced the instrument, was rising from the chair. The words "never fail" seemed to echo from the recesses of the room, appeared to be taken up by the clock in its refrain, *tick-tick, never-fail, never-fail*. The slim, dark man with the brilliant blue eyes smiled at the doctor, and it was obvious that he guessed that the phrase had stuck in the doctor's mind.

"A man may commit all the crimes on the calendar, but one, and get away with it provided he is clever enough or the investigator stupid enough," Bony said gravely. "The exception is murder. Murderers who get away with their crime are fortunate only in that the investigator is stupid. Their escape is never due to their own inherent cleverness. You will understand, therefore, why I never fail to unmask a murderer. I am not stupid."

"You are confident that you will unmask the murderer of Mervyn Blake?"

"I am. I'll tell you why. When you examine a patient and find a case of pneumonia, you know precisely what course the illness will follow. Murder is a disease. The act is the second symptom, the first being the thought in the mind of the murderer. Broadly speaking, every human being who commits homicide will react in the same way and proceed to act along similar lines. When you deal with a case of pneumonia, you take certain steps to arrest the progress of the disease. When I deal with a case of murder, I await the inevitable developments provided not so much by what I discover about the act of murder but by what the murderer subsequently gives me by his acts. If a murderer would only stop still immediately after committing his crime, I might sometimes fail. If a murderer could expunge from his mind the crime he had committed, I should often fail."

"Probably sound philosophy," conceded Dr Fleetwood.

"When I say I never fail to finalize a case of homicide please do not think me vain, nor think I am super-intelligent. Now I must go. Thank you, doctor, for your help. You would, I think, be assisting the cause of justice by delaying the sending of the report to the Coroner as long as you can. I shall personally thank Professor Ericson."

On his way up the road Bony called at the police station, where he found Simes in his shirt sleeves and engaged with his interminable reports.

"Hullo!" exclaimed the constable. "Absent without leave last night and this morning. Where've you been?"

"Visiting relatives," Bony replied, smilingly. "Any news items for me?"

"Nothing. Have you seen the doctor?"

"Just left him. D'you know the result of the post mortem?"

"Yes. What's in your mind about it? Walsh poisoned to cover up the killing of Blake?"

"Perhaps." Bony sank into the vacant chair and rolled a cigarette. "You knew Walsh better than I. Think he was capable of blackmail?"

Simes took six or seven seconds to decide his answer.

"I knew Walsh for a number of years. In spite of that money under his floor, I don't think he would come at blackmail. He was content to live simply, and he earned very good money, sufficient to provide him with plenty of grog."

"Nevertheless, Simes, it would seem that Walsh knew who poisoned Blake, and he permitted the murderer to know he knew and what he knew. I am going back to sit under Miss Pinkney's lilac-trees and read more of that novel by I. R. Watts. I am expecting a call from Superintendent Bolt, and I am also expecting a telegram from the C.I.B., Sydney. Will you be out this afternoon?"

"No. I'll wait for the call, and the telegram. Have you been to Sydney?"

"Yes. Went after Wilcannia-Smythe. He stuck to the story that he didn't know the men who abducted him. They tied him up for the night so that they, or someone in collusion with them, could go through his luggage and take a note-book and pages of typescript that belonged to Mervyn Blake. Wilcannia-Smythe couldn't make any objection because he stole the note-book and papers from Blake's writing-room."

"What the heck was in the note-book to cause all that?"

"I think it was a story of removing unwanted persons with coffin dust. Wilcannia-Smythe swears he knows nothing of such a story, and I'm inclined to believe him. Still, the case is proceeding nicely, Simes, and at any time now we'll get together and write our report on it. How are you with that typewriter?"

"A bit slow, but I can take notes in shorthand."

"Excellent!"

"Think you'll be able to put one over on Snook?" Simes asked, grinning.

Bony turned at the door, saying, his eyes bright, "We already have material sufficient for that most pleasurable occupation. *Au revoir*! Don't miss the super's call. You know where to find me."

Arrived at Miss Pinkney's gate, Bony glanced at the sun, estimating the time to be a few minutes past three. The grandfather clock in the hall was striking the hour as he entered, and he looked at his wrist watch and smiled when he found that his estimate was only two minutes out and that the clock was seven minutes slow.

Hearing his footsteps, Miss Pinkney appeared.

"Oh! There you are, Mr Bonaparte. The kettle's nearly boiling. Where would you like to have your afternoon tea? I have to go out to a committee meeting at the Vicarage."

"Then don't bother, Miss Pinkney," he told her. "I can make the tea all right. I was thinking of having a cold shower and then taking a book to read under the lilac-trees."

"Yes, do. It's beautifully cool there. You have your shower, and I'll leave the tea-tray on the table I took to the lilac-trees this morning. Dear me! I mustn't forget the little notes I wrote of what I have to say about the street stall. Yes, you run along. You must be hot and thirsty, you poor man."

He was under the shower when she knocked at the door and called that she had taken the tray to the lilac-trees and that he was not to dawdle or the tea would be cold, and that there was more hot water in the kettle and he was not to worry about dinner as she would be back in an hour. In order to listen to her, he had turned off the shower, and so was able to hear her quick steps fading along the passage and finally across the front veranda.

Ten minutes later, dressed in open-necked silk shirt and grey flannel slacks, he left the house with *The Vengeance of Master Atherton* in one hand and cigarette makings in the other.

It was then half past three, and the call from Superintendent Bolt could be expected at any minute. To know where Watts lived, or to know who I. R. Watts really was, if it were a pen name, would enable him to advance a step farther. And there were grounds to hope that the reply of the Bogota police to his cabled message would enable him to take yet another step. Meanwhile, he could relax and read *The Vengeance of Master Atherton* for his entertainment.

What a woman was this Priscilla Pinkney! She had placed the table in the deepest shade of the lilac-trees, and beside it was a cushioned chair. The afternoon tea-tray on the table was extremely inviting. The sight of the banana case against the fence beyond the table recalled to mind that late dusk wherein he had stood with her looking over the fence.

The chair was placed just right, the light to pour over

a shoulder that he might read. Then his toes tingled, and a little current ran up his spine to lodge in his scalp. Without haste, he lowered himself into the chair, and putting the book down on the table beside the tray, he proceeded to make a cigarette, his fingers working blindly, for on the ground about the chair and table were the imprints of boots or shoes size seven, the wearer being pigeon-toed and having a corn on the fore-part of the right foot.

Miss Pinkney had been wearing a size five shoe with Cuban heels.

The man who wore the size seven boots or shoes had placed his feet over the tracks made by Miss Pinkney when she brought the tea-tray, placed it on the table, and arranged the chair.

CHAPTER TWENTY-SEVEN

Putting it Over

THE prints on the soft cinder path came from and returned to the hole in Miss Pinkney's back fence.

Bony completed the manufacture of his cigarette, applied a match to it with casual deliberation, and then became interested in Mr Pickwick, who was lying full-length along a branch overhead. Having called Mr Pickwick, and been acknowledged by a soft "mirrill", he rose from his chair and strolled to the fence. He looked through an opening between the palings into the neighbouring garden.

There was no man to be seen there. On the rear veranda of the house were three women. They were seated at afternoon tea. Mrs Blake was entertaining Ella Montrose and Nancy Chesterfield. Between the house and the fence the sunlight was a glare upon the lawn, and Bony felt sure that were he to raise himself to look over the fence and along it he would not be observed by those on the veranda.

The man who had visited Miss Pinkney's garden within the last several minutes could hardly have passed out of Mrs Blake's garden without being seen by one of the ladies on the veranda, and he might well be crouched just beyond the fence or be concealed on the far side of the writing-room.

Bony hauled himself up by the tree branch on which Mr Pickwick was lying, and swung himself slightly forward so that he brought his feet to the fence and then could look right along it within the deep shade cast by the trees. There was no one there.

Only Mr Pickwick had seen the man, and Mr Pickwick was not at all happy about it. When Bony dropped back again to Miss Pinkney's garden, the cat still declined to come down.

"Another stupid killer," murmured Bony. "It's enough to make the sun go out."

Picking up the tray, he started off for the house and was almost at the kitchen entrance when Constable Simes came running round the side garden.

"The super's on the phone," he cried.

"Ah! Good! I'll come along at once," Bony said. "Here, take this jug of milk and the sugar basin. I'll bring the pot of tea. The tray and cakes will be all right on the step. Come along! And don't spill that milk or the sugar out of the basin."

Two men, a truck driver, and several women were astonished to see Constable Simes and a slim, dark man running down the road and holding to their fronts a teapot, a milk-jug, and a sugar basin. Before Constable Simes realized the incongruity, he was being ordered to take extreme care not to upset the milk-jug and the sugar basin over his office desk, and from them and the teapot he looked up to see Bony slump into his chair and seize the telephone.

"Yes, Bony here, super. Good! Oh! So that is who I. R. Watts is, eh! No, I am not greatly surprised. Oh, yes! Yes! Ah, but then, you see, one adds a chance word or two to another chance word or two, and it makes sense. Yes, life is moving along nicely. I shall begin my report on the investigation this evening. I may begin it this afternoon. Thanks, super."

Having replaced the instrument, Bony rose from the chair and regarded Constable Simes with eyes that positively shone from a face, otherwise devoid of expression.

"Take the phone, Simes. Ring up Fleetwood. Ask him to come here at once."

He stood in the doorway whilst Simes rang the doctor. Beyond the doorway ran the length of the veranda fronting the house and in turn fronted by the little garden of flowers. Simes could see Bony's fingers slowly clenching and unclenching. The back was straight and the shoulders set square. He could not see the dark face—the lips lifted slightly, the nostrils gently quivering, as though they smelled blood or the scent of the hunted.

"The doctor says he will come directly he has completed his examination of a patient," Simes announced.

He thought Bony had not heard him, and he was about to speak again, when Bony turned and came swiftly back to the desk. He drew the visitor's chair to it and sat down.

"Get your paper and pencils," he said. "We'll begin the report."

Simes took to his chair and from a drawer pulled out foolscap and set it on the blotter, picked up a pencil and waited with the pencil poised.

"Date it today," Bony said, the sharpness gone out of his voice. "Head it the usual way—to Superintendent Bolt from Inspector Napoleon Bonaparte. Sir, Reference, death of Mervyn Blake on night of 9th November and other matters. Having on 3rd January, approximately two months after Mervyn Blake died, accepted from you the commission to investigate the circumstances of Blake's death, I studied your departmental official file and the summary of the case prepared by Inspector Snook. On the following day I conferred with Senior Constable Robert Simes, stationed at Yarrabo, bringing into discussion all—underline "all"—the circumstances under which Mervyn Blake was found on the morning of 10th November.

"Mervyn Blake was discovered dead on the floor just inside the closed door of his writing-room. The expression on the features of the dead man, the position in which he lay, and the fact that the door was closed, indicated that he was suddenly seized with mortal illness and had attempted to leave the writing-room for help. The state of his fingers, plus the marks of finger-nails on the door, indicated that the last paroxysm prevented him from opening the door.

"When the body was examined, firstly by Dr Fleetwood and secondly by Constable Simes, it was seen that the rain of the previous night had slanted in through the open doorway and wetted the floor covering about the head and shoulders of the body as well as the dead man's hair and clothes.

"It was assumed by Constable Simes and Dr Fleetwood that after Mervyn Blake died someone entered the room, left the door open, remained in the room for probably a minute or two minutes whilst it was raining, and then departed after closing the door. This theory was countered by another put forward by the investigating officer. The opposing theory was that Blake managed to unlatch the door and thrust it open in his last physical effort, and that subsequently the wind blew it shut. Strength was given this opposing theory by, one, the negative report of the analyst, and, two, by the meterological report stating that the wind velocity that night was twenty miles an hour and gusty.

"That a weather report of conditions in Melbourne, situated on a plain, should be relied upon to indicate the weather conditions at Yarrabo, forty odd miles distant, and partially surrounded by mountains, seems at variance with the practice of crime investigation. On checking up on the weather conditions at Yarrabo, I found that the wind that night was exceedingly light, and at no time could the wind be described as gusty. Therefore the theory put forward by Constable Simes being supported by fact urged me to prosecute my inquiries and to discard the official theory because unsupported by fact."

Bony ceased speaking and lit a cigarette. Simes looked up from his note-taking. His large white teeth were faintly revealed by the hard smile about the mouth.

Bony said, pleasantly, "Off the record, how do you think Mr Snook is going to react to that?"

"It tickles my imagination," replied Simes.

"Well, let's proceed. Ready? Having studied the two theories concerning the rain's slanting in through the open door, and finding that I must adopt the one and discard the other, I proceeded to step forward on the hypothesis that someone entered the writing-room after Blake had died and had withdrawn without giving any alarm or reporting the fact that Blake was dead. The natural question was—why? I found that I could invent several assumptions, if I could delete from mind the analyst's negative report.

"Assuming that someone poisoned Mervyn Blake, then someone entered the writing-room after the poison had done its work in order to remove incriminating evidence. It is feasible that someone entered the writing-room to remove the remainder or the residue of the poison, and that that was contained in the bottle of brandy and the glass upon the writing desk.

"There is in the garage a small cupboard in which was kept battery acid and cleaning materials. No mention is made in the official file of a bottle of brandy and a glass that were in the cupboard at seven thirty on the night of 9th November. The maid, Ethel Lacy, states that at seven thirty that night she saw Blake take a bottle of spirits and a glass from the cupboard, and pour himself a drink. The gardener, S. Walsh, also asserted that Blake kept spirits in that cupboard, and gave him a drink there on several occasions. The gardener was never questioned by the investigating officer. The maid was made hostile by the manner of the officer taking her statement, and either because of nervousness or because of resentment, withheld that particular item of information.

"Having reached that point in my investigation, I had reasonable grounds on which to base the assumption that Mervyn Blake had been poisoned, that the poison had been introduced into his brandy within the writing-room, that after he was dead the murderer entered the writing-room and removed the poisoned bottle and glass and set in their place the bottle and glass taken from the garage. The poisoned bottle and glass removed from the writing-room were buried near the front gate, and subsequently were discovered by the gardener, S. Walsh.

"In view of the negative report of the analyst, it became essential to discover, one, the poison employed, two, the person who employed the poison, and, three, the motive for the act of poisoning. Being convinced that the data in the official file was incomplete and that the summary of the case was based on erroneous deductions from the available evidence, I found it necessary to proceed cautiously. It was—"

The report was interrupted by the telephone. Simes answered the call, and announced that the post office had received a long telegram from Sydney addressed to Patience, care of the Police Station.

"There's no delivery, and no one about the P.O. who could bring the telegram," Simes said. "Shall I slip down and get it?"

"Do. Meanwhile I'll think up a few more telling phrases."

When Simes returned, he was accompanied by the doctor. The telegram was dropped on the desk by Bony, who had received it from the constable, and who said, "Doctor, I regret having to ask you to come here, but things to come are taking shape, and a recent event will hurry them forward. I want you to make an examination of the tea in that pot and the milk in the jug, to ascertain if there is or is not some foreign substance in both or either of the liquids."

The sparse grey brows rose a fraction.

"Get me two glasses, Bob," he requested, and then said when Simes had gone out, "What do you suspect?"

"Coffin dust," replied Bony.

"Ye gods! Where do these things come from?"

"They belong to Miss Pinkney. They contain the liquid part of my afternoon tea. Now, now! Don't think what you are thinking. Miss Pinkney is fully exonerated by her own shoe tracks."

Dr Fleetwood accepted the glasses from the constable. Putting one down on the desk, he filled the other from the tea-pot and held it to the light coming strongly through the window. Within the amber liquid floated a cloud of whitish particles. The doctor's grey eyes gazed steadily into the inquiring blue eyes. Then, taking up the milk-jug, he poured a little of the milk into the second glass, wafted it about the inside of the tumbler and then peered at the film of milk upon the glass.

"There doesn't seem to be anything wrong with the milk," he said, slowly. "The tea is full of—a foreign substance of light specific gravity. It is certainly a substance resembling the powder which Professor Ericson and I examined. The tea was made by Miss Pinkney?"

"Yes. It would be made in her kitchen at Rose Cottage."

"Then that foreign substance would not have been contained in the water from her tap. At least, I cannot think so. Do you wish me to make an analytical examination?"

"If you would be so kind."

"Very well. Get me a cloth, Bob, so that I can disguise these utensils from a curious public." When Simes had departed for the second time, the doctor asked another question.

"This is a filthy thing," he said. "Have you any idea who is doing it?"

"I have sure knowledge who murdered Mervyn Blake, who murdered Walsh, who tried to murder me," Bony replied. "I'll telephone you early this evening, and you may be present to hear my report being dictated to Constable Simes. Meanwhile, *au revoir*, and thank you. Perhaps you will be in a position to be definite when we meet again this evening."

"I hope so. Thank you for letting me in on this. I am a nervous wreck through the powerful stimulant of curiosity."

Having camouflaged the teapot and jug with the teacloth Simes had brought, Dr Fleetwood departed, and Simes said, "What do we do next?"

"First we shall pay a visit to the Rialto Hotel," replied Bony. "Immediately following that visit we shall make another. Bring your handcuffs. It's just possible you may need them. Ah, the telegram! Permit me." Bony quickly scanned the eight or nine sheets recording the message from the Colombian Police at Bogota. Then he said, "Yes, we may proceed, Simes, to finalize this Mervyn Blake Murder Case."

CHAPTER TWENTY-EIGHT

The Charge

"You will do well to remember, Simes, always to practise the virtues of patience and courtesy," Bony said when they were driving back from the Rialto Hotel. "Always remember today, and how courtesy and patience paid dividends in our interview with Ethel Lacy. Keep ever in your mind the superiority of the Bonaparte methods over those of Snook. Practise what I practise, and you will one day control a murder investigation."

"I don't fancy my chances," growled Simes.

"On the contrary, I believe your chances are excellent. You have intelligence, and also you possess a gift of greater value even than intelligence, that gift being imagination. Our poor friend Snook is excessively intelligent. He has pertinacity, but he lacks the imaginative man's perspicacity."

"I think I know what you mean," Simes said. "Well, do we drive into the station garage?"

"No, proceed to Miss Pinkney's cottage."

The constable's eyes narrowed, but he made no comment. Bony did not speak again until they stopped outside Miss Pinkney's gate.

"Come with me. I have something to show you," he said, and Simes had to accept it as an order, for the voice was no longer soft and languid. He followed Bony through the gate, and skirted the house to take the path leading to the lilac-trees. Having reached the table and the chair, Bony signalled him to stop and himself proceeded to the fence, where for a moment he looked over. On returning to Simes, he instructed him to study the ground about the table. Simes stared at the ground, took a step forward and went down on one knee.

"The pigeon-toed man's been here," he said.

"To put coffin dust into the tea brought here for me by Miss Pinkney whilst I was having a shower," Bony supplemented. "He is now on the other side of the fence."

The constable stood up.

"Good! I'll get him."

"Wait," Bony ordered. "I have first to ask Mrs Blake a few questions. We'll go through the fence into her garden. Fetch the banana case and put it over two of the boot-prints —the left and the right. Later we'll make casts of them. That's right. Now you will observe how Napoleon Bonaparte finalizes a murder investigation."

Simes braced himself and followed Bony into Mrs Blake's garden.

"Don't be impatient," he was urged. "Pigeon-toes cannot escape."

It was then that Simes saw the three women seated on the open veranda. As he accompanied Bony across the lawn to the veranda steps, he noted the curious faces of the women, each of whom he recognized. For him they were of no consequence in the balance against the pigeon-toed man. He followed Bony up the steps and halted.

Finalizing a murder investigation, indeed! Bony was merely paying a social call.

"Good afternoon, Mrs Blake, and Mrs Montrose and Miss Chesterfield," he said, bowing and smiling. "Please forgive our intrusion, for the reason is a compelling one. May I ask for the favour of a private interview, Mrs Blake?"

The three women rose, Ella Montrose to say, "Come along, Nancy."

"Stay," Mrs Blake said commandingly. "I cannot understand why you have called—in the company of Constable Simes, Mr Bonaparte." She smiled faintly before adding, "One could surmise that you are not what you have represented yourself to be. What do you want of me?"

"I have to confess that, although my name is Napoleon

Bonaparte, I am a Detective-Inspector of the Queensland Police Department," Bony said, easily. "The reason for my stay here at Yarrabo has been primarily due to a request made by the Victorian Criminal Investigation Branch to examine the circumstances under which the late Mr Mervyn Blake died. The questions I wish to ask you concern those circumstances."

"That being so, my friends need not withdraw. Let us all sit down."

Mrs Blake was the first to resume her seat. Mrs Montrose sat next to her, and Nancy Chesterfield regarded Bony with wide eyes as Simes brought two chairs and placed them so that Bony and himself were facing the women.

"May I smoke?" Bony asked, and Nancy Chesterfield reached for the box of cigarettes on the table, which bore the remains of afternoon tea. "Thank you, Miss Chesterfield. Ah! Well, now, I'll proceed. Mrs Blake, on 9th December you withdrew from your bank in Melbourne the sum of one hundred pounds. The sum was paid out in one-pound notes. Why did you withdraw such a large amount?"

"For expenses, household and such like. What an extraordinary question!"

The voice was steady and the inflexion of astonishment real. Simes, who recognized instantly what lay behind the question, was equally astonished. His gaze rose from a pair of worn gardening gloves on the veranda floor to Mrs Blake's face, to note the dark brows drawn close in a frown and the dark eyes fixed in a stare of bewilderment.

"I understand that you pay your current expenses with cheques," Bony said, and Simes glanced swiftly at the other women and then down at Mrs Blake's feet. A sensation of chill swept up his spine to lodge at the base of his head. Mrs Blake's feet were tucked in under her wicker chair, but they could not be concealed. Mrs Blake was wearing a pair of man's shoes, and the size was almost certainly seven.

In conjunction with the canvas gardening gloves, it was a feasible assumption that Mrs Blake had been gardening when Mrs Montrose and Mrs Chesterfield had arrived, and these being old friends, she had not bothered to change her footwear. But then, some women did wear old shoes at gardening. But then—

"It seems that you doubt the truth of my answer to your question, Mr Bonaparte," Mrs Blake was saying, and when again the policeman's gaze rose to her face he saw thereon a faint flush.

"I'm afraid I have to, Mrs Blake. You see, the hundred one-pound notes you drew from the bank were found under the floor of Sid Walsh's hut—after—Walsh—suddenly—died. I suggest that you gave the hundred pounds to Walsh because he had learnt something concerning your husband's death. Your husband died of the effects of poison placed in the bottle of brandy from which he drank after he retired to his writing-room on the night of 9th November."

Mrs Blake moved her feet, and the others became conscious of the constable's rude stare at them.

"Good gracious!" she exclaimed. "I suppose you have proof of what you say?"

"Yes, I have the proof," Bony replied, quietly. "Perhaps it will be better to place it before you in the form of a story, quite a long story, since it begins several years before the war."

"And it concerns me?"

"Of course, as Mr Blake's widow. I still think it would be as well for these ladies to withdraw."

"No, I don't think so," Mrs Blake said. "I am sure they will be interested in the story you have to tell."

"Well, then, to begin," Bony said, stubbing out his cigar-rette. "In 1936 a Dr Dario Chaparral, of Bogota, Colombia, visited Sydney, where he was entertained by several literary people, he himself being an author of some renown. Through-out that visit Dr Chaparral did not travel beyond Sydney and so it was that Mr and Mrs Mervyn Blake and Mrs Montrose travelled to Sydney to meet the doctor in the house of Mr Wilcannia-Smythe. Subsequently a correspond-ence was begun between Dr Chaparral and Mrs Blake, and in one of her letters to Dr Chaparral Mrs Blake asked him if he knew about a little-known poison that she could use in the plot of one of her stories. He wrote back and told her of an extensive belief in his own country that the dust collected from the frame of a long-buried corpse will, if administered to a living person, inevitably kill. In some parts of his country such is the belief in the efficacy of this material that persons having homicidal intent will go to great lengths to procure it.

"Mrs Blake did use this method of poisoning in her novel entitled *The Vengeance of Master Atherton*."

"Mrs Blake never wrote such a novel," asserted Mrs Montrose, her eyes suddenly blazing. "That book was written by a person named I. R. Watts."

"I. R. Watts is the pen-name used by Mrs Mervyn Blake," Bony said with slow deliberation. "The royalties earned by the novels of I. R. Watts are submitted in the taxation returns signed by Mrs Blake."

Ella Montrose leaned forward and placed her hand on Mrs Blake's arm. Her voice was low and vibrant, her eyes were living coals.

"Is that true, Janet?" she asked. "Janet, is that true?"

Mrs Blake raised her eyes from her gardening gloves to look at Mrs Montrose. She nodded without speaking, and Mrs Montrose turned away to regard Bony.

"Later, when it was known that Dr Chaparral was to visit Australia for the second time, Mrs Blake asked him to bring a sample of the poison material, known colloquially as coffin dust, on the grounds that she was a collector of curious substances and bric-a-brac, and Dr Chaparral imported some of the coffin dust by making an opening in several ping-pong balls, inserting the dust, and resealing the openings with white wax.

"Dr Chaparral visited Victoria and stayed here at the beginning of last year. I may be wrong, and I hope I am, in believing that the idea of murdering her husband did not occur to Mrs Blake until some considerable time after Dr Chaparral's visit."

"Janet!" The name was whispered by Mrs Montrose. "Janet—are you listening? It's not true, is it? It isn't true? Janet—is he speaking the truth?"

For the second time Mrs Blake raised her face to look at Mrs Montrose. Again she did not speak, and again looked down at her gardening gloves. Mrs Montrose went limp, and with anguished eyes looked at Nancy Chesterfield.

"Sometime during the evening of 9th November, Mrs Blake slipped away from her guests and poured a quantity of coffin dust into the brandy in her husband's writing-room," continued the voice, which had now become terribly emotionless. "It was necessary to remove the remainder of the poisoned brandy before Mervyn Blake was found dead the following morning, Mrs Blake knowing her husband's drinking habits so well as to be confident that he would drink most of the brandy in his writing-room before he went to bed.

"Accordingly, several hours after everyone had retired, she left the house and proceeded to the garage, where her husband kept another supply of brandy and a glass inside a cupboard. That brandy bottle and glass she carried to the writing-room, being careful not to leave her fingerprints on either utensil. She found her husband lying just inside the door. It was raining, and the rain slanted in through the doorway and fell on her husband's head and shoulders and on the floor covering. The bottle and glass from the garage Mrs Blake exchanged for the bottle and glass on the writing desk, and these she took away and buried near the front gate—for Walsh, the casual gardener to discover. To leave the door open whilst she groped her way over the body of her husband, to reach the writing desk and make the exchange of bottles and glasses, was the first vital mistake Mrs Blake made."

"Must you go on?" Nancy Chesterfield cried, and Mrs Blake spoke.

"Yes, he must go on. The sun must set. We must all die—some time. I've been dying for years. Oh yes, he must go on."

"I will pass to the night of 3rd January of this year," Bony continued. "That night Mr Wilcannia-Smythe entered Mervyn Blake's writing-room and stole a note-book and typescript containing the collection of anecdotes related to

Mr and Mrs Blake by their guests. The next day Mrs Blake, having occasion to enter her husband's writing-room, found proof of Wilcannia-Smythe's theft in the form of his initialled handkerchief, and the absence of the note-book and type-script. On the terrace of the Rialto Hotel, she accused him of the theft, and he refused to restore the articles to her. Subsequently, in collusion with Mrs Montrose, she abducted Wilcannia-Smythe late one evening when he was out walking, and they took him to a lonely place and securely bound him to a tree where he was not found until the next morning. Meanwhile, in acknowledgement of many little kindnesses shown to her by Mrs Blake, and urged by her dislike of Wilcannia-Smythe, the maid, Ethel Lacy, employed at this time at the Rialto Hotel, ransacked his luggage and found the stolen memoranda, which she returned to Mrs Blake.

"Wilcannia-Smythe it seems, is a singularly mean person, considering the fact that he was often Mrs Blake's guest and a friend for many years. It appears that he valued the collection of stories as plots for his future novels, and it would appear that Mrs Blake also valued it on similar grounds. It might be, too, that the collection contains the story of the coffin dust.

"Anyway, the important point in what appears to be a side issue, is that when engaged in abducting Wilcannia-Smythe, both Mrs Blake and Mrs Montrose wore male clothing and male shoes. The imprints of their shoes left on the ground that night were easily followed.

"The imprints of Mrs Blake's shoes were plainly to be seen about the hut inhabited by Sid Walsh, the casual gardener, who died the other night. He also died from the effects of coffin dust placed in the whisky he was drinking.

"It will be suggested that Walsh possessed incriminating information and successfully blackmailed Mrs Blake. I shall be able to state that Walsh said he was giving up work. Precisely when and where Mrs Blake suspected I was an investigating officer, I cannot say. She decided to remove me, and the chance occurred only this afternoon. Miss Pinkney left afternoon tea for me on a table just on the other side of the dividing fence. After Miss Pinkney left the tea on the table there, Mrs Blake slipped through a hole in the dividing fence and emptied a quantity of coffin dust into the teapot."

"Did you see her do it?" Nancy Chesterfield asked, her eyes wide with horror.

"Mrs Blake did what I have described," Bony said. "On the ground about the hole in the fence, and from that hole to the table, are the imprints of shoes Mrs Blake wore when she and Mrs Montrose abducted Wilcannia-Smythe and when she visited Sid Walsh's hut to remove the poisoned spirit bottle—the same shoes she is wearing now."

From Mrs Montrose came a soft, whimpering cry. She rose with feline grace to stand straight with bent head, her eyes blazing at the seated Mrs Blake. When she spoke her voice was husky with anger.

"I could forgive you, Janet, everything but the one thing. I could forgive you for killing Mervyn, I could even admire you for the courage you must have had to do it. But I cannot forgive you, and I never, never shall forgive you for being I. R. Watts, to smear our Australian literature with common fiction, betraying poor Mervyn, and the rest of us, who have worked so hard and sacrificed so much."

Mrs Ella Montrose stepped back, turned and went down the veranda steps, followed the path to the far end of the house and so passed beyond the alert eyes of Constable Simes.

Miss Nancy Chesterfield, the Cosmic Blonde, supposedly tough, left her chair and occupied that vacated by Mrs Montrose. She leant towards the motionless Mrs Blake and placed her hand lightly upon her arm, saying, "Why did you do it, Janet? Why did you kill Mervyn?"

CHAPTER TWENTY-NINE

The Defence

"As you know I killed my husband, I'll tell you why I killed him," Mrs Blake said. "I'll tell you because, long ago, I resolved not to fight if ever I were found out."

The deep bosom lifted a fraction, pushing back the shoulders. The fine feminine head went upward as the wide mouth and the firm chin were recast by strength, leaving nothing of weakness. The wide-spaced dark eyes beneath the deep dark brows became occupied only with Bony. Her voice gained steadiness.

"When I married Mervyn Blake, I loved him greatly," she said. "He was brilliant, his mental capacity was remarkable, and we were bound by interests that normally should have enabled us to bridge all gulfs likely to open before married people. These interests were literary, for he was writing his first novel and I had published a number of short stories and a volume of verse.

"Six months after our marriage, my husband completed his first novel. He was very proud of it, and it was a severe blow when the publishers sent the manuscript back. I made certain suggestions about the story, to which at first he refused to listen. Eventually, with bad grace, he adopted them and the novel was accepted for publication.

"The book was well received by the critics, who praised its literary qualities and predicted a great future for the author. The praise went to his head and seemed to alter his character to an astonishing degree. In his mind was born a grudge against me for the suggestions I had made to eliminate his faults, but he accepted my assistance with his second and third novels, which were also published and were fairly well received.

"The knowledge that his work was not entirely his own became a canker in his mind. I came to see it clearly. He craved for adulation; he craved for power. He was ruthless in the employment of the means to realize his ambition. He used to tell me that the successful men are those who have learnt to use others. He would say that for a fellow to blow his own trumpet is fatal, and the wise man persuades others to blow it for him. It was a creed that returned him handsome rewards of a sort, for he was a man of fine address and knew how to be charming.

"Then he failed. His fourth and fifth novels were rejected by publisher after publisher. He had refused me even the opportunity to read the manuscripts and offer suggestions about them, and he knew that without me he could not stand. I knew he never would unless he devoted all his spare time to the novelist's craft instead of dissipating his energies in social activities, literary societies, and the like, writing critiques and generally concerning himself with criticism.

"Then came his sixth novel. With this he permitted my assistance, and it was published and received good notices. This further proof that he could not stand alone embittered him still more, but he resolved to resign the university appointment and devote all his time to literary pursuits and to courting friendship with those in the literary world he thought might be of use to him.

"Within months our financial position was alarming, and it was then that I showed him the manuscript of my first novel. He condemned it out of hand, taking pleasure in putting me in my place, telling me that my story was loosely written, badly constructed, melodramatic. We quarrelled bitterly about it, but in the end we compromised in my use of a pen name. The book was financially a great success, and I. R. Watts became a well-known name up and down the Americas and over all of Europe.

"At this time, my husband had teamed up with Wilcannia-Smythe, and each of them was influential in the literary

217

circles of his respective State. My novel and those that followed it were scorned and jibed at as being mere commercial fiction, a term they employed for the work of most Australian authors who would not acknowledge them as leaders of literature.

"The money came in, the money earned by I. R. Watts, and the money housed and clothed and fed the great Mervyn Blake. The money provided him with the use of a car. The money replenished his bank account every month with fifty pounds. The money enabled him to invite famous and influential people to my house. He became famous—locally—as an author and critic, on the money earned by my commercial fiction, which he condemned publicly, which his friends condemned, and which was read by nearly all nations of the world. My work became something that could not be mentioned in polite literary circles. His novels were acclaimed as fine contributions to the national literature by people whose work he in turn praised with equal fervour.

"Well, that's what it came to. I ought to have kicked him out. I ought to have told the world that his novels would never have seen print had it not been for my collaboration. I ought to have told the world all about him. If ever a human dog bit the hand that fed him, it was my husband. For my love he returned hate. For my money he returned abuse. For the gifts of my mind he returned jealousy. Oh no, I didn't kick him out. I would not return to him such a kindness as that. He wanted me to divorce him and go on paying him the fifty pounds a month. I would have been a simpleton. I had him, and he knew it. Without the money earned by I. R. Watts, he was finished with his social climbing, and with his ambition to gain honours. He knew I had him fast, knew that once his friends knew he was living on the earnings of I. R. Watts he would be more greatly shamed than if they found that he was living on the earnings of a woman of ill fame.

"Let him go, indeed! I just loved to see him squirm, to let him see the contempt in my eyes, to let him see there, too, the knowledge that I could bring him down with a word. He would get vilely drunk, and then with cold and studied sarcasm would lash me with abuse, with insults, with filthy innuendoes, saying that I thought only of grasping at cheap popularity, and that I was pandering to the low instincts of the common herd. Once he knocked me down with his fist and then kicked me as I lay stunned on the floor. That was a long time ago, and it was then that I decided to remove a horrible excrescence battening on my life.

"For years I have carried on a large correspondence with notable people abroad, for one does not produce successful novels merely out of one's head. The mind must be refreshed and fertilized with the inspiration of other minds. Thus it was that, after having met Dr Chaparral, I opened a correspondence with him. We exchanged information concerning our respective countries, and in one letter he told me that a compatriot had been tried for the murder of his wife by giving her coffin dust. As you stated a little while ago, I used that method of killing in my *Vengeance of Master Atherton*. And, as you said, I persuaded the doctor to bring some of the coffin dust when he came again to Australia."

Mrs Blake paused in her narrative. Hitherto her voice had been coldly impersonal. When she spoke again, the note of earnestness had crept into it.

"I have spoken the truth, Mr Bonaparte," she said. "I shall continue to do so. You must believe I speak the truth when I say that Dr Chaparral never had the slightest suspicion of why I wanted him to bring me some coffin dust. I told him I should like a sample of it to add to my collection of curios sent me from all parts of the world.

"The dust was contained in five ping-pong balls so that it would not be questioned by the customs officials. He gave them to me one afternoon when the others were out or resting. It was on this veranda. They were taken from his case in which he kept his bats and table net, and accidentally, I let one drop and it bounced clear of the veranda and simply vanished. I never found it. But that left me four balls half-filled with the dust of a corpse.

"The four balls I kept in my own safe, and I allowed the weeks and the months to pass by without using their contents. Possession of them gave me a wonderful feeling of power. I would look at my husband's sneering face, and feel it. I would watch him talking charmingly with a notable guest, and know that when I wished it he would die, that he lived only so long as I wished him to live. I would see the hatred in his eyes and be calm in the knowledge that he was mine to destroy. I would meet his insults with a soft smile, and that would infuriate him the more because he could never be sure why I smiled. I let him live on only because I wanted to continue to enjoy the exquisite sense of power given me by the contents of those four ping-pong balls.

"It was on the afternoon of the day before our house party was to assemble to meet Mr Marshall Ellis that my husband again knocked me down. He was reasonably sober, so there was no possible excuse. I merely smiled because he was strutting about and throwing out his chest and boasting how he, with the help of Wilcannia-Smythe, would hoodwink Marshall Ellis, who was coming to survey Australian literature. My husband then clearly proved himself to be a monomaniac. I shall do this, and that, he said. Through Ellis I shall become famous in London. And so on and on, until I smiled and he knocked me down.

"And so, as Hitler is said to have bitten the carpet in his rages, so would this great and immortal Mervyn Blake bite the dust—my precious coffin dust.

"When staying here, Dr Chaparral related to me the highlights of the trial of the man who murdered his wife with coffin dust. It was given in evidence that the husband believed his poison would act slowly in a person of sober habits, and swiftly in one addicted to alcohol. I had not the mind to poison slowly. Having decided to kill my husband, I wanted death to come to him with reasonable swiftness. The constant upsets had affected my work, to the extent that my last novel was only doubtfully accepted by my publishers. That could not possibly go on, and my husband knew it. He knew that the creative mind cannot continue to create if it is continuously clouded by upsets and mental storms. He told me so, told me he was destroying my gift and would never rest until he had done it.

"Knowing that when the house party assembled, he would begin a bout of drinking in order to quicken his mind, I decided to wait until he was well inflamed with alcohol. When I dragged myself up from the floor that afternoon and wiped the blood from my mouth, I smiled at him in the way he didn't like. My blood was in my mouth, and coffin dust would be in his—I hoped, grittily between his teeth.

"And then, when the excrescence was removed from my life, I should write as I. R. Watts had never written before. I should declare myself as I. R. Watts and accept the tributes I. R. Watts had earned. I should come into my own and the second-rate novelists like Wilcannia-Smythe and his fellow crawlers would crawl to I. R. Watts.

"Yes, Mr Bonaparte, I did all you said I did. I opened the door of the writing-room and stepped over the body of my husband. I carried no light. I exulted, for the evil was stamped flat on the floor. I left the place and hurried to the front gate, where I buried the poison bottle and the glass, and it was then I remembered I hadn't closed the door, and I went back and did it.

"A month afterwards, when Walsh was working in the garden, he asked me to lend him two hundred pounds. When I told him I wouldn't think of doing any such thing, he slyly said it was a pity, since he had always liked working for me, and that he would have to give the police the brandy bottle and the glass he had found buried near the gate. He told me that on the night Mervyn Blake died he had been in the garden to dig up three bottles of brandy my husband told him he had buried as a reserve, and he had seen me go to the writing-room, and looked in after I had left and actually struck a match and saw my husband's body, and then had seen me go to the gate and bury something, and finally followed me back to the writing-room to see me close the door.

"I gave him a hundred pounds, and told him that he would never get any more. But he came back for more, and there was only one way to deal with him. Wearing these old gardening shoes, I studied his habits after dark. I used to watch him through the windows of his hut. Every night he'd read and drink spirits from a bottle. He never drank water or anything with it. Then, during the afternoon of the day before he worked here last, I opened a bottle of whisky and poured some of the dust into it, and then, having carefully resealed the cork, I buried it in the garden. When he came the next day I ordered him to do certain work at which he would be sure to find the bottle. I watched him find it, watched him hide it in his shirt and take it to where he left his case and coat.

"That night I watched him drink from the bottle. He drank almost two-thirds before he lay down and slept. Then I stole into the hut and searched for the bottle and glass he had found near the gate. Both bottle and glass were inside an old portmanteau. I took them, and the whisky bottle I had poisoned for him, leaving on his table an empty bottle and another with a little untainted whisky left in it."

"And the drinking glass on his table?" murmured Bony.

"I knew nothing about the glass. I never saw him drink from it. He did have a visitor the night before. Then the next danger arose in you, Mr Bonaparte. When you visited me that afternoon, you did not convince me you had come from South Africa, not completely, anyway. You see, I have been corresponding with Professor Armberg for several years, and never once did he mention in his letters a tribe called the N'gomo. After you had left us, I referred back to Nancy's paragraph about you, and I wrote to Mr Lubers asking him to find out what he could about you. He rang up Inspector Snook, and Inspector Snook told him what you are and why you are staying at Yarrabo."

"Did he, indeed!" Bony softly exclaimed, and Simes sucked in his breath. "Please go on. What next?"

"This afternoon I was gardening on the far side of the writing-room," Mrs Blake continued. "I heard Miss Pinkney talking to her cat, and I could see her through the fence. She was placing a tea-tray on a small table just beyond, and as I had seen you there before having your afternoon tea I felt sure you would come to take it this afternoon. So I fetched the coffin dust, and crept in through the hole in the fence and put some of it into the teapot. If you go to the doctor very soon, he will probably save you. I have nothing against you—not now."

"It will not be necessary, Mrs Blake, because I didn't drink the tea," Bony said, his face expressionless, and a little soreness in his heart at his failure on the point of the N'gomo natives. "You see, I saw so plainly the imprints of your shoes about the table, and to and from the hole in the fence. And then I saw you seated here, wearing men's shoes.

"That was the proof leading to you, but not the culminating proof. I have found in many cases a tendency for important events to take place in rapid sequence once I have begun to put the puzzle together. Within an hour of knowing who left the tracks on the hill-side about Walsh's hut, and about my tea table, I was informed who I. R. Watts is, and for whom Dr Chaparral brought coffin dust into Australia. Why did you persuade Mrs Montrose to assist you in abducting Wilcannia-Smythe?"

"The note-book was a treasure chest for any writer," Mrs Blake replied. "It belonged to my husband, but the contents were contributed by people entertained on my money. When I discovered that Wilcannia-Smythe had stolen it, and when he refused to give it up, I wrote, at the Rialto that afternoon, to Ella Montrose and asked her to visit me. I did think of Martin Lubers to help me, for he has been a real friend for many years, knowing that I am I. R. Watts and giving me constant support. Then I realized that his career would be damned if what I proposed to do became public property, and so I chose Ella. We disguised ourselves in some of my husband's old clothes.

"I didn't prosecute Wilcannia-Smythe for theft because he knows I am I. R. Watts, and because he knows just how my husband treated me and why. If he had made it all public in revenge for my prosecuting him, the finger of suspicion might have been pointed at me.

"He didn't prosecute us, because he was a thief, and because I could reveal all the rottenness of his school of literary criticism. So we were equally strong. Ella disliked him on personal grounds." Mrs Blake looked down upon the hand still resting upon her own, and she said, "Take your hand away, Nancy, you mustn't touch me." To Bony, she said, "You have a brain, Mr Bonaparte. When did you first suspect me?"

"After seeing your husband's portrait on the wall of your writing-room," he answered without hesitation. "The other pictures were placed symmetrically, and the frames were exactly the same. That containing your husband's picture was a trifle smaller, though of the same wood. Behind it the wall colouring had faded less than the general surface, proving that a larger frame had hung there. When I learnt that your husband's picture was not included in that gallery as late as the date of his death, it suggested that you did include it to avoid remark upon the absence of it in such a collection of well-known writers and poets."

"You are quite right, Inspector Bonaparte," Mrs Blake conceded, and abruptly stood up. "I did think that the doctor's suspicions might be aroused, and that the police might send a clever detective to go through the house and question us all. You see, I was right. They sent you, and they say, don't they, that you never fail. I failed, because you never do. I know, too, that your case against me is much more complete than you have indicated. I shall not attempt any defence. I am too tired, too desperately tired." She turned to Nancy Chesterfield.

"I'm glad I killed him, and I want you to believe it, Nancy. I hope that during those last moments, when he frantically struggled to open the door, that he knew I had poisoned him. I hope that as the light of his life flickered and went out, that as he slipped into the pit of death, he remembered how he had been turning down the light of life for me—turning it down slowly for more than twenty years."